Falling for Colton

JASINDA WILDER

FALLING FOR COLTON

ISBN: 978-1-941098-44-8
Copyright © 2015 by Jasinda Wilder

Cover art by Sarah Hansen of Okay Creations. Cover art © 2015 by Sarah Hansen.
Formatting by Champagne Formats

This book is for you, the reader, for everyone who has fallen for Colton with me.

One: What Kind of Choice Is That?

I DON'T WANT TO GO HOME; I CAN'T GO HOME. I DON'T dare. Not with this report card in my hand. If Dad sees this report... Fuck. There's no way I'm going home. Hell no. I mean, I know he's going to find out eventually, but I might as well put off that shit for as long as I can.

Up front, the dumbass teacher is still droning on about fucking gerunds, whatever the fuck those are, even though the bell is literally ten seconds away from ringing.

Angrily I stuff the envelope into my bag, crumpling it down into the very bottom, placing my stupid remedial English textbook on top of it. Stupid thick-ass fucking book, full of useless bullshit.

Fucking words, man. All those words, a book full of fucking words. They gave me this big-ass book as part of a remedial class I take because I can't fucking read. I mean, come on, how much sense does *that* make? Stupid goddamn motherfuckers.

Like, if a private tutor couldn't help, I don't think remedial classes with big fucking books will help, either. It's not like I don't care or like I'm not trying. I *am*, I just…can't read. Mom and Dad spent thousands of dollars on that tutor, and it didn't get me anywhere.

I zip the backpack closed and toss it over my shoulder, letting it hang by one strap.

Fuck it.

I stand up and head for the door, not about to wait for the bell.

"Mr. Calloway. We aren't done here." The teacher is short and gumpy, thick around the middle with skinny legs and arms. He's bald with a few wisps of hair pulled from one side of his scalp to the other. Like, what the fuck? Who does comb-overs? And why?

BRRRRRRIIIIIINNNNNNGGGG! I'm saved by the bell, literally.

I flip him off, Detroit-style, thumb out, fingers bent at the second knuckle. "Yeah, we are."

He's writing a detention slip before I've finished speaking. "Here you are, Mr. Calloway. For the *third* time this week." He extends the detention slip toward me as the other students file out, some of them looking at me with a mixture of pity and frustration. They've all seen this many times before.

I snatch the slip out of his hand and crumple it into a ball, toss it at him and nail him in the forehead. "You're wasting your time. I'm not going to that detention any more than I went to the other two this week, twat-face. Why don't you just write me one for every fucking day, huh? In fact—" I grab the book of slips off his desk and toss them at him. They bounce off his chest. "Just sign them all, or I can throw the whole book away, and we can skip this bullshit."

He glares at me, red in the face, embarrassed. "Why must you be so antagonistic?" he sputters.

I shrug. "Why must you be such a dick?"

His expression hardens. With a huff, he starts toward me, grabs me by the elbow, and we lunge toward the door. Problem for him is that I've got thirty pounds of muscle and four inches of height on him. I dig my heels in and he's jerked backward.

He squeezes my arm and pulls again. "The office, Mr. Calloway. *Now.*"

I grab his hand and pry it off, twisting his fingers until it hurts. I hold him like that for a second, and then toss him aside like a ragdoll. "Keep your fucking hands off me."

He sputters. "You—you can't—"

I get in his face. "You-you-you—you can't touch me either. You know who my father is. If I tell him you grabbed me you're done. But you know something? That's not gonna happen. Because if you touch me again, I'll rip your skinny-shit arm off and beat you with it. Now. I'm leaving. And I'm not going to fucking detention, so you can just go ahead and report me to Dr. Shitsky. That way, I'll get suspended and then I can stay home for a few days and jerk off."

"You're disgusting."

"So are you." I smack him on the back hard enough to make him flinch. "Glad we had this talk, twat-face."

"Stop *calling* me that!" He sounds like a little kid—he was probably picked on when he was younger.

Shit, *I'm* picking on him right now, and he's a grown-ass man and I'm only seventeen.

I walk out of the classroom without a backward glance. I'll show up for school tomorrow, but I'm guessing I'll have a little interview with the principal, the good Dr. Chizinsky—aka Dr. Shitsky. He'll send me home for the tenth or eleventh time this year, and that'll be that. I mean, there's got to be a limit to the number of times you can get suspended in a single year, right? Apparently not. Or not for me, since good ol' Dad is a senator.

The second I leave the school property I begin thinking about the muffler I'm upgrading on my '67 Camaro. I'm not done yet, so in my mind I go through the next steps as I'm walking home. Having this hobby is the only thing that takes my mind off school. And it gives me something to do out of Dad's crosshairs. Whenever he's home from Washington he's riding my ass about fucking everything: grades, detention, suspensions, my job, applying for colleges.

Like I'm fucking going to college. Haha—that's a good one. If the idea wasn't so lame it would be funny. He honestly thinks I'm going to fucking *Harvard*? I'm in a podunk high school in rural Michigan, and I'm barely passing, and he thinks I can go to a goddamn Ivy League university? I've lost count of the number of arguments we've had about it. I know he can probably pull strings and shit and get me in despite my lousy grades, but I'm just *not* going. I don't know what I *am* gonna do when I graduate, but it's sure as shit not gonna be college.

I cut through the woods between the high school and the main road separating the school from my subdivision. A familiar route. I think I've actually worn a literal path between the trees, I've gone this way so many times over the last four years. I've even got a little hideout, an old tree with a rotted-out hole near the base, just big enough to hold my stash. I hang out here and smoke, drink, and basically avoid going home. Anything to avoid Dad's disappointed glare and Mom's...mom-ness. She's always so anxious to please Dad and I know she's afraid of making me angry because she just can't handle conflict, and I have a hell of a temper.

I halt in front of my tree, toss my backpack to the ground, and sit down beside it. I reach up into the hole, into the little cubby I've dug out up in there. It's just big enough to hide a pint of cheap whiskey, a little baggy of pot, a packet of papers, and a lighter. I don't dare keep this stuff at home or in my backpack, but I sure as hell can't live without it.

I take a swig of whiskey and hiss as it burns its way down, and then I roll a joint. Leaning back against the tree I puff on it lazily, relishing the sensation of having a floaty head and loose, heavy limbs.

God, I really don't want to go home.

But fuck it. I can't avoid the place forever. So I might as well get this over with.

Time to man up.

I stash my goodies and make my way out of the

forest, not really paying attention to much of any-thing as I jog across the busy four-lane road, and hop the wall between the road and my subdivision. There are wide-open spaces here on this side of the wall, acres of manicured green grass mowed in smooth arcs, with the houses way off in the distance, all fac-ing inward.

As soon as I land a fist connects with my skull, sending stars bursting in my eyes and pain lancing through my head.

I stumble backward, bumping up against the wall, blinking, and shaking off the pain-haze. I drop my bag and face them.

"You fucked my girlfriend, Calloway," Preston snarls.

I grin at him. "And she was a pretty fucking sweet lay, too." It's four on one, so taunting them may not be the smartest thing, but hey—no one's ever accused me of being the sharpest crayon in the toolbox. "Got that fine ass of hers bent over in the backseat, and man…I fucked her *senseless*, bro."

"You fucking asshole!"

I lift my hands as if I'm innocent. "Hey, man, it's not my fault she's not getting it good enough from you."

Fucking Preston, fucking Doug, fucking Brady,

and that motherfucking piece of shit Dane. Football jocks. Dickheads extraordinaire. Jealous pricks.

Well, maybe jealous is the wrong word. I don't know what the right word is, but whatever it is, they're it. They're all mad as hell at me because not only have I fucked all of their slutty-bitch girlfriends, but I've kicked each of their pussy asses more than once.

But now they're all here together. And they're all pretty fucking big. And pissed off. And they've got the jump on me.

My ears are still ringing and I'm blinking to clear my vision—sucker punches are tough to shake off. I assess the situation: Preston to my left, near the wall—he's the one that sucker-punched me—Brady and Doug in front of me, and Dane to my right. They're all wearing their stupid varsity letter jackets in May like the pretentious douchebags they are.

Fuck.

I lunge for Dane first because I hate his ass the most—not for any particular reason, just because he's a stuck-up preppy douchebag pretty boy, and I disagree with his existence on a fundamental level. I connect with his jaw and he spins and stumbles. I pull off another jump-lunge-swing, and I connect again in the same spot. Say goodnight, Gracie. He's on the ground now, crying.

Well, not crying, but moaning.

Preston is behind me with his arm around my neck, Brady has one of my arms, and Doug is hammering punch after punch into my gut, bam-bam-bam.

Fucking hurts.

But Doug is a pussy.

I kick him in the nuts and he stumbles back, clutching himself, making a little squeaking noise. I jam my elbow into Brady's chest, but take a shot to the cheek, another to the lip, and a third that smashes my nose open. I'm seeing stars now. Dizzy, aching—fuck. Brady is the toughest of all of them, the one who can actually fight for half a shit. Preston is squeezing my throat as hard as he can, but I've got my chin between his arm and my windpipe, so he can't actually choke me. I lash out at Brady again, because he's the one to worry about. I catch him somewhere between his eye and cheekbone with a wild left, and he's distracted enough that I can now deal with Preston.

Fucking Preston Fairchild. He's the most pretentious of all of them. Pretty-boy cocksucker. I reach up behind me and grab him by the spiky, gelled, faux-hawked blond hair and smash my head backward into his nose. Blood runs sticky and warm down the back of my neck, and then he lets go of me. I pivot in place, stumbling, dizzy, and then rocket four lightning-fast jabs at him, left-left-right-*left*, one-two-three-four to the face. Nose, cheekbone, jaw, nose. One more, a smashing left hook to his nose again, just to really fuck up his face.

Dude's shit is so broken he'll be marked for life.

Brady is still there, but he backs up, hands lifted. "I'm good, man."

I spit blood. "Fuck you, bitch. Come at me."

He shakes his head. "We've rumbled before. No thanks. I got no beef with you."

I laugh, my tone bitter with sarcasm. "You know Shelly sucked my dick under the bleachers last week?" I must have a death wish. Brady could give me a serious run for my money in my current condition. "And then I fucked her in her car, had those bangin' cheerleader legs up over my shoulders and everything."

His gaze darkens. "Yeah, I know." He waves his hand dismissively. "She was a slut. She's sucked half the dicks in the entire school. I don't know what I was thinking, dating her ho ass."

"I don't either."

He snorts. "You fucked her too, man."

I shrug. "Well yeah, I mean she's hot—slutty, but hot. I ain't about to turn down easy pussy." I point at Preston, who is on the ground, clutching his nose, writing. I'm bleeding too, but I just let my shit bleed. "Now *his* girl, man…she was tight as hell. I'm not sure he ever actually tapped that ass, it was so tight."

"She bleed?" Brady asks.

I shake my head. "Nah. Not that I noticed."

"You know what? Whatever. I don't care." A shrug. "Like I said, I'm good, man. You come at me, I'll take you down. But I'm good if you are."

I'm not that much of a glutton for punishment that I'm willing to ignore the olive branch he's offering. "Tell your pussy-ass friends to leave me alone."

He turns away from me, ignores me, and then helps his friends get up.

I grab my backpack and jog away. Fuck that. Fuck them.

I make it to the end of my street before I slow down. My T-shirt is soaked with the blood that is still sluicing out of my nose. My eye is swelling shut, and I'm pretty sure my lip is split wide open. I run my tongue over the stinging lump on my lip; sure enough, I taste blood. Shots to the face hurt, man. I can take body shots all day long and not be fazed, I've packed on so much muscle over my torso that someone has to really hammer hard to get through. But there's no way to toughen up your face. Your lips will split open. Your eyes will swell shut and turn black—and then yellow and purple and green. Teeth will get loosened. Nothing you can do about that shit.

Okay, maybe I lied: my fucking stomach hurts like a bitch, man.

But I've learned all this the hard way. I've been in lots of fights this year, which accounts for the nearly dozen suspensions I've had since September. I'm a big guy naturally. At seventeen, I stand six foot three in my socks. I work out a lot, because what else is there to do in this bullshit little town? So I'm pretty fucking ripped, which invites trouble, especially when you add in the fact that my attitude leaves something to be desired. Basically what I'm saying is, I'm fresh out of shits to give, seeing as I've got all I can handle just trying to pass my classes and keep my dad off my ass.

I cross through backyards, hop fences and sneak into my house via the back door. All is quiet. There is no sign of Dad or Mom, so I take the time to grab a bag of frozen peas, a can of Coke, and a handful of those crunchy peanut butter granola bars that end up leaving a pile of crumbs with every bite.

I almost make it to my room. Almost.

"Colton? Honey, is that you?" Mom is calling from the hall bathroom.

"Yeah." I shove my bedroom door open. "Got a lot of homework. I'll grab dinner later."

She's after me, though. I turn away as she approaches, pretending to dig in my bag so she won't see my face.

"You sure you can't come down for dinner?"she asks as she stands in the doorway to my room. "It'll be ready in less than fifteen minutes. We're eating early 'cause Kyle is going to a pool party with his baseball team tonight."

I shrug. "Nah." I lift the granola bar. "I'm good."

"You can't eat just a granola bar for dinner, Colton." Mom still hasn't spotted anything...maybe I'll be able to avoid the have-you-been-fighting-again bullshit after all.

"Sure I can. Lots of homework to do. I'll be down later, Ma." I toss a history book on my desk, kick the chair back and sit down. As I hunch over it I see that blood is dripping onto the book—*pit-pit-pit-pit-pit*.

She sees it. Damn. "Colt? Are you okay? Are you bleeding?"

"Just bumped my nose. No big deal." There's a box of Kleenex on the desk. I wad up a handful and stuff it against my nose. "I'm fine."

"Let me see." She grabs my shoulder and turns me around. Gasps. "Oh my god! Colton Henry Calloway! What the hell happened to you?"

"Nothing. I'm fine, really." I jerk away, turn

around, and glance at the history book that sits un-opened, a silent reminder of the fact that I can't fuck-ing read.

"Were you in *another* fight?" She kneels beside me and we are face to face. She prods my nose and my eye. Her hands smell like onions and fancy hand soap, and I can't help but notice the pain and concern in her eyes.

"You're getting bleach on me, Ma. You're not helping." I pull my face away. "I'm fucking fine."

"Watch your language, Colton. What *happened*?"

"It's nothing, I handled it. I'm fine." I need to move, to do something.

I grab my backpack and start yanking shit out of it. Which, stupidly, includes the report card.

"You got your report card?" Seeing it lying on the desk, she reaches for it.

I want to snatch it away, rip it up. But I don't. "Yeah."

I dab at my nose with the red, sodden ball of Kleenex. I try to ignore her and pretend I don't care. I ignore her as she opens it, ignore her as she unfolds the paper and reads it. I ignore the way her shoulders begin to sag.

"I thought you were going to do better this se-mester, Colton?"

"So did I." I hurl the blood-soaked wad of tissue across the room.

It splats wetly against my closet door, leaving a reddish-pink trail on the white wood as it slides down and hits the floor.

Mom watches this happen. "Really, Colton? That's disgusting." She waves the report card. "I'm sorry to say it, but your father is going to be—"

I rip the paper from her and wad it up, chuck it angrily away. *"Very disappointed,"* I finish for her, mimicking my father's stentorian voice. "I know. What a fucking surprise *that* will be."

"Colton—"

"Is he home?"

"Yes, but I think—"

"Mom, I think you should go find something else to do." I walk across my room, un-crumple the report card and push past her. "You're not going to want to listen to this."

"Maybe you should wait until after dinner—"

"He's not going to be any less disappointed in me on a full stomach, Ma."

She just sighs. "Maybe you should change your shirt first?"

I glance down. My Rage Against the Machine T-shirt is heavily stained with my blood. I shrug. "It doesn't matter."

Since there's nothing more she can say, she lets me go in silence.

Dad is down in his office, which is no surprise: on the occasions when he's at home, the great senator is always in his office working.

A public servant's work is never done, son, he'll say.

Yeah, well, neither is a father's, but what do I know?

I hate his goddamned office. The French doors from the foyer open inward, revealing a battleship of a desk. It's made of polished dark wood, spotless but for a few things: computer, keyboard, mouse, a desktop blotter/calendar, and a fancy silver pen in a stand. Bookshelves line the walls from floor to ceiling, filled with hardcover copies of classic literature along with four-inch-thick law tomes in equal number. Thick pile carpeting underfoot. Blinds drawn to keep the room cool and in constant shadow. An antique vinyl record player sits under his framed degrees from U of M, Brown, and Harvard. Yeah, he's got an Ivy League doctorate, but he doesn't talk about it very often. He doesn't go by Dr. Calloway. He's humble that way.

As I enter the room I see his face is lit by the computer screen, a whitish glow on his classically handsome features; he's a real silver fox, my pops. Even home on break, he's dressed nice enough to stroll into any five-star restaurant. Pressed and creased tan slacks, crisp white button-down, slim navy tie.

We couldn't be any more different. I'm in baggy khakis—which have blood, ink, and oil on them—and a bloodstained rock band T-shirt. I've got tattoos on my biceps and on my forearms. I've got diamond studs in my ears. My hair is shaggy, uncut, messy, and sweaty.

Shit, my eye is black, my lip is split, and my nose is crusty with dried blood.

He glances up at me, frowns. "Don't bleed on my carpet, son."

"Yeah, thanks, I'm fine." I cross the carpet, lift the hem of my T-shirt and dab at my nose with it—the shirt comes away dry, so I guess I'm not bleeding anymore. "Here." I toss the report card on his desk and turn to go.

"Wait." It's a command, the sharp crack of a man accustomed to being listened to.

I stop with my hand on the doorknob, hearing the paper crinkle as he smooths it out on his desk. I can see the motion in my mind's eye, palm sliding over the paper, pressing it against the desk compulsively; he hates mess, hates things out of order. Everything I am, basically.

"This isn't acceptable, Colton." He says this with a long-suffering sigh. "We agreed you were going to apply yourself this final semester."

I don't bother arguing. I don't bother pointing out how many hours I've spent in my room, studying, doing homework. I *have* applied myself. I guaranfucking-tee you I've worked harder than anybody else in the entire school. I've worked my ass off just to get *those* grades. But he doesn't see that. He doesn't care.

"Calculus, C plus. Not bad." Of course he's going to go over every single grade, and make a snarky-ass comment about each one. And I just have to stand here and take it. I'm shaking with anger. Ten more seconds. I'll listen to his fucking bullshit for ten more seconds and then I'm out of here. "History of Western Civilization, D-minus. Barely passed that one. Fundamentals of Reading and Comprehension, E-minus. Lowest grade there is. I mean, it takes talent to get a grade that low. Jesus, Colton. How do you manage that? It's baffling."

"By being fucking *dyslexic*?" I spin back to face him, palms slapping on his fancy-ass desk. "What part of that don't you get, cocksucker? I—*cannot*—READ! It doesn't matter how hard I try—and I fucking swear on your dead mother's soul I've worked like a dog my entire life—I'll never be able to read the way you can.

It's not laziness, there's something wrong with my brain that can't be fixed."

"You're just lazy. You're blaming your failure on a minor disability that could be easily overcome if you cared to apply yourself." He's not even fazed by my shouts, doesn't even hear me. My vulgar insult doesn't register. He's used to them by now. "Let's see…Human Anatomy, C. Independent Study in Advanced Automotive Repair, A plus. Economics, D."

I twist the knob and pull open the door. "Finished?"

He stands up; I hear casters rolling on the plastic mat underneath his chair. "No, I'm not finished."

"Too fucking bad. I don't wanna hear any more." I haul ass for the back door, for the old barn at the back of the property.

He follows me. "Get back here, Colton Calloway. I have more to say to you."

"You always have more to say, you old windbag. I quit giving a shit a long time ago." I turn and walk in silence across the manicured backyard, through the hedge and into the stand of woods hiding the barn that is my workshop.

I feel him behind me but I don't bother looking back. I hover over the combination lock securing the only door to the barn, twist it to the correct numbers, and yank it free. I push aside the latch, squat, and shove up the roll-up door. I switch on the lights, which flicker-flicker-flicker, then catch with a hum, bathing the workshop in a fluorescent white glow. The exhaust system for the Camaro is laid out in pieces on the workbench. A brand new Flowmaster American Thunder. Once this bitch is on my Camaro, it'll be even more powerful and a shitload louder. This baby will snarl like a damn lion. Not as good as a custom exhaust system would be, but that's a little out of my reach just yet.

I go to work, pull the cover off the Camaro, toss it aside, grab the tools I'll need along with one of the exhaust parts, then I lay down on my roller board. I slide under the Camaro, which is pulled up onto a set of blocks to allow for a few more inches of clearance.

Dad just watches me for a while. "If only you could apply yourself to school the way you do this car." He sounds honestly morose. Sad.

I don't stop working. "It's not about applying myself, Dad. If I wasn't applying myself, those grades would all be E's. If I wasn't applying myself, I'd be captain of the football team. I'd be playing ball with my friends right now—shit, if I wasn't applying myself, I'd *have* friends. If I wasn't applying myself, I wouldn't spend four or five hours a day on fucking homework.

I don't go to bed until after two in the morning, Dad. Doing homework. And then I'm up again at eight, and I spend my lunch breaks in the library, studying. I see a tutor on Wednesdays…" I trail off with a sigh. I don't know why I'm telling him this. He knows all about it. He just doesn't care. "I'm fucking trying. I'm sorry my best isn't ever going to be good enough for you."

"You spend all your time in here, working on this car."

"Because it's the only thing in my life that I actually enjoy. It's what I'm good at."

"But you're a Calloway. You're *my* son."

"Nothing wrong with working a trade, Dad. I can take apart an engine and put it back together with my eyes closed. I can name every single part of a car, from bolts to headers. I can custom tune any car you put in front of me."

"That's great, Colton, but it's no kind of future for any son of mine." He sighs. "I just wish you could be more like your brother. He's had straight A's for the last three years in a row, and he's *eleven*."

I'm tempted to throw this fucking ratchet at his head. I take a few deep breaths so I don't end up in jail for patricide; and, yes, I do know what patricide means. "Well, I'm sorry I can't be more like your pre-

cious perfect golden boy, sweet little Kyle. I'm sorry
to be such a *disappointment* to you."

I note his lack of disagreement with my last
statement. Or the one before it, for that matter. Kyle
is perfect, and I'm a big disappointment.

I hear him exhale a breath of resignation. "Well,
even with these grades, I'm sure with a generous do-
nation and a few phone calls, I can still get you into
NYU or Harvard."

I laugh out loud. "Harvard? You still honestly
think that? You must smoke more pot than me if you
think that's ever going to happen."

Silence. He's trying to decide whether or not
to address my blatant admission that I smoke pot.
"You're going to college. Or you're on your own."

"Fine by me. I can make my own way."

"I'm serious, Colt. You'll get nothing from me
if you don't pursue your education. Not a dime. And
you cannot take anything I've paid for. Which includes that car."

Fuck him. I built this car with my own two hands
from a rusty pile of shit in a junkyard to the mint beauty she is now. I've paid for every single part and tool
with money earned changing oil and mowing lawns
and shoveling driveways and cleaning out cars and
mucking horse stalls. He paid two thousand bucks

for the shell and the seized-up, rusted-out engine. It didn't even have a transmission. It was more rust than metal or paint. And he's gonna take it from me if I don't go to a goddamned Ivy League university?

Fuck him.

"I have personal assurances from the deans of Harvard, NYU, and Stanford that you'll be admitted as long as you apply by February at the very latest.

"Congress is back in session soon, but I expect you to submit your applications and the appropriate paperwork, including the essays, for the three universities we've discussed." A pause. "You have three months from the graduation, Colton. Three months, and you'll either head to college or you're on your own."

I'm still under the car but I hear him leave the barn; hear his feet crunch on gravel drive.

Except for the buzz of the fluorescent lights the barn is awash in silence.

He's serious, deadly serious. Either I go to an Ivy League college, or I'm disowned.

What kind of choice is that?

Two: So Much For Choices

I GRADUATED, PASSED ALL MY CLASSES EXCEPT THE READING for dummies bullshit. And I didn't apply to any colleges, obviously. And I spent the summer cruising in my Camaro, working for Mr. Boyd—the Automotive teacher and the only adult who I've ever actually liked—with his summertime hobby, helping him restore a classic car. I learned a lot from him and he paid me pocket money, which I saved. Well, except for cigarettes and pints of whiskey and pot.

It was a good three months. Dad was gone most of the time, trips to Washington for who knows what reason. Mom left me alone and Kyle was away at football camp for most of the time, so I was on my own, which was cool with me. I kicked it with Lacey Myles for most of the summer. Hot stuff, that girl. Dumber than a box of rocks, but hot. Mouth like a Hoover. Apparently she had no problem with the fact that I'm a rougher sort of guy. Maybe it was the reason she kicked it with me in the first place—to get a taste of the wild side and stick it to her rich-ass parents. I mean, it wasn't because of my stellar sweet-talking skills, that's for damn sure. I was an asshole to her most of the time and that never changed from day one, so she can't say she didn't know it going in. I basically just picked her up at her house, watched her big juicy titties bounce around as she hopped down those four steps from her fancy front door to the sidewalk, and watched her hips sway as she approached my car. She always did this thing where she bent over at the waist, leaned into the open passenger window and gave me weird little wave where she wiggled her fingertips at me. I liked it, though, because she basically fell out of her shirt while she did it.

We would grab a bite to eat—another reason I liked Lacey is that she didn't give a shit about things like chivalry, so she paid for meals seeing as she was loaded, even though I always said I'd get it because, despite being an asshole, I'm not a *complete* asshole— and then we'd cruise around in the Camaro. Maybe head way down to Woodward Avenue for a while, or

Gratiot. Eventually, we'd find a quiet spot somewhere and she'd help me with my belt and I'd help her with her shirt, and she'd swing over and ride me like she was practicing for barrel racing at the rodeo.

Honestly, she was a sweet little thing. Never gave me shit. Never expected anything more from me than what I was offering, which was a ride in my car, a swig off my whiskey and a puff of my dope, and a ride on my cock. We didn't talk much. We just cruised, smoked, drank, and fucked. But when she did talk she was sweet. She was just…ditzy. Not actually stupid, I don't think, just…a bit of a space cadet—the reason there's a stereotype regarding blondes.

But all good things come to an end. Lacey got ready to head off to MSU, probably to major in fellatio and journalism. Dad came home for the last break before the congressional season really kicked into gear in September. My complete dismissal of his demands for college apps three months ago teed off our big rumble. I knew I'd bitten off a pretty big chunk by refusing to apply to college; I was choosing disownment. Sucks. I was going to lose the Camaro, too, and that was, honestly, the hardest part to swallow.

At least they weren't selling it to some jackass, though. Dad clearly respected my skills, even if he didn't approve of them for "a Calloway", since he'd decided to give my Camaro to Kyle when he turned sixteen.

I even have a little talk with Kyle about it. I'm working in my shop, tweaking things here and there, and in comes Kyle, fresh from football camp. Skinny little shit, all of eleven, almost twelve, black hair cut tight to his scalp. He'd be a good-looking son of a bitch, though, you can already tell.

He tugs a stool out from underneath the workbench, turns down my Metallica CD, and kicks his feet. I know he's there, obviously, but I also know he's got something to say, and will spit it out when he was ready. He never comes out here to my shop; no one does unless they have to, but Kyle especially. I caught him in here one day when he was nine or ten, messing with my tools, trying to help probably. I don't know. I do know he'd fucked up a brand new set of spark plugs, though, and I lost my shit, told him I'd kill him in his sleep if I ever found him out here again.

A few minutes pass, and Kyle just watches me work, kicking his feet.

Finally, I set down my wrench, turn to face him, arms crossed over my chest. "Well? Whaddya want, kiddo?"

"Are you leaving?"

I shrug, nod. "Yeah."

"Why?"

I sigh. "Hard to explain. Dad wants me to go to college, and I want to work on cars. And Dad said if I don't go to college, now that I've graduated high school, I can't live here anymore. So I'm leaving."

"Where are you gonna go?"

"Hell if I know, bud."

"When will you be back?"

I feel that one in the gut; I haven't been the best big brother to this little squirt, but he's a good kid. Better than me, that's for fucking sure. I can only shake my head. "I don't know. Shitty answer, but it's the truth."

"I heard Mom and Dad arguing about you last night."

I cock an eyebrow at him. "Oh yeah? What'd they say?"

"Well Mom is mad that Dad's making you leave, and he was all like 'he's made his bed, now he has to lie in it', whatever *that* means. And Mom is mad because Dad's not letting you keep your car, which I think is bullshit."

"You're not old enough to swear yet, kid." I toss a washer at him, which he catches and throws back, hard. Kid's got an arm, man.

"You swear all the time. And besides, it *is* bullshit.

You did all the work on that car. Why can't you take it?"

"Because Dad paid for the shell. I built the engine myself, put in the transmission, the exhaust, the stereo, the seats, everything. But he paid for the shell, so he technically owns it. I could take all that stuff out, but then I'd have the parts for the car and nothing to put them in. Doesn't make any sense to wreck a work of art out of petulance, you know?"

"So what's gonna happen to it, then?"

"You'll get it." I shoot him a grin I don't really feel, but I can't hold anything against Kyle since he's innocent in all this.

"I will? Really?"

"Well yeah. You're gonna be sixteen in a few years, and you'll need a car. This way, they don't have to buy a new one. Bonus for you is, you'll have the sweetest ride at the entire school. Bitches are gonna be tripping over themselves to get a ride in it, bro."

Kyle frowns. "You shouldn't call women bitches, Colt. It's not nice."

I throw a hex nut at his head, not gently this time. "Neither am I, if you hadn't noticed."

Quick hands catch the nut, toss it aside casually. "You could be. You don't have to be a jerk all the time."

I rock back, stunned. "You think I'm a jerk?"

He shrugs. "Well, not to me, mostly. But then, you barely notice I exist most of the time. But you're a jerk to Dad."

"That's because he's a jerk to me. We don't see eye to eye on a lot of things, Kyle. Hopefully you'll never have to understand that."

I sigh, tug open the driver's door, gesture for him to get in. He scrambles off the stool and slides into the driver's seat, grabs the steering wheel with one hand, the shifter with the other.

"Man, this is so cool!" He grins at me. "I can't believe I'm gonna get to drive this!"

"You better take care of it, Kyle. She's a sweet ride, but you gotta take care of her. Any problems, Mr. Boyd will be able to help. He's the auto shop teacher at the high school. Do NOT let Mom or Dad take it to some fucking piece of shit garage, they'll just fuck it up. Take it to Mr. Boyd. Got it?"

He nods, serious. "Got it."

I hesitate, then spit it out. "Kyle, it's not that I didn't notice you. It's just...I had trouble in school, so I had to work a lot harder than everyone else at shit that comes easy to someone like you. And, honestly, I didn't want to pull you into my mess. I haven't been the best brother. I get that, and I'm sorry."

He meets my gaze, nods. His expression is knowing, and serious, and understanding. "It's okay, Colt. I could always tell that Dad's a lot harder on you than he is on me. It's not really fair, is it?"

I scrub my hands through my hair. "Not really. But he's good to you, so that's all you need to know about. I'm not gonna talk shit about Dad to you, because that's issues between him and me. It doesn't have anything to do with you, so don't worry about it."

"But he's making you leave, and you don't know where you're going, or when you'll be back."

"Pretty much. Although, if I'd let him make me go to some Ivy League university, I could have stayed here, kept the Camaro, all that. But I can't go to college. I just can't. So I made this choice. And like I said, I just hope you never have to understand why I left. Just know...it wasn't because of you, okay?"

A nod. "Okay. It sucks, though."

"It does suck," I agree. "Now scram, so I can finish this."

He unfolds from the driver's seat, reluctantly. Yeah, he'll take care of my baby, that's for sure.

"Kyle?" He looks up at me. "Make sure this gets started and run once a month, or have Mr. Boyd winterize it for storage until you're old enough to drive. It can't just sit here. Since it's gonna be yours, you gotta start taking responsibility for it."

He nods. "I will. I promise." He lunges at me, wraps his arms around my waist, squeezes hard and fast, and lets go. "Bye, Colt."

I don't know what to do with the hug, so I just pat him on the shoulder awkwardly. "Bye, Golden Boy."

An embarrassed grin. "Shut up."

I watch him trot away with the boundless energy of an eleven-year-old, jumping to swipe at a low-hanging branch, tripping over a root and righting himself, kicking an acorn.

It all comes to a head three months almost to the day from graduation.

I'm hanging out on the dock, eight at night, pretty early for me, but Lacey has to leave for MSU first thing tomorrow morning. I've just dropped her off for the last time, and I'm feeling good about our rough and wild goodbye-romp. I'm high, but not too high. Coming down. Smoking a cigarette. Waiting for him, basically.

"Colton. Put that nasty thing out," he says by way of hello. I flick the butt out into the water. "I didn't mean throw it into the lake, you degenerate."

I just wait. Slump lower in the Adirondack chair

and watch the moon glint off the gently lapping waves.

"Well?" He stands behind me, tapping a toe, arms crossed.

"Well what?" I ask, not turning around.

"Which college did you get into?" He says this expectantly. "You had an easy in at three of them. Which one did you decide on?"

Asshole, acting like he doesn't damn well know. Just wants to make a scene out of it.

I scuff the heel of my Wolverine boot on the wood of the deck. "I didn't apply to any of them."

"You what?" I hear him take a step closer. "Tell me I didn't hear you correctly."

I stand up and push past him. "I have an interview, though. It's at Hemingway Auto on Thursday. The owner, Jimmy, does custom tuning on the side, so I'm gonna angle for that."

"We had a deal, Colton."

I stop and jab a finger at him. "No, actually, you issued me an ultimatum—go to college or be disowned. But there's an option C: I get a job, a *good* job doing something I'm really great at. I can get my own apartment in a few months, and you can even pretend I don't exist if you want."

"Why, Colton? Why can't you for *once* toe the

line? Why couldn't you take the opening I provided? I got you into three of the best schools in the country. All you had to do was apply, damn it! The essays didn't even have to be good! You just had to *do* it!"

"I'm not going to fucking college, Dad! I barely passed *high school*! I've got other skills, okay? Why can't you *get* that? I'm not book-smart, but I can do other stuff. There are other things in life besides Ivy League universities and fancy offices."

"Not for you. Not for a Calloway."

"Oh come on, Dad. It's not like we're the goddamn Boston Brahmins, or some shit. We're not some kind of old money aristocrats. Your great-grandfather was from Dubuque, Iowa. He was a farmer. Which, by the way, happens to be a perfectly respectable vocation."

"But my grandfather wanted better. He paid for college himself by waiting tables. He went to Yale on his own terms. Graduated *summa cum laude*, from *Yale*. My father went to Brown. I went to—"

"Yes, I know. U of M, Brown, *and* Harvard. I got it. I've seen the fucking degrees."

"It's about more than a piece of paper, Colton! It's about pride! It's about tradition. It's about making something of yourself, doing something worthwhile with your life!"

I groan, tipping my head back. "I can be proud of myself, too, you know. I can build a car by myself. I'm not even eighteen yet and I can disassemble, repair, and reassemble an engine. I can make something of myself without going to college."

"You're *going* to college." He shoves a hand into his pocket. "I'll call Bill at Stanford. He can probably still get you admitted if you apply by the end of the week."

"I'm *not* going!"

"Yes you *are!*"

I glare at him, shouting, "Fucking hell, Dad! Why? Why is this the only thing you can let me do? Why? Why can't you be proud of me for the things I'm good at instead of trying to force me into a box I'll never fit into?"

"Because you *can* fit, if you just tried."

"But I don't *want* to! I don't *want* to go to college. I hate classrooms. I hate teachers. I hate textbooks and essays and tests. I'm good at cars—I'm not good at school."

"I swear to god…" he groans, just like I did moments ago, tipping his head back in frustration. "If you didn't choose to be so fucking *stupid*. Not to mention ungrateful."

You know how many times other kids called me

stupid, growing up? More times than I can count. I grew up around rich kids, *smart* rich kids. I was the only one who ever struggled academically. The only one who ever got tests back with a big fat red E on the front.

Why are you so stupid, Colt? Did your mama drop on your head, Colt? You're such a dumbass, Colt.

But I never expected to hear it from him, my own father.

"What did you say?" I ask in a near-whisper.

"You're stupid! That's what I said!" He shouts this at me. "You don't have to be, but you are. You're intentionally choosing to be fucking *stupid*! What kind of *idiot* can't even write one little essay? What kind of idiot throws away a free ride to an Ivy League school?"

"I'm not stupid." I sound so small and petulant, saying this, and I hate it. I hate the lump in my throat. I hate the way my stomach aches from how badly that word hurts.

"Yes you are."

"Fuck *YOU*!" I scream it, and follow it up with a wicked right hook.

Dad stumbles backward, clutching his jaw. His eyes are blazing. Blue, like mine. Full of disgust and rage. He comes for me, swinging.

He boxed in college, I remember belatedly. Preppy boy boxing, rules and mouth guards and all that.

He still connects, though, and he packs a hell of a wallop for an old guy. We're scuffling, grappling. I'm about to knee him when I hear Mom screaming, crying. I feel her whack me in the back of the head, hear Dad bark in surprise. We part, panting, and I see that Mom has a big wooden spoon in her hand, the one she uses in the kitchen. She's whacking Dad over and over and over, hitting his head, shoulders and arms.

"Henry! For god's sake, what is *wrong* with you?" She whacks him across the back of his head, *hard*. "He's our son!"

I back away, wiping the blood off the corner of my mouth. "Nothing's wrong with him. I'm just stupid, according to him." I hate the salty sting in my eyes as I turn and jog off the dock.

"Colton!" Mom calls out. "Wait."

I think she thinks this is just another argument, one of the hundreds Dad and I have had on this issue over the last couple of years.

I ignore her pleas. I head upstairs to my room and I dump out my old black Jansport. I shove jeans and khakis and T-shirts and socks and underwear and a couple of hoodies into it. I dig under my bed for the shoebox containing my life savings. One thousand two hundred and four dollars, a pathetically small stack of bills bound up by a rubber band. I stuff that into my bag, as well.

Downstairs, I raid the pantry. A few granola bars, a couple of apples, a package of Ritz crackers, four cans of Coke. It all gets zipped into the backpack.

Mom is at the back door, watching. "Colt? What are you doing?"

"I'm leaving."

"Where are you going?" she asks. She's tearful, clearly upset.

"Don't know. Anywhere but here. New York, maybe."

"Don't, Colton. He didn't mean it."

"The hell he didn't."

"Leave him alone, Olivia." Suddenly Dad's there, watching Mom and me. His lip is split and puffy. His eyes are dead and cold. "Let him go."

"You're just going to stand there and allow our oldest son to run away?"

"He's not running away." Dad eyes me. "He's *choosing* his own way."

"No, I'm not, *asshole*. I'm taking the only option *you've* left me with."

"Colton, don't talk to your father that way," Mom says.

I look straight at him. "He's not my father. He's just the senator. And I'm just an embarrassment."

I glance over at Mom. "You probably won't see me again anytime soon."

"What—what are you talking about, Colton?"

I shoulder my backpack. "I'm *leaving*, Ma. I'm walking out that door and I'm never coming back."

"But Colton, you can't—"

"You can't stop me."

"I don't understand." She's sobbing now.

I sigh. I hate seeing her cry. She's weak, but at least she loves me, in her own timid way. "I know you don't. Talk to your husband. This is on him."

One last time, I beseech my father. "It doesn't have to be this way. You're going to look back on this moment someday and you're going to regret it."

"The only thing I regret is you, Colton."

I run my tongue over my lip and sigh, nodding. "Yeah, fine. Fuck you, too."

I sling one arm around Mom's shoulders and squeeze briefly. "I love you, Ma. I'll see you around." Saying those words really suck and it's difficult, but I have to stay hard, especially right now.

I'm only seventeen. Despite what they might think, I'm not running away. I've been given no other choice. I'm *walking* away and both my parents—

and Kyle upstairs, in his room, peering through his blinds—watch as I close the back door behind me.

Alone.

At first it doesn't seem real. Walking down the road in the middle of the night. My legs hurt. I've walked several miles already, heading further and further south. Somewhere I might find a bus out of Michigan. I have no idea what I'm going to do or where I'm heading. I feel like I'm in a dream. Like I can still go home.

But I can't.

I can never go home again. Because I don't have a home anymore.

I'm a homeless teenager.

Holy shit: I've become one of the statistics you hear about.

A light rain starts. It's warm, blown diagonal by a cool breeze. I don't mind, at first. But then I start to get soaked through and the weather turns cold.

A car drives past and then stops, taillights glowing red ahead. I keep walking until I'm beside the open passenger window. The driver is a woman, mid-thirties, maybe. Obviously not too smart. Honey, stopping for a guy like me, in weather like this, is a risky move. You don't know me from Adam.

But I'm not turning down a free ride. 'Sides, she's

kinda sexy.

"Where are you headed?" she asks.

"Bus station, I guess."

"Hop in."

"I'm wet."

"Leather seats. They'll wipe down."

I shrug, pop open the door, toss my backpack to the floorboards and slide in. Nice car. BMW, new, smells like leather and perfume.

And pot.

I might've just scored in more ways than one.

She's brunette, hair done up in a messy bun, wearing a tight skirt and a low-cut shirt—business-casual wear, basically. Not overtly sexy, but enough to get across the point that she's all woman. Her makeup is smeared and she's got mascara running down her face. She has a wipe in one hand, and she's in the process of wiping the makeup off. I don't bother hiding my perusal. Nice body. Not exactly bangin', but nice. Decent rack, probably a little smaller bare than it looks propped up by that bra—not that I'm complaining.

She eyes me. I've got a hoodie on, hood pulled low, baggy jeans, work boots. I could be anyone. Why'd she stop? I don't get it.

"I'm Helen," she says, extending her hand.

I take hers in mine and shake it, squeezing very lightly.

She lets go of my hand, reaches out and pushes back my hood. Pretty forward, but whatever. I haven't cut my black hair in a while, so it's pretty shaggy and in my eyes. Girls seem to like the way I look, so I know I'm not exactly ugly. And her gaze seems to indicate that she likes what she's looking at.

"Colt," I say by way of introduction.

"How old are you, Colt?" She asks this as she glances out the window to her left and behind, watching for traffic, leaning forward, and then pulls her BMW off the shoulder and onto the street..

What's the right answer, here? Option A, I tell her my real age. If she's smart, that'll be that. End of story. Or, option B, I tell her I'm eighteen, and we have some fun. I feel like the answer I give will tell me what kind of person I am.

Deep breath. Sigh in frustration. "Seventeen, Helen."

"Damn." She smiles as she says this. She obviously had something in mind when she picked me up, even though she couldn't tell anything about me when she stopped.

"Sorry."

She shrugs. "It's okay. It's shitty out there." She

glances at me. "So. Colton. Why are you out here all by yourself, in this weather?"

"Shit happens."

A nod, as if she knows. "Ah. Running away?"

"Not exactly. They know I'm going, they just don't give a shit."

"Ouch."

"Yeah, well…fuck 'em."

Another knowing nod. "Exactly. Fuck 'em." She reaches down into the cup holder and pulls out a glass bowl. And no, I don't mean an actual bowl, like for cereal, but a blown-glass pipe for smoking pot. "Smoke?"

"Hell yeah."

She hands it to me, reaching into the cup holder again for a lighter. Flick the Bic, baby. Ohhh shit, this is good herb. Like, damn near medical grade, probably name brand. I slump lower in the seat and hold the smoke in as long as I can. Wish I'd thought to stop at my tree and collect up my stash before leaving. I'm blinking dizzily as I blow the smoke out, because the THC hits hard and fast. I glance to the side, and somehow the top three buttons of Helen's shirt have popped open. And fuck me if her bra isn't basically see-through. Sheer black lace. Full view of her breasts, pale skin, small pink areolae, flat button nipples. Turns out I was wrong: the bra isn't much but lace, so it doesn't do much supporting, and I can see that she's got a little sag to her tits. Gravity, man. But still, nice tits. A good handful each.

I take another toke, blow it out, lean my head back against the headrest, roll my head to the side and stare. "All right, then." Hand her the bowl and lighter. "Thanks. Good shit."

She grins at me. Glances down, "Them," lifts the bowl and lighter, "or this?"

I grin and shrug. "Both." I blink hard and begin to float, because I'm high as shit. "But I'm still only seventeen, Helen."

"Doesn't mean you can't look." She steers with her knees as she takes a toke.

"True." I watch her inhale and watch the way her chest swells and makes her boobs thrust out. "You probably shouldn't go around picking up guys you don't know off the side of the road. I mean, you got lucky with me, but some other cat you pick up may not have the same manners I do. Not safe, Helen."

She slips a hand between her seat and the center armrest, and brings up a small silver 9mm. "Registered, with a CCW." She replaces it after she's satisfied I've had a good look at it.

I nod and shrug. "Still."

"Thanks for the warning."

We smoke the whole bowl. She's got some stupid-ass pop music playing, but I don't care. We don't talk much as we smoke and drive, which is fine with me. I steal glances at her. I mean, she unbuttoned her shirt so it's not really stealing, is it? I'm not sure what's going on. Or what she wants. This whole thing is surreal; I'm just going with it.

I'm homeless.

I'm in a car with a woman ten or fifteen years older than me. She's got her tits hanging out, we're smoking pot, and she's got a gun. Like…what the fuck?

Is she gonna blow me? Shoot me? Or neither? Maybe she just likes driving around with her boobs out. I really have no idea what to expect next.

She takes me to a Greyhound station in downtown Detroit. The parking lot is basically empty, but she parks in the far back, in a corner, in the shadows. She unbuckles her seatbelt and then turns to stare at me. "Well, here we are. Where are you headed now?"

Pot makes truth come out, I guess. "Anywhere. I'll take the first bus I can afford."

She licks her lips. Eyes me. "How about I make you feel good, before you go?"

"Why, Helen?"

"You want the truth?"

I nod. "For sure."

"I'm lonely. I'm married, but my husband cheats on me. He doesn't love me, and I don't love him. It's a marriage of convenience. He's rich, which makes me a trophy wife. I don't know if I want to leave him, because I like having money. I like having a nice car and a big house with a closet full of expensive clothes. I know it's totally shallow, but…I was a runaway too once, so I know what it's like to not have anything."

"So you're lonely. You pick up homeless runaways and get them high and blow them?"

She laughs, a breezy titter. "Oh hell no. Just the really fucking sexy ones."

"Oh." Not sure what else I'm supposed to say. "Thanks, I guess."

"So." She reaches under the steering wheel, raises it up out of the way. Then she tugs the bra down under her breasts, baring them. Damn, they're nice. "Lean your seat back. Hands off and let me do all the work."

Shit. How can I say no? "Okay."

I find the button on the side of my seat. I tilt it back as far as it'll go. I get comfortable and then tuck my hands under my head and watch as she leans over the console. She tugs the hem of my hoodie up and unbuckles my belt. Pops the button of my jeans, and lowers the zipper. She glances up at me, a lopsided smile on her face. She really is getting off on this. So fucking weird. I watch as she tugs my boxer briefs away from my stomach, and pulls them down. I lift up and she works my jeans under my ass. I'm hard, way hard.

"Damn, Colt. You're a big boy, aren't you?"

"If you say so." I grin, though, because I most girls I've hooked up with have made similar comments.

She wraps both hands around my cock and flutters her touch up and down. Jesus, she's good at this and it feels damn good. She doesn't spend much time using her hands, though; bending over me, her tits brushing my thigh, she takes my cock into her mouth. Hot, wet. Tight—god*damn*, this is the best blow job I've ever gotten. She sucks hard, then backs away and licks me. She looks up at me, blinking, big green eyes telling me she's finding something in this. A smile, then she licks her lips, and puts her mouth on me again. Takes me deep, real deep. I've never had a girl deep throat me before; high school girls aren't much for technique so much as eagerness and fun. This is…a whole new level.

"Fuuuuck." I can't help the groan.

"Yeah?"

"Fuck yeah."

She hums as she goes down on my cock. I watch and feel myself hardening in her mouth as she sucks and bobs, using tongue and lips and teeth. The humming drives me crazy.

She backs off and wraps her hands around me. "Tug my hair twice when you're about to blow, okay?"

I nod. "Got it."

She leans closer, her eyes on me. "And Colt? You can move, if you want. Use your hips. I can take it."

With her mouth on me again I have no chance to respond. I can't help doing what she said, working up with my hips, fucking her mouth. She hums, or maybe it's moaning. Whatever, it feels damn good. She reaches back and brushes flyaway hair out of her face, but doesn't lose her rhythm. She's really going to town, now, bobbing fast and furious. I don't want this to end, because it feels so fucking good. And, because in the back of my head, I know once it's over, I'll have to get out of the car and face the fact that I'm alone in the world.

But for now, I'm getting my dick sucked.

And damn, I need this.

I feel come surging in my balls, and I reach down, gently tug a lock of her hair twice. When I do this, she moans and goes lower. Lifts in her chair and angles her head down, takes me as far as I can go, so deep her nose touches my belly. I can hear her breathing through her nose, groaning a little. Her hands are on my thighs, gripping tight. Bobbing, backing away an inch or so and then back down, she repeats the rhythm hard and fast. My cock has to be filling most of her throat. I almost feel guilty for what that must feel like. But she's doing it voluntarily. So…

"Ohhhh Jesus, Jesus-fuck." I tug her hair again.

"Mmmmhhhmmm," she moans.

She takes my hands and places them in her hair. She'd told me not to touch, so I didn't. But now she's put my hands in her hair and I'm going for it, pulling at her gently. Harder, then involuntarily as I get ready to blow my load.

"Ohhh holy…fuck…" I groan.

I come, then, hard. So fucking hard. I hear Helen gulp, and then she backs away and takes the rest of my come, swallows it, goes back down, taking me deep, swallowing so I can feel her throat muscles rippling tight around my cock. Fuck, this feels good.

Finally, I'm done, and Helen is sitting up. Her tits hang and sway.

"I feel like I should return the favor," I say. "That was fucking incredible."

She runs her wrist across her mouth and licks her lips. "I'm glad you enjoyed it."

I lean my head back and sigh. Then raise my seat and adjust my pants, buckle and zip. "For real. Lift your skirt up. I'll help you out, too."

She shakes her head. "No, thanks. I'll flick my bean later, and think of you. I'll use my vibrator and pretend it's you."

"Sure?"

"I'm sure. That was for you."

"Why? I still don't get it."

"I can't do much to help you. Give you a ride; give you some good memories to hold on to. Like I said, I've been homeless. I wish I could do more for you. This…was what I could give you. And besides, I enjoyed it too."

"Well…thanks."

She hands me the bowl, which is just about cashed, but has one hit left in it. "Hit the bowl one last time. For the road."

I hit it, inhale, and hold it. I take one more glance at her tits, and blow out the smoke. Reach for my bag; twist the strap in my fist.

She tugs her bra back up and buttons her shirt. "Remember me."

"Couldn't forget if I wanted to." I lean toward

her, giving her a hug. "No more picking up homeless boys. Even with the gun. And leave your husband."

She just waves her hand. "I probably never will. He cheats, I cheat. But I will agree to no more homeless boys."

I shove the car door open, step out, and then sling my bag onto my shoulder. "Bye, Helen."

"Bye, Colt. Be safe. Watch your back."

She waits until I'm in the station before driving away.

I have a moment, then, in which I wonder if that really just happened. I'm nice and tingly down below, which is a nice reminder that, yes, it did indeed just happen.

The departure board presents a challenge, since I can't read for shit and all the words are really tiny. I end up having to swallow my pride and ask a cashier at the ticket booth for departure times.

The only bus leaving any time soon is for Toledo in ten minutes. Twenty bucks.

Not very far, but better than sitting around here. Digging in my bag for the cash, I pull out a few extra bills so I don't have to keep doing this. I pay the fare, then go to wait outside at the bus stop. I think of Helen and her nice tits and her mouth.

Again I wonder why that happened. I mean, how

fucking lonely does a woman have to be to do that? It actually makes me kind of sad, thinking about a beautiful woman like Helen being lonely enough to pick up a random stranger off the side of the road and suck his dick like that. That's pretty fucking lonely.

The bus shows up, and I stumble on. I'm high as fuck, and it's lovely.

The trip is not long—a little over an hour—and I soon find myself sitting in the Toledo Greyhound station. It's then that the munchies hit me. I forget about that for a minute and wonder where to go next. I think there are buses leaving for New York, Philadelphia, Florida, Texas...I have to really focus on the board just to make out individual city names, and again, end up having to ask someone to tell me the times and destinations. Here, though, the cashier is a jackass, some cranky old codger who just shoves a printed schedule at me.

I pull out a granola bar, and then another, and I'm conscious that I should probably be sparing with my food since it's little enough, and it's all I have. A thousand bucks won't last long.

Instead, I eat an apple and stare at the bus schedule. The letters and words are a jumble to me, but finally I am able to identify the words *New York*.

New York. Why not? I mentioned it as a throw-away comment to Mom, but…

Fuck it. New York it is. I buy a seventy-seven-buck ticket for New York. The guy at the counter tells me the bus is leaving at eleven tonight so I've got a bit of a wait. There are a few magazines in the waiting room but, shit man, I can't fucking read. And that only serves as a depressing reminder about why I am here in the first place. I choose a magazine with a picture of a sweet-ass hypercar on it. I have to focus on the words very carefully and block out the sounds around me, block out the distorted voice on the PA, block out everything. Just to figure out the fucking title.

Mot—Mot…Motor…Tre…Trend? Motor Trend?

That only took like five fucking minutes to figure out.

I flip open the first page and even by squinting and focusing I can't figure out any of the words I'm seeing. The words are too damn small, and there's too many of them. The letters distort and twist and then vanish. I turn the page and there's a photo of a sexy blonde standing beside a sweet custom classic Charger. Man, I could do that. I could build that car. I could polish the body and paint it, I could fabricate brand new chrome bumpers and strip the engine and rebuild it, put in a killer six-speed manual and a custom exhaust, something growly and snarly that'd give that bitch some serious legs.

I daydream: my own shop. Racks and racks of tools, fucking towers of Craftsman toolboxes, a couple hydraulic lifts, some long benches and big-ass tables for laying an engine out in order...I could do it. If I had the money, I could do it.

Dad could've floated me the seed cash, and I could've done it. Started small, and then built it up myself and paid him back. But fucking no.

Go to college, Colton.

You're stupid, Colton.

You're an idiot, Colton.

I must have dozed off, because the next thing I hear is the PA squawking. I make out the words "... New York...." and lurch to my feet, rubbing my eyes. I swing my bag over my shoulder and head for the bus.

It's full. I'm lucky to be just barely making the last boarding call. There's only one open seat, next to a nasty old toothless white guy who smells heavily of booze and cigarettes. I take the seat, settle my backpack on the floor between my legs, and within moments the bus is rumbling and moving. The overhead lights go out, and then the only light comes from the little reading lights dotting the interior. Most people are trying to sleep.

It hits me about an hour later: Toledo is only an hour from Detroit, and Detroit is only an hour or so from home. It would have been so easy to make it back home without too much trouble. But I'm two hours from Detroit now, and when I get off this bus again, I'll be in New York City. Turning around at that point won't be so easy. This is fucking permanent, man. I'm by myself.

I'm alone.

I'm homeless.

Three: Winners and Losers

IT'S FUNNY SOMETIMES HOW SUBTLE DISASTER CAN BE.

The bus ride is easy. I sleep for most of it. I wake up at one point and drink a can of Coke, and eat another apple, and another granola bar. I'm almost out of food and I've been gone for less than twelve hours. I'm down to a package of crackers and one can of Coke.

The bag containing the rest of my money lies at the bottom of my backpack. I zip the backpack and stuff it between my legs. I keep it near me at all times, zipped up tight.

I drift back to sleep and wake up as the bus is squealing to a halt. I blink, rub my eyes and pull myself together. It's late morning, and I'm in New York

City. I stand up, grabbing my backpack, and then I notice that the zipper is open, just a little. Not a lot, but enough that I notice. This is weird, because I know I had closed it. And it's the little things, right? Whenever I close my backpack, I always zip it all the way to one side or the other, because that way if things shift inside the zipper won't accidentally rip open. I had that happen once in sophomore year. I had all my books with me because my locker was in the farthest upper ass-end of the school and I wasn't about to schlep up there after every class. I'd gone to shoulder my bag and it had popped open and spilled everything everywhere. Embarrassing. So after that I always zip it closed to one side. Never at the top.

And now, the zippers on my backpack are up top, in the middle and open just a bit.

The dude pushes past me and hops off the bus real quick, disappearing into the crowd of the Port Authority bus station. The speed with which he flies past me and off the bus lights a little fire of suspicion. So I sit back down and open my bag.

I see crackers,

A can of Coca-Cola,

Clothes,

But no cash.

FUCK.

"FUCK!" I shout it out loud.

"Excuse me, young man. No call for that kind of language." An old black woman, graying dreadlocks tied back by a large rubber band, looks at me.

"Sorry. But that asshole stole my money." I gesture at the seat where he'd been. "Or someone did."

She gives me a sympathetic look. "I didn't see nothin', honey. Sorry."

I want to cry. I don't, I can't, but if I could, I probably would. "People, man. Fuckin' people."

She shakes her head, her thick queue of hair swinging. "Hard luck. Sorry, honey." And then she's gone.

No one else says anything, or even bothers to look at me.

I'm broke. Totally broke. I dig into my pocket and find a single crumpled five-dollar bill.

Alone in New York, homeless, and now broke with five bucks to my name.

Nothing to do but handle it, I guess. I trudge off the bus and scan the crowd for the old guy, but he's nowhere to be seen. The crowd of people is like nothing I've ever seen before. People of every age, race, and size mill in a never-ending sea, and finding one face, even one I knew well, would be impossible. So finding one man I hardly noticed when I first boarded the bus? Impossible. Besides, he's probably long gone by now, with my cash.

I follow the crowd out of the station and onto to the main road, ignoring the hustlers trying to take advantage of kids exactly like me: young, homeless, and scared. I may not be book-smart, but I know better. I push past them, pretend they don't exist.

For a second I lose my breath. Reality hits *hard*.

I'm in New York Fucking City. The road is a river of cars, many of them the iconic Yellow Cab. The sidewalk is crammed with people. The noise is deafening. Engines, horns, brakes, voices. A whistle sounds off to my right, and I turn to look, see a policeman blasting on his traffic whistle. I follow my instincts and end up at the intersection of Eighth and West Forty-second. I have no idea what that means, or where in the city I am.

Where do I go? What do I do?

I'm hungry. I'm used to eating a lot more than granola bars and apples and shit. I work out a lot, so I'm used to bulking up on protein shakes and eggs and meat, lots of protein to pack on the muscle. I have to shit. I'm tired.

What the hell did I get myself into?

How the hell am I going to survive? My throat is tight. My chest aches and my eyes burn. I only slept fitfully on the bus, so I've been awake for…shit, almost two days.

I tell myself to calm down. To think. Be rational. I can *do* this.

The first thing I need to do is get a job. This is the Big Apple, there's got to be a garage or something where I can pick up some work. Changing oil, sweeping floors, shit, anything. I'll clean toilets.

First thing, though, is to start walking and find a garage.

One foot in front of the other, I follow Eighth Avenue and just keep walking and watching. I end up in Central Park, which is beautiful and interesting, but not what I need right now. I walk back out to the city itself, along a street I think is called Central Park West. I have no clue where I'm going so I start turning up streets at random and end up on…Sixty-fourth. I stop at the corner of Broadway. The real fuckin' Broadway. And, for a moment, as I take in the lights and the people and the magic, I forget why I ended up here in the first place.

At little further up the block I see a sign that, after some puzzling, I make out as "Emergency Auto Repair", and I go in.

Leaning thick forearms on scratched counter is a big, bald white guy. He's got tats, earrings and is wearing blue coveralls. "Help you?"

"Yeah, I'm looking for work. I've got a lot of experience with automotive repair, I can take apart and reassemble—"

"Not hiring. Sorry." He pushes upright and crosses his arms over his chest.

"For real, I can do it blindfolded. I'll work the desk, I'll clean the floors—"

"Said we ain't hiring, kid. Fuck off." His stare is cold, flat.

"Do you know anybody who is?" I ask, aware that I'm pushing my luck.

"No. Scram." He moves as if to come around the desk, which tells me this won't end well for me if I don't leave *right now*.

I leave and end up retracing my path back south, this time walking along Columbus, where I see another auto repair shop on Fifty-fifth. This place has a different vibe. Behind the counter is a woman with limp dishwater blond hair, a rough-looking lady who's obviously seen better days.

"Hi. I'm looking for work." I start talking before she's even acknowledged me or said hello.

She doesn't even bother to look up from the computer screen. She's wearing glasses, so I can see in the reflection that she's playing solitaire. "Piss off, kid."

"I need a job, ma'am. I work hard, I know engines—"

"We're not hiring. Unless you got a car that needs fixing, go away."

I leave and keep walking, but I have no clue where I am or where I'm going. Lost. Tired. Sore feet. Hungry. Scared. And then I have an idea: I'll find a phone book with Yellow Pages, and start looking up all the garages and repair shops in the area.

I duck into the next doorway I see—it's a Chinese restaurant. I ask to use their phone book and the little old Asian guy tosses it to me without a word. I take it and sit down at an empty booth. I take a deep breath and summon all my attention, then I flip open the four-inch-thick book.

Fuck. Tiny-ass words. How the hell are you supposed to read this shit? Jesus. I turn to the Yellow Pages but it takes for-fucking-ever to find the auto repair section, and even longer to copy the addresses down on the scrap of paper I asked for. My handwriting looks like a five-year-old's. Childish scribbles and scrawls.

All told, it takes me over half an hour to find and copy out five addresses and phone numbers.

I ignore my exhaustion and hunger, mainly because I don't really have a choice. After leaving the restaurant, I stop at a little kiosk on the sidewalk that sells magazines and cigarettes and such and ask for a map. The young Hispanic guy behind the counter says he doesn't sell maps but tells me to try a hotel, which sometimes have tourist maps. So I go in search of a hotel and finally find one. The map they give me is basically a cartoon, but it provides me with a basic understanding of the layout of the island of Manhattan, I realize; it's probably better for my illiterate ass than a real map, to be honest. Maybe I should venture out of Manhattan and try to look for work in another area—maybe Brooklyn or the Bronx.

Tomorrow, I decide. That's a long-ass walk, I'm guessing.

In the meantime I manage to find the five auto repair shops on my list. They are scattered across the city, dozens of blocks apart. I spend hours and hours just walking, but not one person will even give me the time of day.

Not hiring, kid.

Sorry, we got all the help we need.

Piss off, kid.

Come back in a couple years.

Go away, kid.

It's late evening by the time I decide I have to sit down before I pass out. And that's when I start to wonder where I'm going to sleep tonight.

Central Park, maybe? It's big, so there's got to be somewhere I can catch a couple hours of sleep.

Of course, when I finally decide to try it, I'm a half-hour walk away. By the time I get there I hurt all over, and then I have to hunt through the park for somewhere to crash. There are people everywhere, even at this time of the night, walking, running, biking, rollerblading, in couples and alone and with dogs. I see a cop on foot, friendly looking, thumbs hooked into his gear belt. Smiling at people, waving, just strolling through the park.

Okay, correction, Central Park is fucking mammoth. I've been walking these damn paths for what must be an hour, and I'm totally lost. There are a lot of paths and a lot of open space.

Dark is coming on fast. There are fewer and fewer people around and eventually I feel like the only person around. Then a few more late-night types emerge—a guy on a bike passes me, wearing a helmet with a light attached, a runner with a headlamp, a couple walking a huge dog, each carrying flashlights.

Finally, after much searching I find a bench located in a shadowy alcove, under a canopy of trees. Before me I can see the tops of the towering buildings—tiny squares of light peeking up over the tree line in the distance.

I toss my backpack on one end of the bench, lay my head on it, curl up and try to get comfortable.

Fuck, it feels good to lie down. My feet ache. My stomach growls—I haven't had a proper meal in two days.

I miss home: a real bed, real food, shit, I even miss Kyle, just a little.

This is the last thought I have before sleep takes me away from my aches and pains and the deep loneliness I feel.

Whack. "Yo, wake up, man. Can't sleep here." *Whack.*

Each *whack* is accompanied by a sharp, painful smack of a hand to my shoulder. I roll, sit up, and I'm blinded by a flashlight, a body behind it, a cop. Blackness behind him, silhouetting the angles of his cap.

I shield my face against the blinding flashlight. "All right, all right. Can you get that out of my face?"

He lowers the flashlight and shines it at my chest, the bench, my hands. Checking for weapons, maybe. His hand isn't quite on the butt of his gun, but near it. Ready to palm it and blast me, probably. Or maybe not.

"Up." His voice is deep, and judging solely by the sound of his voice, I'm guessing he's black. "Get a move on, man. Outta the park."

"I don't know the way out of the park," I say.

He shines the beam of light to his left, illuminating a cross-path in the distance. "Take that, it'll lead you out."

"Okay, thanks." I shoulder my bag as I stand up. I stretch and work the kinks out of my back.

"Must be new here if you're tryna sleep on a bench in the park." He's making small talk, waiting for me to get moving.

"Yes sir. Just got here yesterday. Today, whatever."

"Nowhere to go?"

I head toward the path he indicated. "No sir. On my own." I may be a teenager, but I was raised by upper-class parents, and they taught me to show respect for cops. Saying "sir" is ingrained.

"Between you and me, kid, you ain't gonna catch any sleep on a bench. Find an alley, or under a bridge somewheres. Watch your back, but you gotta better chance that way."

"Thanks, Officer."

He watches me as I turn onto the path, and then I see his light flick off, and he keeps walking. Humming a song, a tune I recognize from the radio.

The city streets are better lit than the park, but

it's not the rural night landscape I'm used to. No stars, no silence, no crickets. I used to sit out on the dock back home, late at night, listen to crickets and owls and the waves, and stare up at a sky full of stars. Now I'm in the big city, and the only sounds are cars and horns and ambient urban blare.

I have no choice but to walk and walk and walk.

Again, I'm not sure where I'm headed. I'm just walking to stay awake. Walking to be doing something.

Several hours later the sky turns from black to gray and begins to lighten, and I'm still walking. Trudging like a zombie. I crossed a long-ass bridge at some point. Water way below, girders above, semis and taxis roaring past. I'm not in Manhattan anymore, but I'm not sure where I am. The buildings are smaller—there are no highrises here. I notice more graffiti on the walls. Fewer taxis. Security bars on the windows, not as many lights, more trash in the gutters.

Barely past dawn, I see a tall, thin black guy wearing mechanic's coveralls cross the street ahead of me, carrying a lunchbox. He's got big bright purple headphones on his ears, the cord trailing down into the open front of his coveralls. He has a bit of a limp, and I can see that his eyes are scanning his surroundings, his head constantly swiveling. He sees me approaching him and halts, tenses.

He tugs the headphones down around his neck.

"What'chu want, man?"

"You're a mechanic?"

"Yeah, why?" He's still tensed, hands in his pock-et. Probably fingering a weapon.

I keep my hands on the straps of my backpack so they are visible. "I'm looking for work. I know cars, I know engines. I'll do anything."

He backs up. "Can't help you. Sorry, man. I just got work myself. Change the oil and shit. They just hired me, probably won't hire nobody else."

"Fuck." I back up, lift my chin at him. "Thanks."

"Yeah, man." He watches me over his shoulder as he walks away.

I keep walking. The gray dawn turns to day, and I'm miles and miles from where I started—that bench in Central Park. Early morning quickly turns to noon, and in that time I've changed directions, asked for work at three more garages. It's all I know, and it's all the talent I have to offer. I don't think much of my chances of applying for anything else. Applications mean writing. Mean reading. Answering questions. *Name a time you provided excellent customer service*. I re-member that from the application I had to fill out for Mr. Boyd. He made me fill it out, I don't know why.

So I'd know how, I guess.

I spend the day walking. The entire fucking day. It ain't like the neighborhoods are labeled or anything, so I've got no clue where I am. I'm in a worn-down area, not quite a ghetto but, being white, I stand out for sure, especially in broad daylight.

Near sundown, I see a guy struggling to get a couch onto a moving van by himself. How he got it this far, I don't know. It's a big-ass leather couch, and it looks heavy as hell.

"Hey man, need help?" I ask, approaching him.

He sets the end down, wipes sweat off his forehead. "Sure." He hops up into the moving van. "Grab the end, lift it up."

I help him get the couch into the moving van and positioned against the wall.

He hops down. "Thanks."

I follow him and we lean back against the truck. "No problem," I say.

He eyes me. He's Hispanic, short and thick, with a sleeveless shirt revealing tats from shoulder to knuckles. "I got some other shit to bring down. My boy was supposed to help me, but he bailed on me. I'll toss you a ten-spot if you help me with the rest."

"Fuck, man, I'll help you for some *food*. I ain't eaten in a few days."

He digs into the hip pocket of his baggy shorts, the hem of which hangs to mid-shin. "Sucks." He pulls out a pack of cigarettes. "Smoke?"

I take one, and he lights mine and then his own with a plain silver Zippo lighter. We smoke in silence, and then he tosses his butt out into the road and indicates for me to follow him. His apartment is two floors up, and he's got his shit packed in boxes, all piled in his living room, a stack of framed posters near the door, a recliner to match the couch, a big TV wrapped up in a comforter.

I spend an hour helping him get his stuff onto the truck. When the apartment is empty, he digs in his pocket and hands me the rest of his cigarettes, his Zippo, and a ten-dollar bill.

"I'm about to do a nickel at the pen, so I got no food to give you. Puttin' all my shit in storage."

I extend the Zippo back toward him. "You wanna keep your lighter?"

He shrugs. "It'll just get taken when I turn myself in." He holds up his hand, and I clap palms with him, lean in, bump shoulders. The thug-hug, I think of it. "There's a bridge a few blocks north. Good spot to crash."

"Thanks."

He climbs up into the moving truck, rolls the

window down, and rests his arm on the door frame, ink covering his forearms and knuckles. He drives off. I never even got his name.

He leans out of the window, about twenty feet away. "Yo, man! Check the bottom of the pack!" Then he turns the corner, and he's gone.

I bring out the pack, nudge aside the last few cigarettes, and see that he's stashed a nugget of pot at the bottom. Enough to tip a couple smokes. Score.

I head north and see the bridge he mentioned. It's just a little overpass; two lanes with a gap between them letting down a ribbon of light. Steeply angled concrete walls rise from the road underneath to meet the bridge overhead, leaving a low, narrow ridge at the top where the two structures meet. Tags mark the concrete, overlapping black and red paint in dramatic swirls and lines and arcs, indecipherable unless you know what you're looking at. Glancing around for traffic and onlookers, I find things empty for the moment. I climb up the concrete wall and, at the top, the bridge is so close and low that I can't stand up straight.

There's a pile of newspapers in the middle of the ledge; most are ripped and torn and stained, obviously having been there a while. Good enough. I lie down on them, put my head on my backpack, and tuck my hands into my armpits. Curl up.

Dark. Cool. Not quite cold, but enough to make me sit up, dig in my backpack for a hoodie. I tug the hood over my head and lie back down.

Concrete, even cushioned by newspapers, isn't comfortable.

I manage to sleep, though.

For a while.

I'm woken by a vicious kick to my back, knocking the wind out of me. "My spot!" A shout, guttural, enraged. "Get outta my spot!"

Another kick, but I'm already moving, rolling, knees up to protect my stomach and nuts. Take the kick to my shins, make out the face of an old, grizzled white man with a long dirty gray beard. My shins scream from the kick, but I'm up, on my feet, backpedaling.

The old bum lunges at me. "My spot, motherfucker! Stay out of my spot!"

I'm dazed with sleep, breathless from the kick to my back, dizzy and faint with hunger.

Rage suffuses me. "Fuck you, old man! I found it. I'm sleeping there."

We crash into each other. He's skinny and wiry, but strong. Hard. Knees and elbows and fists crack into me, ramming into my gut over and over and over. I tense my muscles and take it, shove him back, lash out. Normally, this old man would be down in seconds, but I'm literally faint with hunger. Three days, maybe more since I've had something decent to eat. No sleep but for a few winks here and there, all of it interrupted. Hours of walking. I'm not at the top of my game.

But I'm desperate. I *need* to sleep.

So I fight hard. It's messy, man. He's a tough old fuck, takes the body blows and gives 'em back just as hard. He smashes my nose with his forehead, and I'm bleeding. I manage to get a knee up and shove it into his groin, a dirty move, but shit, this is about winning. It's about survival. I'm not sure he won't kill me if I lose. I can't lose. Don't dare lose.

Red stains my vision, and my eye hurts. My eyebrow is split open. I blink the blood away and see that the old dickhead is slowing down, hobbling. I remember vaguely nailing him in the thigh, a move I learned the hard way: if you get nailed hard enough in the right spot in your thigh, it'll fuckin' cripple your ass. Now I rush him, both fists swinging in hard sloppy haymakers, one crushes into his cheekbone, the other his ribs. I feel something crack.

He coughs, stumbles, trips, and slides down the concrete. He comes to rest against the pillars separating the road from the embankment.

I watch. He moans, stirs, but doesn't get up.

Shit, that could be me down there.

I watch for another minute, and eventually he gets up, slowly. Stares up at me. Throws me the finger, but hobbles away, vanishing into the shadows.

I lurch back to my spot. My hard-won spot. I lie down again. The world spins worse than being drunk. Everything hurts.

I'm fading fast, but something keeps me awake. I hear a footstep.

Goddamn it. I just want to sleep.

"Hell of a fight, man." The voice is deep and slow, a ways off.

I sit up. Peer blearily into the shadows. "Yeah."

"Ol' Bruce has been in that spot for years. Seen him wreck some folks to keep 'em off." Flame spurts, an orange glow appears. Smoke wreathes upward; the glowing cherry illuminates a round, black face, white teeth.

"I just needed somewhere to sleep. He kicked me while I was laying here."

"I ain't said nothin'. Bruce is a miserable old fucker. Hates everybody." The glow brightens, tobacco crackles.

I light my own smoke, stay where I am. Fought

for this spot, not giving it up easily. I feel an urge to defend myself, to fill the silence. But I don't.

Eventually the other guy tosses his cigarette away and I sense he is considering something. "Wanna make a hundred bucks right quick?"

"Doing what?" I ask.

"I'll show you."

I know better. I'm cursing myself for an idiot even as I stand up and follow the guy. I'm gonna get shot. Rolled. Something. I mean, this is really stupid.

But it's a hundred bucks. With a hundred bucks I could get a motel room and sleep in a bed.

Not much I won't do for a hundred bucks, at this point.

So I shoulder my bag and follow the guy, leaving the spot I just fought somebody for. He leads me out from under the bridge, and an orange streetlight reveals him to be a black guy about five years older than me, wearing baggy black jeans, Timberland boots, a black T-shirt, black Yankees ball cap turned on an angle, tilted, over a stretchy headband. He walks with a confident swagger. Doesn't look back to see if I'm following—he knows I am. He's muscular, heavy-set, but deceptively light on his feet. And as I'm following him, I notice the way the back of his T-shirt hangs over his jeans, revealing the handle of a pistol in his waistband.

What am I getting myself into?

Shit.

He leads me off the main road and down an alley. Shit, shit, shit. I'm for sure about to get killed. I slow down, putting space between me and the other guy.

He notices. "Hey, man. Keep up. I ain't gonna do nothin'."

"Like you would tell me if you were?"

He laughs. "Got that right." He gestures at an old Buick. "Get in. We goin' for a drive."

I slide into the passenger seat. The car smells like old car, cigarettes, pot, something harder, crack maybe. He starts the car, and the engine turns over immediately. He revs the engine, and it responds with the deep bass snarl of an engine definitely not original to the Buick.

"What you got under the hood?" I ask.

He glances at me, shrugs. "350. I had my boy hook me up."

Meaning, he don't know much about the engine but what his friend told him. There are all kinds of "350" engine blocks, varying by year, original manufacturer, bore, stroke, a whole bunch of shit. Saying it's a 350 is like saying it's a V-8—a little vague.

The outside of the car doesn't look like much, a

little beat up, rust on the edges. The inside is comfy, that old velvety material on the seats. Custom stereo receiver and speakers, probably some big-ass woofers in back. It's not the prettiest car on the block, but that engine snarl has the sound of some beefy power, so I'm guessing this old babe can move.

He pulls his car down the alley, navigating without headlights until he hits the main road. The radio is silent. When we're moving down the road, he flips on his lights, twists on the stereo. Rap thuds low, bass vibrating heavily.

A glance at me. "I'm Eli."

"Colt." I watch the buildings pass by, and we drive through the occasional intersection. It's late, the middle of the night. I could be anywhere in New York City right now, and he could be taking me God knows where. I'm such a dumbass. "Where are we going, Eli?"

A white-teeth grin, sidelong glance. "Why, you nervous, white boy?"

"Hell yeah." I say it with a laugh, but it's true.

"I got'chu, man. You wouldn't be in my car if I was gonna cap you." A pause for effect. "That shit is messy."

I glance at him, but this doesn't seem to be a joke. "Right."

He's still not telling me how I'll be making this quick hundred bucks but I don't push it. We drive for a long time, winding through one neighborhood after another, cruising slow. He seems to know exactly where he's going, but he isn't in a hurry to get there. He's always watching his surroundings, eyeing the few people on the sidewalk. He watches the intersections carefully as he cruises through them.

I'm jittery. Nervous. Scared. Knee bouncing, hands curling into fists and uncurling, palms sweaty. My stomach growls loudly.

"Hungry?" Eli asks.

"Been a few days," I admit.

"I got'chu." This seems to be a stock response for Eli, the meaning varying by context.

I watch the digital clock on the stereo receiver. I got in the car at 1:28 a.m.; we've been cruising slowly for almost an hour now. A few minutes later Eli pulls into an alley between two mammoth buildings. It's not really an alley, I realize, so much as just a space between them. Both buildings are old warehouses made of corrugated iron walls with rust streaking down the sides. The windows up near the roof are all smashed and jagged. Glass crunches under the wheels of the Buick. Eli flicks his lights off and on twice, quickly, and then leaves them off. In the distance, the single circle of light from a flashlight winks twice in response.

We roll forward very, very slowly. Eli reaches behind his back, wiggles the handle of his pistol, but doesn't pull it out. My heart is in my throat. The air feels thick and tense.

"Leave your bag. Nobody gonna mess with it in my ride." Eli glances at me as he pulls to a stop, seemingly at random. "I got your back. Don't talk to no one, and stick with me."

"A'ight." It comes out like he'd say it, drawled urban slang.

Eli shoots me a look, but doesn't say anything as he climbs out of his car, tugs at the back of his shirt to keep it from tangling in the butt of his gun. He peers over the roof of his car, and I follow his gaze and see wide doors, pulled open. The doors are big enough to need two guys to open and close them. Lights glow inside, and I hear voices. Cheering, jeering. Thuds. Smacks. *Oohs* and curses. Through the open doors I see a huge crowd forming a ring. I see movement through the milling bodies and a flash of skin. I hear the distinctive crunch of fist meeting meat.

This isn't good.

Not good at all.

We're barely through the doorway when a big

Latino dude emerges from the shadows. He extends his fist, and he and Eli touch knuckles.

"'Sup, Ruiz?"

"Eli." Ruiz glances at me. "Who's this?"

"Colt." Eli tilts his head at a staircase along one wall near the open doors. "Gonna head up there for a minute."

"Two more ahead of you." Ruiz says this as if Eli should know what it means, and Eli just nods as if he does.

It's all very vague, meaningful glances and silences are exchanged. I don't know what to think, but I can guess.

Two more—meaning there will be two more fights, and then I'm up, I think.

Eli leads the way up the stairs, which level off at metal grating forming a catwalk to a large platform overlooking the warehouse. Thin railings form a fence around the perimeter of the platform, and there are couches on two sides and a few tables. People mill around, most are men, and most of them are black or Latino. There are only a few women around, and those are topless and carrying trays. This is quite a set-up. Eli approaches the small crowd on the platform, maybe twenty people in total. A huge beast of a man separates from the crowd, a black guy whose overall dimensions resemble an industrial freezer. He's got diamonds glinting in his ears and sparkling on his fingers.

"Eli. What's good?"

"Found a fighter." Eli doesn't look at me, but he is obviously referring to me.

"He any good?"

"Took down Bruce over by my crib."

A nod. "A'ight, then." A glance at me. "Have a seat, man." A thick finger flicks at a couch.

Eli nods at me, so I head toward the nearest couch, threading between the bodies. I feel stares. I seem to be the only other white person up here besides one of the girls. I watch Eli, who confers with the big dude for a minute. A crook of that forefinger, and one of the topless serving girls trots over, listens, and then nods and jiggles away.

A few seconds later, that same girl finds me on the couch, hands me a bottle of beer and a sandwich wrapped in white butcher paper. A wink and a shimmy of her tits at me, and then she's gone, weaving through the crowd, ignoring hands that freely grope and grab. The sandwich is the best thing I've ever eaten, thin sliced roast beef and cheddar cheese and mayo, lettuce, tomatoes, onions. Fuck, it's good. I have to force myself to go slow, and to sip at the beer.

I haven't forgotten why I'm here.

When I'm done, I wad up the paper and toss it onto the nearby table, then take my beer and stroll over to the railing overlooking the fight. The crowd is huge, hundreds of people. Silver duct tape forms a large square on the concrete floor, and there's another layer of tape around that, forming a perimeter to separate the fighters from the crowd.

One fight just ended, I think. There's blood spattered on the floor. The people in the front row of the crowd have red spots and speckles on their shirts. Money is clutched in pumping fists. The crowd parts, and Ruiz pushes through, leading two other guys. A wiry Middle Eastern guy in his mid-twenties, and a much bigger and much younger black kid.

Ruiz shoves them to separate corners. Points at the Arabic dude and addresses the crowd. "Ibrahim. First fight." Points at the black kid, who's maybe a year older than me. "Julius. Nine fights, seven wins, two losses. Julius is favored. Place your bets."

The fighters bounce and shake hands while the crowd shouts at Ruiz, who makes his way around the front row, collecting cash and handing out slips of paper with numbers written on them. Ones or twos, it looks like. Assuming "1" is Ibrahim, pretty much everyone expects Julius to win.

The fight is short and brutal. Ibrahim is slow and tentative and he only gets in two good hits, right at the start. Julius allowed them, I think, just to get a feel for his opponent's punching power. After those two initial shots, Ibrahim gets destroyed. Just...wrecked. Julius is a whirlwind of fists, going in hard and fast, all jabs like jackhammers. Ibrahim goes to his knees, coughing, spitting blood, holds up a hand; Julius lays him out anyway with a smashing left hook. Ibrahim goes down in a messy spray of sweat, saliva, and blood, a tooth clattering to the concrete.

Nobody helps Ibrahim up. Nobody offers him anything to stop the bleeding. He has to climb to his feet on his own, spitting out red gobs. He manages to drag his carcass out of the ring, ignoring the jeers.

Eli appears beside me. "You're up next, Colt."

"What happens if I lose?" I ask.

"Don't," Eli says.

"But if I do?"

"Win, I'll give you a hundred and a place to sleep, under a roof. Lose, you get nothing. You walk out of here on your own two feet, and that's that. You'll be lucky to walk out of here if you lose, though." He glances at me. "Hundred is for the first fight. More you win, more you make per fight. Julius pulled down three grand for that fight."

"Big jumps," I point out.

"I don't back Julius. He's quick and brutal, but I think someone is gonna drop him for good sometime. He is too cocky."

I don't want to know what that means. The response didn't really answer my question, though. "So I fight once tonight, and make a hundred if I win."

"Yeah. You can fight more than once in a night if you win, and if you want. You win, I'll back you for another, hundred and fifty."

I'm feeling good considering the circumstances. I don't feel hungry anymore, and the beer was nice and cold. I'm wired, now. Adrenalized.

Eli smacks me on the chest with the back of his hand. "Come on, white boy. You're up."

I follow him down the stairs. Eyes follow me. Money changes hands. I'm hot, now. Sweating. Shaking. Feverish. My hands tremble.

When I'm through the crowd, my heartbeat ratchets into a frantic pounding. All I see is eager, blood-lust gleaming eyes, and sweaty faces. Mostly men, but there are a couple of women in the crowd, as well. They're all howling. I strip off my hoodie and hand it to Eli.

I feel something sticky on my face, under my nose. I'd almost forgotten about the fight with Bruce, the bloody nose. I wipe at it, but it's crusted on. I swing my arms, stretch my pectorals. Tense my abs, relax, tense. Bounce, jump. Ribs are a little tender, but nothing too bad.

Adrenaline has me vibrating, bouncing.

Ruiz pushes through the crowd, and the man behind him is a fucking giant. White with blond hair and brown eyes and prison tats. Six-foot-six easily, broad as a barn, shirtless, heavily muscled. Not like a body builder, but like the guys who compete in Strongest Man competitions: heavy slabs of muscle under a layer of fat. The kind of guys that are hard as fuck to hurt.

Ruiz points at me. "Colt. First fight." He gestures at my opponent. "Al, fifth fight. Four wins, one loss. Al is favored. Place your bets."

Al's eyes are eager. He's looking forward to this. He curls his fists, smacks them together, knuckles cracking on knuckles, then grins at me.

Fuck me.

Ruiz glances at each of us, and then steps back. "Fight."

Four: A Bed For the Night

AL SWAGGERS TOWARD ME. HE EXPECTS TO DEMOLISH ME, clearly.

And I'm not sure he's wrong.

I can't think like that, though. I'mma fuck him up.

Al swings first, a slow hard haymaker that would have taken my head off if it had connected. I see it coming a mile away, though, and duck under it. I smash my left hard as I can into his ribs, cutting the punch up and putting my weight into it, twisting into it. That hit should have at least winded him, but he just grunts and grins and lifts his knee into my chest. I stumble backward, wheezing, backpedaling as Al lunges for me.

Okay, so he really telegraphs his shots.

Again, I'm able to move outside the swing, and this time I land a fist on his jaw, and I *know* he felt that shit. Didn't like it, either. He shakes it off, but I'm not done. I'm inside his swing, but I have to be quick. I bet this big boy could pound the life right out of me, if he got hold of me. Two jabs, right-left, quick as I can. Nose, broken; lips, split. Back up, dance back, and let him swing. Stay in range until he's committed to the wild haymaker.

But shit, he ain't as stupid as I thought.

He lets the haymaker go wild, but as I'm ducking in he rams his knee at me. I take the knee to my stomach and taste bile. I can't breathe. Fuck. He's got a big left hamhock of a fist whistling for me, a straight shot I can see coming but can't quite manage to move away from. So I take it. I taste blood in my mouth and spit it out. Fuck, that hurt. But I'm blooded now, and pissed. I curl as many undercut jabs into his diaphragm as I can, as hard as I can, chain-lighting shots right where his ribcage meets in a V unshielded by muscle. That winds him and sends him stumbling. I follow, dribbling blood and saliva from my split lips. I swing my forehead at him and connect a ringer to his chin.

Hint: head-butting someone hurts you, too.

We both stumble back, dizzy. I recover first, but only by a matter of seconds. My right meets his cheekbone, high and hard, and his left hits my ribs, low and hard.

Then mayhem ensues. I close in and hammer my fist without art or technique at his face. Body shots won't do shit to take this beast down, so face shots are all I can hope for. He's hurting, but his punches still have killing power behind them and he can take a hell of a beating. I take one to the nose and feel it break.

But then I get in an uppercut to the jaw and he stumbles and hits his knees.

This is not an arena in which mercy is rewarded.

Like Julius before me, I show none. I piston my fist into his temple, and he topples over.

The crowd, I suddenly realize, is going crazy. That was an upset. Al was favored by a fuckload, I think, and I just lost a lot of people a lot of money. I glance up, and Eli is smirking, a fat blunt in his fingers, a bottle of top-dollar brandy in his hand. A nod; I did good.

I'm a hundred dollars richer for taking a hell of a beating.

I spit blood onto the floor and grimace as I suck in a breath. That motherfucker could hit *hard*. I push through the crowd, ignoring howls and jeers and curses and insults, and go outside under the smog and into the shadows.

The shakes hit me.

"That was some good shit, man." Eli has followed me out; he hands me the blunt, and I toke it long and hard. "Al was favored by a long shot."

"I'm guessing most don't make it more than few seconds with him," I say while holding the smoke in my lungs.

"Nope. He swings wild like that, and if you don't get out the way, you done. I seen him wreck some motherfuckers with that first hit."

"I believe it. I fought guys like him at school. The football jocks back home hated me. They'd sic the linebackers on me in the locker room after gym class. You gotta mash up their faces to knock 'em down."

"Well, you knocked his ass down." He hands me five twenty-dollar bills. "You done, or you want to try for another hundred?"

I eye the brandy in his hand, and he sees me looking, lets me take a swig. Burns so good, baby. Dizzy, a few aches. Still spitting blood. "How long until I'd be up again?"

Eli turns sideways, facing the open door. "Hey, Ruiz! When's the next opening?"

"Julius is going again, then Hector…" a pause,

"Marshawn, and two new guys. Then we got Jesus ready to go but nobody to fight him."

Eli glances at me. "Jesus in four rounds. Twenty minutes or so."

"I'll take him."

Eli lifts his eyebrows. "You sure about that? You ain't seen Jesus fight, yo. He ain't no joke."

I'm money-hungry and feeling rash. "I'll take my chances."

A shrug, a gleam of amusement in his eyes. "A'ight then." He pivots to shout at Ruiz. "My boy Colt here got the spot against Jesus."

A bark of laughter. "Man, your boy has some co-jones. Jesus is *mean*."

This talk isn't making me feel good about my decision. They're making Jesus out to be worse than Al. I better stay warmed up. I drop to the rough as-phalt, bust out thirty pushups, slow and steady, hold 'em on the downbeat for two seconds, push back up slow. I jump up, do jumping jacks until I'm panting and sweating, then drop to the ground again and do mountain climbers until everything aches and shakes. I rest a minute and just breathe, then drop to the ground, do a single pushup, swing my torso up and plant my feet between my hands and leap as high ver-tically as I can, land, and drop down to do another pushup. I repeat the sequence until I'm gasping.

Eli watches with amusement. "What the hell is that bullshit?"

I peel my shirt off, wipe my face with it. "It's how you stay ripped without a gym."

Eli eyes my abs, which, admittedly, are pretty ripped. When you're bored as fuck and sick of doing goddamned homework but you can't leave your room, what do you do? Work out till you pass out. At least, that's what I did. Got some dumbbells and installed a pull-up bar in the barn. Honed my routine so I could work on isolating parts of my physique. They were mostly all bodyweight routines since I never really had access to a proper gym with machines. I mean, there was one at school, but there was no fucking way I was gonna spend one more damn second in that hellhole than I had to, and no way I was gonna ask Dad to buy me freeweights or some shit, nor was I gonna spend my money on them.

Pair an hour-a-day workout routine with a tendency to get in fights, multiply that by a healthy dose of rage, and what do you get?

Me, ready to wreck some shit.

Jumping jacks and spaceman jumps, and then Eli is handing me a bottle of water, which I down. The hit of dope and swig of brandy have been burned away for the most part, so now I'm just loose and limber, sweaty, beefed up.

Ruiz sticks his head out. "Colt's up next, *ese*."

"Man, I ain't'cho fuckin' *ese*, Ruiz." Harsh words are accompanied by a grin and a slap of palms, a gesture at me. "Come on, man. Hope all that jumpin' around got you ready for this shit."

Ruiz grabs me by the shoulder, shoves me forward, pauses, reaches out and takes a short, lean, wiry Hispanic dude—whom I'm assuming is Jesus—by the back of the neck, shoves us both toward the crowd, which parts to let us through. Once in the ring, Jesus does the pre-fight bouncing, fake swings and jabs. Rolls his head on his neck. He's not ripped, but he's lean. Hard. Ugly, beady eyes, nose too big, jutting jaw and a permanent snarl on his face. He's fought already tonight, judging by the split lip and crusted blood under his nose.

I don't bother bouncing or jumping, this time. I simply roll my shoulders, spit pink, flex my fists. Eye my opponent.

This is going to be nasty.

Ruiz is between us. He gestures at Jesus. "Jesus, fifteen fights. No losses. Heavily favored." Motherfucking shit—not good at all. "Colt, one fight, one win."

He glances at both of us. No mention of rules, now that I think of it. "Fight." He steps back.

Jesus is on me before the word has left Ruiz's lips, before he's even stepped back all the way. Hands wrapped around the back of my neck, knee flashing like a jackhammer, bashing into my stomach—one, two, three times. Steps back, launches a straight right rocket that catches me on the chin, sends me backward.

Fucking hell. Can't breathe, and that chin-shot was a bitch.

But I ain't one.

Let him come at me, step inside his next punch, wrap my right arm around his left elbow and under his armpit, lock it out. Step sideways, lifting up. Right hand is a wrecking ball on Jesus's ribcage, battering, battering, battering. He's in agony, but takes it without a sound. Makes like he's gonna punch me with his right hand, but switches tactics at the last second, jabs his thumb at my eye. I manage to turn my head aside at last second and merely get the skin under my eye socket ripped open by his thumb. Blood sluices freely and hot down my face, and I curse in surprise. This lets him jag his knee into my kidney, which forces me to let him go. He doesn't back off, doesn't take a second to catch his breath. Just comes right at me, snarling, grinning, and punching like a machine gun. Hard and fast. Most land on my stomach and sides, which I can take for a good bit. Tense, backpedal, curl in, feel his skinny bony fists hammering at my abdomen without letup.

I time my hit between punches, twist away, feel his fist smack against my back, and then I'm pivoting on my heel, swinging my fist around in an arc, putting momentum and all my weight into the swing. My fist lands on his liver like a fucking Mack truck, and he gasps breathlessly, curses in Spanish, lurches forward. I follow in, growling, grunting as I land blow after blow to the same spot. Liver, liver, liver, until I'm sure he'll be pissing blood for a week. When he staggers, finally, I swagger in, smash my forehead right near my hairline onto the bridge of his nose.

I feel a crack and then I see stars.

Jesus goes limp and collapses to the ground, bleeding from both nostrils.

I'm hurting, now. Bad.

I back away, chin lifted high, watching as Jesus writhes on the floor.

The crowd is silent, now. Or nearly so, silent but for murmurs of shock.

I'm gonna feel this tomorrow.

But then I'm out of the ring and Eli is handing

me an old ratty blue hand towel and another bottle of water.

I hold the towel against my cheek. "He tried to gouge my fuckin' eye out."

"Ain't no rules in here, man. In big money prize fights Ruiz might tell you no biting and no gouging, but that's about it."

"How much is big money?" I ask, pacing in circles outside the warehouse.

Eli eyes me, passing me another roll of twenty-dollar bills. "About two months ago we had a big-ass prize fight. Sleek Zeke versus Lil Nasty. Over a mil exchanged hands in that fight. Both fighters took a base of twenty k, and Nasty won so he got the prize, another eighty grand."

"No shit. A hundred grand?"

"Nasty quit fighting after that. He was the best I ever seen, that mothafucka. He probably cleared a good half-a-million in prize money over his career. A hundred fights, only lost once, and that was to Sleek. It was a rematch. Hell of a fight. I pulled in a good quarter-mil myself, betting on Nasty."

"A quarter of a million dollars? You shittin' me?"

"Hell nah, man. I don't joke about money."

"But you drive a Buick and live in the ghetto?"

"A fast as hell Buick, and you ain't seen my crib."

His voice is hard. "And if you think that's the ghetto, son, you don't know shit. I'd watch your ass, talking that shit, white boy."

"That's just a lot of money, you know? That's get-the-fuck-out-of-here money."

"Fuck that, dog. I'm a New Yorker, born and bred. I'll live and die up this bitch. I don't want out, I just want *up*. Na'mean? Uptown, son. A big ol' mothafuckin' pad with some sexy-ass bitches to go in it."

"Hear that, man."

Fist on flesh, shouts.

Ruiz appears, a pinner joint between thumb and forefinger. "Puff on that shit, *ese*." He hands it to Eli, who inhales deeply, and then hands it to me. Ruiz watches me smoke. "You up for one more?"

"Another fight?" I ask, stupidly.

Ruiz takes the joint back from me and tokes on it, laughing. "Yeah, man. Another fight. Julius wants another one. He owes somebody money, I think. Needs quick cash."

Julius. That'd be a pretty brutal fight, and I'm already hurting. But fuck it. "Two hundred and I'm in."

Eli bobs his head side to side. "I dunno, man. Julius might have your number."

"Fuck that. I can take him."

"You better win, then, I'm putting two hundred

down."

"How much you win off me so far?"

A smirk and a laugh and a nod. "Five large."

"Exactly." I dab at my face with my thumb, and note that blood is still trickling from the gash in my cheek. "And I'm the one fighting."

Eli just shrugs. "A'ight then. But you better win."

"I will. And when I do, I get five hundred for my next fight."

"You ain't fighting again tonight. You and Julius are the big finale, dog."

"I wouldn't fight again tonight anyway. I think Julius is going to put the hurt down. I'll take him, but it'll hurt."

Eli eyes me with something very much like respect. "You crazy, white boy. Bruce, Al, Jesus, and now Julius?"

"Got nothin' to lose," I say. It's the damn truth. What else am I going to do? Walk aimlessly around New York?

"You fightin' Crazy Bruce for somewhere to sleep, you're probably right." He extends his hand, thumb pointing up, and I slap my palm against it. "You got a deal. You win against Julius, I'll put five hundred down for your next fight."

This is pushing it, even for me. I'm exhausted. I

haven't slept in I don't even know how long. I've got a broken nose, throbbing ribs, a cut cheek, and bloody knuckles. And I'm going in for another fight with a known bruiser. I really must be crazy. Fuck, I *know* I am. I'm hurting bad, man.

It keeps me from contemplating my existence, at least.

I lean back against the rear quarter panel of Eli's car, spit blood, lean over and blow blood and mucus out of my nose. I spit some more. I bridge my fingers over my nose and bring my palms together. I take a deep breath, hesitate; this shit does *not* feel good. Pull my hands downward slowly toward my chin, groaning, dizzy from boiling pain as the broken cartilage realigns. I have to sink to the ground, sitting on my haunches until the dizziness passes.

"Didn't get blood on my ride, did you?" Eli asks. I don't think he's joking.

"No," I grunt. "How long do I have?"

Ruiz vanished at some point, but now he reappears. "You're up, Colt."

No time at all, apparently.

I push up, bounce on the balls of my feet and shake my hands, roll my head on my neck. "Lead the way, Ruiz."

Julius is already waiting in the ring, flexing his

fists. He's got puffy eyes, split lips, bloody knuckles and a deep gash over his eyebrow. He's lost his shirt, too. We're evenly matched, I think, just in terms of size. He might be a few pounds heavier in muscle, but I'm pretty sure I've got a longer reach. He's got the experience on me, though. And I doubt he's missed any meals recently.

I'm running on rage, determination and desperation now.

Ruiz steps between Julius and me. "Keep your teeth in your mouths, the both of you. This is the last fight of the night, so make it good." He addresses the crowd. "You know who's who by now. Julius has twelve fights, ten wins and two losses. Colt has two fights, no losses. Julius is favored. Place your bets." He finishes collecting the money, twists a rubber band around the stack of cash and shoves it in his back pocket, and then steps between us again. Glances at each of us. Steps back. "Fight!"

Julius is careful. He doesn't come out swinging at me, just edges forward, head down, fists up. The crowd is crazed, and I hear my name called a few times. Not everyone is betting on Julius, then. That makes me feel a little better.

We circle a few times, and then I lead in, left jab. Quick and dirty, a feeler. It glances off Julius's barred forearms, and I follow it with another, and a right cross. The cross connects, reopening his eyebrow. Pisses him off. He abandons his careful approach and charges in, blood-frenzied. I tuck my chin against my chest and bring my fists over my face, backpedaling and ducking and weaving under the barrage of blows. Most batter against my forearms, one grazes the top of my head, another finds its way to my side. He doesn't quit, though, just keeps hammering blow after blow on me, punching like a madman, and some of them connect painfully.

Enough is enough.

I duck my head and lunge for him, knock his fist aside and crush both my fists at once into his chest. My head cracks against his, but my fists meet his chest, and he's toppling backward, both of us shaking our heads. Julius recovers first and gets in a full, hard hook to my eyebrow, splitting it. An uppercut to the jaw, knocking me backward, cracking my teeth together. He follows through, the bastard, hooking a fist into my gut. Fucker is tough, and he hits hard.

I'm dizzy, I ache. I hurt. I can't take another hard hit or I'll fall, and once that happens, I'm done. So I don't let it happen. I dance back out of range, blink against the dizziness of the pain and breathe through it. I'm growling through it, snarling like a bear, chest heaving, shaking my head to clear my vision, all but foaming at the mouth. Julius is charging for me, a bull on the loose. I swivel aside at the last second, sucker-punch him in the back of the head, send him sprawling. Leap on him, straddle him, turn him over and crash my fist against his face again and again, feeling his knee bludgeoning my spine, his fists battering against my sides.

I get in half a dozen good hits before he bucks me off, rolls away, and lurches to his feet. I power up and forward, going after him, refusing to let him get away, refusing to go on the defense. He's bloody, wobbly, but still fierce. I go in with fists and knees, bashing and driving him to the edge of the ring. He's edging away, trying to buy time to shake off the damage. I see nothing but Julius, hear nothing but my own ragged breathing. He's backing away from me, wiping at his face, trying to clear his vision, and holy fuck is this guy a hard-ass motherfucker. Not many guys can take this kind of beating and stay upright.

I have a vision of me, bloody, the loser, rattling around the city alone, hurting, hungry, exhausted, money stolen. I have a vision of sleeping under bridges, stealing scraps from rats and pigeons. Fuck that.

We close in together, almost clenching one another, both of us bleeding like stuck pigs. He hooks another hard left into my gut, and that's his undoing. I intentionally accept the gut-shot, tense and wince at the smack of his fist into my abdomen. It was a gambit, taking that hit. I'm about done in, but if I can take one more gut-punch, if I can get close enough, inside his wicked fists, and pummel him, I think I have a chance to end this.

As his fist is buried in my gut, I'm already swinging. Not for his stomach, though. Up, to his ribs. Like with Al. You gotta be tactical, sometimes, pinpoint that shit. I rock him up and back with a brutal blow to his diaphragm, another, and another. All as close to the same spot as I can get.

He staggers, gasping. I have to finish it. Follow through. I spit blood and step toward him. He's too proud to lift a hand in surrender, and he knows that in this ring there is no mercy, and he wouldn't show it to me if the tables were turned.

I swing my right once more. I don't hold back. It's not a finisher, but it's enough to put him down.

The swing leaves me staggering. Drooling. Coughing, blood stringing to the floor from my lips. Julius is on the ground, on his side, face on the concrete, gasping and gagging. Spitting so he doesn't choke.

I got mad respect for Julius. I drag myself step by

step over to him. Stand over him. He's wary, expecting a kick, maybe. I don't know. I extend my hand to him, and after a suspicious, baleful stare, he raises his hand and grasps mine. I haul him to his feet, and we stand a few inches apart. Staring at each other. Assessing.

"You a hell of a fighter, dog," Julius says. His voice is way deep, the sound coming from the bottom of a well.

"You too, man." I grin. "Let's not do this again any time soon, huh?"

He laughs and we walk—stagger, really—out of the ring. "No shit. That fuckin' hook to the chest, man…that shit's a killer."

We leave the building together. Eli is there, peeling bills off a roll, smoking a blunt. The huge black guy from up on the catwalk platform is there too, the diamonds in his ears and on his fingers glinting in the moonlight. Huge and silent, hands in his pockets, just up to the knuckles, head tilted to the side.

"Ya'll are homies, now, huh?" he asks.

Julius steps away. "Hell nah. Just respect, man."

"He beat yo' ass." The huge man steps forward. Clearly unhappy. "You *lost*, dog. I had ten g's on that shit."

"Hey man, it coulda gone either way. If I'd'a gotten one more hit in, he'd be done too."

"But you didn't."

Julius is nervous. The air is still, cold and hard. I don't dare speak or move or even breathe too loudly. Eli is the same, blunt in his fingers coiling smoke up, up, up, not smoking it now, just holding it. Watching. Waiting. There's violence in the air. Not fists and broken noses, but holes in the chest and dead eyes.

"Come on, man." Julius just stands there, wiping at the blood trickling from his nose with his thumb. "I'm ten and three, Train. I won't lose again."

I swallow hard, my throat thick. I can see a similar conversation happening between Eli and me. This isn't boxing. It's not MMA or the UFC. It's back alley, underground, nasty. No rules but those set in place by the dudes running it. Like Train, there. Staring at Julius, holding the younger man's fate in his hands. You lose, you could die. Not in the ring, but outside, afterward.

"I back you, I expect you to win," Train says. "I don't back losers. I let those first two losses go since you was new. You ain't new no more. I ain't gonna let any more losses slide."

"I got you." Julius just breathes, not yet daring to relax.

Train shoots a look at Eli. Digs in his pocket, pulls out a thick stack of cash. "Guess I owe you this."

"I told you he was a fighter," Eli says, slowly taking the money from Train and tossing it into the open driver's side window.

"Sho did." Train eyes me, now. "He could go large. I'll buy him from you."

"Buy me?" I can't help asking.

Eli shoots me a meaningful look. "Shut the fuck up, white boy. Lemme handle this." His eyes move to Train. "Nah, man. I found him, I'll back him."

"Change your mind, lemme know." Train shuffles back into the building. "Get outta here, Julius. Go see Johnny tomorrow. Learn some shit."

Julius nods, backs away, shoulders sagging. When Train is out of sight, Julius pivots away, rakes his hands over his closely shaved scalp. "Shit, man. Shit. Shit. I was about to piss myself, no joke."

I don't know what to say. "Got tense there for a minute."

Eli puts the blunt to his lips. Takes a long drag. "Train don't fuck around."

"So if I lose too many times, will you shoot me?" I ask Eli.

"I might, dog. I might." He doesn't sound like he's joking. Doesn't look like it, either.

"Guess I'd better win, then."

Julius jerks his chin up at me. "I'll be seeing you,

Colt. Good fight."

"You too, Julius."

When Julius is gone, Eli shakes his head. "Man, I thought Train was gonna blast him for sure. Be a hell of a waste. That kid is quick. Loss like that one'll make him careful, take him down a peg. Good for him." He hands me four fifty-dollar bills. "This is yours. Four hundred in one night, your first time in the ring. Not bad, white boy."

"Yeah, well, I'm not in Kansas anymore, am I?"

"You from Kansas?"

I'm not sure if he's joking. "Um, no. Detroit. That was…it was from a movie."

"Oh yeah, with the lion, the scarecrow, the tin dude, and that white bitch with the red shoes. The fuck's it called? *The Wizard of Oz*, ain't it? I seen that shit before." He pinches the cherry off the blunt, puts the roach into a baggy and then into his pocket. "So what's that supposed to mean, you ain't in Kansas anymore?"

I shrug. "Just that I can't afford to lose, can I?"

Eli laughs. "I was just fuckin' with you, man, I wouldn't shoot you for losing."

"Good to know." I'm not sure I believe him. "Hey, man, I'm done in. I need to crash somewhere."

"I got'chu." He glances to the side, someone in

the shadows beckoning to him. "I got some business for a minute. Try not to get in trouble."

Eli vanishes into the shadows, and I'm alone in the alley.

But not for long.

The girl who brought me the sandwich slinks out of the doorway, this time wearing booty shorts and a tanktop sans bra, no tray. She's...I don't know what she is, ethnically. Mixed, maybe. Dark curly hair, the kind of skin that could be tanned white girl, Italian, Mexican. Dark eyes with heavy makeup. A fuckin' bangin' body, ass that won't quit, tits for days. Real tits, too, judging by the way they jiggle. I hold my ground, leaning back against the wall, letting the aches fade. She comes straight up to me, leans back against the wall beside me, digs a cigarette out of her cleavage.

"Got a light?" she asks, glancing at me sideways.

"Sure." I snap open my recently-acquired Zippo, light her smoke.

"Thanks."

"No problem." I watch her smoke, watch the way her tits swell in her shirt with each breath.

She flaunts them to make a buck, so I'm not real concerned with getting caught staring. Besides, the looks she's giving me, I think she's got something in mind. And just let me say, no matter how hurt I am, I'm never too sore to get down with a sexy chick.

Finished with her smoke, she pushes off the wall, turns away from me, walks a few steps, then turns her head back to look at me, a playful smile on her lips, eyebrow quirked. It's an invitation if I've ever seen one, so I push off, follow her. Up the stairs to the catwalk, across it to a door leading to a makeshift kitchen. Not much but a deep fryer, an industrial refrigerator, a rolling counter top, and a shelf with some dry goods. Another door leads to an office, a battered metal desk, a filing cabinet, and a leather couch new enough to look out of place.

She closes the door behind me, pivots around me, puts her back to the door. Looks up at me. "I don't usually like watching the fights, but you make it sexy, somehow." Her voice is low, sultry.

"Oh yeah?"

She reaches for my belt. "Yeah. *Real* sexy. Had me all hot and bothered, watching you fight." She's got my cock out, and she's stroking it slowly; not wasting any time, clearly. "The way you took hit after hit after hit…"

She times the strokes to the rhythm of her words, has me bucking and moaning within a few seconds. I let her go to her knees, watch her wrap those plush lips around me, watch her suck. Let her suck for a minute, until I'm worked up, and then I pull away.

"I wasn't done," she protests.

"Yeah you are." I pull her to her feet. "I'm not coming down your throat."

She moans as I tug her tank top off, whimpers when I lick one erect nipple. "No? Where, then?"

I make quick work of her shorts, get her naked. Spin her in place, smack her ass hard enough to leave a mark, leave it quivering. "All over this."

"There's condoms in the desk."

I don't think about what the convenience of that means, because it doesn't really matter. This girl—whose name I don't know and won't ask—knows what this is as well as I do. I find the stash in a drawer of the desk, all sizes, all kinds. Take one, open it, roll it on.

She's been busy while I'm engaged in rolling protection on; her fingers are at her pussy, sliding in slick, quick circles, getting herself there while standing up, feet wide, shoulders back against the door. I watch for a second, because that's fucking hot.

"You wanna take over, Colt?" she invites.

"Nah. Watching you is fun."

This gets me another sexy little grin, which quickly fades as she gets closer and closer, hips starting to buck, eyes fluttering closed, thighs trembling with a nice little shake.

I wait until it looks like she's gonna pop any second, and then I grab her hips. Pull her to me. Knock her fingers out of the way, take over, finish her off with a quick, harsh, rough stab of two fingers into her slit, thumb against her clit. She comes with a quiet shriek, and I slide into her while she's coming, push in deep.

Fuck hard, slamming her against the door. She braces her hands on my shoulders, lifts one foot to hook her leg around my waist. I grip her under her ass, lift her off the ground, and then buck up into her, hard, so hard her head snaps back and her tits jounce beautifully.

But I've been through too much over the past few days to be able to sustain that for long, so I let her down, pull out. Spin her around and bend her over the arm of the couch. She puts her palms on the cushion, leans over so her face is down, ass up, lifted up on her toes. Jesus, she's eager. I slide back in, and fuck, she may not be tight, but she's wetter than a slip'n'slide, and doesn't seem to mind my palm whacking across her ass cheek. I pound her like that, harder and harder and harder, until I'm close to coming.

And then I pull out, strip the condom off, and

jack myself with my fist, shoot my come all over her big round ass, splatting dripping rivulets of come on her spine, her ass cheeks, and down the crack.

There's Kleenex on the desk, so I take a moment to clean her up; I'll take easy sex, but that doesn't mean I'm a jackass about it.

She tugs on her clothes, eyeing me curiously, as if no hookup has ever bothered to do that before. "Didn't have to do that," she says.

"I make a mess, I clean it up. It's basic decency."

"Well, thanks." She buckles my belt for me, almost wistfully. "You fuck even better than you fight."

I give her a cocky grin. "Thanks." A horn blares outside, Eli getting impatient, probably. "Got to go. Thanks for a good time."

"Thank *you*." She winks at me. "You want more, find me at the next fight. I might even bring a friend or two, next time."

Ho-ly *shit*. "I will for sure take you up on that."

"I'm Raquel, by the way."

Another honk, this one longer. "Really got to go. My backer is getting antsy. Nice to meet you, Raquel."

I duck out the door, jog through the kitchen and across the catwalk to the exit.

Eli is waiting in his rumbling Buick, and I join him, lowering myself into the passenger seat.

"Where'd you go, dog?"

I lean back in the seat, blowing out a breath. "Business," I mutter.

Raquel is moseying out the exit, sees me through the open window of Eli's Buick, waves at me, a wiggle of all five fingers.

Eli laughs. "Ohhhh, *that* business. Got all up in that, did you?" Another laugh. "You do *not* waste time, do you? Damn, son, that was quick. Raquel don't mess around with the fighters, usually."

Another long, slow cruise through the streets, a heavy bass line thudding from the woofers in the trunk. We don't go back to the bridge where I tangled with the old homeless guy. We head somewhere else. Not sure where, but it seems familiar. Low buildings, graffiti on the walls, chain link fence around basketball courts, dilapidated tenements with crumbling brick stairs and battered intercom boxes. The highrises of Manhattan are barely visible to my left, far in the distance, tall rectangles in the early morning haze. Eli pulls to a stop in front of an apartment building. He gets out of the car and unfolds his frame, tugging at the tail of his shirt. He swaggers up to the front door and jerks it open. The intercom buzzers are all broken, no names, just graffiti in black marker.

There are flickering lights overhead, a battered

staircase, an empty bottle of cheap malt liquor in the corner. A used condom. The foyer stinks like piss and smoke and food grease and old building. Eli hops up the stairs and up another flight to the second floor and heads to the third door on the left. 2B. He doesn't knock, he just opens the door to reveal a smoky haze in the room. There's a chill pebbling my skin. The place is pretty bare bones—a low table in the middle of the room, a threadbare couch under a window and another perpendicular to it. There's a small kitchen, pots and pans on the stove, crusted and stinking, dishes in the sink, carryout containers on the counters, bottles of beer and liquor everywhere.

A black girl lounges on the couch, mostly naked, wearing a tattered robe loosely tied, showing bare breasts and a thong. A metal pipe smolders on the coffee table. Judging by the smell, she's not smoking pot.

"Maisy," Eli mutters. "Wake the fuck up."

"'M'awake." She stirs, swivels her head to stare balefully at me, and then sees Eli. "Whozzat?"

"Colt. He's gonna crash a few nights. Don't give him any shit."

"Got anything good for me, Eli?"

"Nah." Eli blows out a frustrated breath. "I think you high enough, bitch. Maybe tomorrow."

"Fine. Fuck you too."

"Watch that shit, Maisy." Eli shuffles side to side. Eyes me. There's history between these two, but I really don't want to know what it is. I'm too tired to care. "Take the room on the left. Lock the door."

"Okay." I hobble, sore and tired and hurting and hungry and lonely and scared, toward the hallway.

"I'll be back later. Don't go nowhere."

"I need food."

"Maisy. Got anything to eat?" Eli asks.

"I ain't his bitch. He can look for hisself." Maisy takes a long hit off the pipe, holds the smoke, blows it out with a cough, and flops back on the couch, draping her forearm over her eyes.

"I'm just asking if you *have* anything here for him to find." Eli shakes his head in disgust. "You gotta lay off that shit, Maisy. It ain't doing you any favors."

"Live your own fuckin' life, Eli. We don't roll together no more. Remember?"

Shit is getting tense.

I back away from the living room. "I'll be fine until you come back."

"Just look around. She may have something to eat. She's so fuckin' high, she won't give a shit what you do." He rubs the back of his neck. "Wish I ain't brought you up here. All she do is get high and wanna argue."

She's staring at Eli, eyes heavy-lidded, glazed. Not sure she's seeing anything.

"Should I, like, check on her or something?" I ask.

Eli waves a hand in dismissal. "Nah. She'll be fine. I make sure she don't have enough to kill herself with. Dumb bitch can't help herself." He yanks open the front door, steps out. "I'll be back later. Stay here, for real. Like, stay in the room and mind your business." *Bid-ness,* he says it.

"Okay." Not sure where else I would go. I don't know where I am. I have a little cash now, but not enough to get a place or a ride.

When Eli is gone, I wait in the hallway for a while, watching Maisy. She's cashed out, lying on her side, eyelids almost closed, her arm hanging off the couch, wrist limp. When I'm sure she's really out of it, I head into the kitchen. Fucking nasty up in here, man. Mold is growing on the dishes. The stink is enough to turn my stomach. Doesn't leave me very hopeful that there's any edible food to be found, but I poke through the cabinets and fridge just in case. Some old cans of beans that expired six months ago, boxes of Jell-O that expired over a year ago, some moldy bread, a jar of peanut butter that seems okay, some grape jelly in the fridge, the rim crusted with hardened jelly.

Peanut butter and jelly, no bread. A carton of milk, so old and soured that the sides are bulging. Orange juice in the same condition.

How does this girl survive?

I find a box of Cheez-Its on top of the fridge that aren't too stale, so I settle on those and spoonfuls of peanut butter. I find a dusty juice glass in a cabinet, rinse it out, fill it with tap water. Spoonfuls of peanut butter, handfuls of Cheez-Its. This is familiar. I'd often be doing homework so late into the night that I'd miss dinner, and then I'd sneak down into the kitchen in the middle of the night and scrounge for food. Often, dinner would be granola bars, fruit, a PB&J, crackers, leftovers, anything I could find and eat quickly without having to work at it. Not because I was afraid of cooking or that I didn't know how, but because of my brother. Kyle. The golden boy. Back when I was fourteen, fifteen, sixteen, he was in elementary school, and god help me if I woke him up. Precious perfect boy needed his sleep, you know? That's envy talking, though. I always had to be up at the crack of dawn to walk my ass to school, to finish homework, all while Kyle got to sleep in, get driven to school. Not his fault, but I sure was jealous.

Not that I'm bitter toward Kyle, though. I mean, for real. He's a good kid. That's the problem: he's *good*.

Smart, well-behaved. All A's in school, athletic, great at baseball and football and soccer *and* school. Five years younger than me, a world between us. I mean, when you're eleven and getting shit on for being stupid, your six-year-old brother is kind of periphery, you know? And there's a world of difference between boys at that age anyway, but with having all I could do just to get anything close to passing grades at school, I pretty much never saw him. And I think my folks were fine with that. Afraid my brand of dumb was catching, maybe. Afraid I'd infect poor Kyle with my stupidity. The embarrassment. That's how Dad saw me, and Mom never dared challenge him openly on it.

Okay, maybe I am a little resentful of Kyle. I just got fucking sick to death of hearing "Why can't you just be more like Kyle?"

I don't even know why I'm even thinking about him right now since I've got a few other things on my mind.

When I'm as full as I can get, I check out the bathroom, thinking maybe a shower would be nice. I lower my backpack to the cracked, stained linoleum on the floor, perusing with distaste the foul mess of the bathroom. Girly shit everywhere. Hairspray, makeup, brushes, a million random bottles containing who-the-fuck-knows-what, a garbage can near the toilet overflowing with condom wrappers, wadded up balls of toilet paper probably containing the used contents of the discarded wrappers, several used and sloppily-wrapped…girl time-of-the-month products.

Fucking nasty.

Jesus, this bitch is a slob.

The shower isn't much better. A shower curtain that was once white, but is now orange from hard water stains, mildew dotting the bottom. Or maybe it's just flat-out mold. More bottles, a hard, crusty old rust-colored washcloth permanently folded over the faucet. A thin sliver of soap in one corner. I don't see any clean towels but there is a damp one hanging off the corner of the bathroom door. I check the cabinet under the sink. Curling iron, a bag of barrettes or something like that, clips of some kind, and little rubber bands. More boxes of tampons, a box of condoms, and…shit, a baggie of drugs, long white crystals, probably meth. Haven't ever and won't ever touch that shit. At least there's one clean towel under the sink, faded blue, folded in sloppy quarters.

I shut the bathroom door and lock it. I turn on the shower and run it hot—as hot as it'll go, which isn't very—and rinse off. I scrub my hair, and hiss and wince at the sting of the soap on my face. The cuts in my eyebrow and the split lip and the corner of my nose and my cheek all hurt like hell. I scrub my body and, shit, that hurts too. I've got a fuckload of bruises on my torso, chest, stomach and sides.

Finally, I'm clean. I dry off, put on clean clothes and shove the dirty ones in my bag and hope I get a chance to do laundry at some point.

Finally, I look at myself in the mirror; dude, am I busted up. My face is a wreck, both eyes are black and nearly swollen shut, my lips are puffy and split, and my nose is still crooked despite my attempts to reset it.

But I've got four hundred bucks in my pocket.

Was it worth it, getting the shit beaten out of me?

I can buy my own food, now. Maybe, if I take another couple fights and make some more cash, I'll be able to afford my own place. A room somewhere, at least.

I hang the towel I used over the shower curtain bar, drag my fingers through my thick shaggy hair and try to untangle it a little, and then I exit the bathroom.

Maisy is still passed out. She hasn't stirred. She's lying on the couch with her tits hanging out and her robe rucked up around her ass. She's snoring loudly.

Eli said room on the left, so naturally I peek into

the room on the right. Nothing in it but a twin bed, a bedside table and a stack of cash rolled up and rubber-banded together. The curtains are closed. But it is the one clean room in the apartment.

I don't want to draw any false conclusions, but I have an inkling as to how Maisy affords the apartment and the drugs.

I close the door, and try the room on the left. It is totally empty except for some barbells and dumbbells in one corner, and a bare, piss-stained mattress on the floor. No blanket.

Fuck it. It's a bed and it's indoors.

I lock the door behind me, shut off the light, and lie down. Once again I stuff my backpack under my face and wrap my arms around it.

I'm asleep before I've taken three breaths.

Five: Power From the Earth

WHEN ELI SAID HE'D BE BACK LATER, APPARENTLY HE MEANT a lot later. Three days go by. He'd told me to stay put, but I had to eat. Plus, my guess as to what Maisy does with her time, besides doing meth, was correct. There are grunts coming from the room across from mine at all hours. Maisy completely ignores me. I stay in my room at all costs, only sneaking out in quiet moments to piss, maybe, or grab a cup of water and another handful of Cheez-Its. But eventually, I'm too hungry. I have to go out and find something decent to eat. I have to.

I shoulder my backpack, placing the bulk of my cash rolled up tight and stuffed into a rolled-up pair of socks, hidden way down at the bottom. I keep two twenties in my pocket. I memorize the address as I walk out of the building and hang a left. I remember seeing a couple of fast food places on the way here and I head toward them.

I make it three blocks.

Crossing the parking lot beside a laundromat, a big black SUV with shiny, spinning rims tears into the lot and stops in front of me and blocks my progress. I back up slowly, hands in my pockets, heart pounding. Six guys get out, all of them black, all of them big, hard looking, scary as fuck. They swagger, each of them wearing bright white Jordans or spotless tan Timberlands, do-rags around their heads or hanging from pockets.

"You in the wrong 'hood, dog," one of them says.

"What'chu got in that bag?" says another.

Shit. Shit.

My heart is in my throat. Adrenaline pumps like fire in my veins. This bag is all I've got. Some dirty clothes, some crumbled crackers, and $375. They will have to take it literally over my dead body.

I stand my ground and say nothing. They spread out in front of me in a semi-circle. I swivel my head, trying to keep my eye on all of them at once.

Six on one. I don't like these odds.

This is gonna fuckin' hurt.

One of them swaggers closer to me. "Tyrell asked what you got in your bag, motherfucker."

"Clothes. Nothing else." I let it slide a little, ready to drop it and swing.

"Bullshit."

"It's just fuckin' clothes, man," I say. I swing it in front, unzip it a little, show him. "Just dirty clothes."

He snatches it, or tries to. I jerk it back, snatching it from his grip. I see his punch coming, dodge it, smash my fist as hard as I can into his throat. He gurgles, and shuffles backward.

I know what's coming next. I dance backwards, drop my bag and stand on the strap. They're closing in, all five of them. One swings, I dodge it and return the punch, but another fist is incoming at the same time and I can't dodge both. I ain't Jackie Chan, that's for sure. It's a sucker punch to the back of my head, and it sends me sprawling. I roll, catch a kick to the kidney before I can get back up.

It gets nasty, after that.

I give all I've got. I lay them out, knock teeth out of skulls and balls up into crotches. I take knock after knock and keep getting up. I'm drooling blood and feel a tooth loosen. I gasp for breath, peering blearily, woozily at the scene around me. I'm sagging, staggering. One of them is standing over me. He shoves me, kicking me as I fall, sending me flying. I can't fucking breathe.

Another kick. Seeing my bag, I grab it and haul it to me, curl around it. Kick after kick, rattling my bones and jarring my organs.

I hear a petrifying sound: a metallic slide, followed by a *click*. A gun being cocked.

"Leave his ass, dog. He ain't shit."

"Knocked my fuckin' tooth out, the hell I'mma leave him alone."

I scramble away, each movement an agony. I roll to my knees, struggle to my feet and spit more blood. All six are on their feet, staring at me. They're all hurt and bloodied; I held my own, motherfuckers.

The one in front has a silver pistol in his hand, and it's aimed at me. This is none of that movie bullshit where some thug holds the gun at a stupid sideways angle. He steps up to me, jams the barrel into my chest, grinds it hard. I stand my ground.

Blood pools in my mouth, and I spit it at my feet. Meet the gun wielder's gaze. Wipe my chin on my arm. Stare him down. All but daring him to shoot me, basically.

"Come on, man. He ain't worth it. Just a cracker in the wrong 'hood. Leave his ass." The speaker urges his friend backward. I lift my chin. I'm scared fucking chicken, very literally shaking in my boots. But I don't show it. I continue to stare them down, holding my bag in one hand. I spit more blood.

I swear I'm about to get shot.

But then an engine snarls and tires squeal. Eli, in his Buick, slides to a halt beside me and jumps out. He draws his pistol smoothly, holds it out, swinging it to point at each of the other guys in turn.

"Ya'll know me. Back off. Ya'll wanna start some shit with me, you're startin' shit with Train. Back... the *fuck*...off." He says the last part through clenched teeth, stomping forward like he's got a dozen armed friends at his back, rather than just bloody, fucked-up me.

They all back up, get into their SUV without turning their backs on Eli. He doesn't lower his pistol until the black SUV is out of sight.

And then he whirls on me. "I fuckin' told you stay put, motherfucker!"

"And you've been gone three days, Eli! There ain't shit to eat in that place except fucking crackers, man! I'm hungry! I haven't anything except that sandwich before the fight in over a week. I gotta eat."

"You playin'?"

"Why the hell would I lie about that? You think I'd be fighting homeless bums for somewhere to sleep if I had anywhere to go? You think I'd venture out here on my own if I didn't have to? I know what's up. I knew I'd probably get jumped, and I did. But I gotta fuckin' eat, and I didn't know when you'd be back. I couldn't wait for you."

"You a crazy-ass motherfucker, you know that, Colt? They'd'a shot you if I hadn't shown up."

"Almost did shoot me." I have to collapse backward against Eli's car, sagging, breathing hard, clutching my ribs where they ache.

"You done fucked things up good, man. There's a fight tonight. A big one. I got you booked to fight this cat named Moreno. He's big trouble, real tough-ass mo-fo. I got a grand for you, bet five G's on you to beat his ass. And now you go and get your ass kicked. What the fuck am I supposed to do now, man? I can't back out."

"Just get me something to eat. I'll fight him and I'll win. Just get me food and let me chill."

"You just got your ass handed to you by six dudes. You gonna fight anyway?"

"I can't afford to turn down a thousand bucks, Eli. I need my own place."

He chuckles. "What, Maisy's ain't cuttin' it for you?"

"Between the meth and the tricks, no, not really."

Eli makes a surprised and unhappy face. "That dumb bitch is hookin' again? I told her to quit that shit. I told her I'd take care of her."

"Didn't get the memo, I guess. Seven or eight in the last three days."

His expression hardens. "I'm cuttin' her shit off, then. She ain't gettin' shit from me, if she wanna turn tricks behind my back. Dumb-ass bitch." He tucks his gun back into his waistband. "You need anything from her place?"

I shake my head. "I got my bag. Wasn't about to leave it there."

"Smart." He jerks his head. "Let's go."

I climb gingerly into his car, sag back against the velvety upholstery. Just breathe, let him drive wherever he's taking me. I must have dozed off, because I start awake when the engine shuts off. I rouse myself and glance around. Yet another part of New York, similar to everywhere else Eli's taken me so far. Whatever. It doesn't matter where I am.

There's a Chinese carry-out place, a gym, a liquor store, and a cell phone store, all in a row in a single building with apartments above. Eli leads the way to the door leading up to the apartments above the stores. Narrow stairway, wood-paneled wainscoting, the smell of Chinese food permeating the space.

There is a short hallway with two doors, one on either side of the hall. Eli knocks on the door on the left and waits. I hear several locks being unlatched, then the door cracks open.

"Eli, 'sup, dog? Who you got with you?" Deep, deep, deep voice. Chasmic, syrupy.

"Rhino, this is Colt." Eli steps aside so the person on the other side of the door can see me. I see nothing but inky skin and pot-reddened eyes and brown irises, a hint of scruff on a chin, a slice of forehead, a shaved head. "Colt, this is my boy Rhino."

"He a fighter?" Rhino asks.

"Yeah. On the come-up. Needs somewhere to crash, and some technique."

"Looks like you just lost a fight."

"There were six of them," I say.

A nod, understanding. Six-on-one is nasty odds for anyone. "You in trouble?" he asks, his eye on me, on my bruises and cuts.

"No."

"Nobody looking for you?"

I shake my head. "Nope."

That's the sad truth, too. There isn't anyone looking for me. They just let me go. Because I couldn't meet their standards.

The door closes, a chain slides, unhooks, and the

door opens again. "C'mon in, y'all."

Holy fucking hell. I see why he's called Rhino. Six-seven at least, probably close to four hundred pounds. Huge motherfucker. Scalp shaved bald, goatee scruff, gold chains around his neck, rings on his fingers. He's wearing a pair of gym shorts and nothing else, displaying a physique that scares me a little. Or a lot. A layer of fat, but under that is enough muscle to deadlift a car off the ground. Tattoos, a dragon on his right arm, skulls, lettering, a face and "RIP" in tag lettering. Bullet hole scars, knife scars and a burn scar on his left forearm.

Rhino settles into a sagging La-Z-Boy recliner, the hinges and springs squeaking. There's a brown couch, fuzzy and scratchy, the fabric pilling, cushions faded and dented by decades of butts. Eli and I sit down. A blunt the size of a stogie smolders in an ashtray on the battered coffee table, and Rhino lifts it, takes a drag. Extends it to Eli, who smokes it and hands it to me.

"So why you stashin' your boy here, Eli?" Rhino asks.

"Gotta go somewhere. Tried him at Maisy's, but she back to hoein' herself out again, so that ain't gonna work."

I really don't know why Eli is doing this. Or why

he cares.

"I just need somewhere to crash for a few nights. A couple fights, I'll have enough for my own place." I take the blunt as it circles back to me.

Rhino chuckles. "Couple fights and you done, huh?"

"That's the plan."

"That's a stupid-ass plan." He laughs again. "That ain't how this game works, man. You don't just quit. Especially not once the money starts addin' up."

Eli seems fidgety, nervous. "So, you in?"

Rhino lets the smoke roll out of his mouth in a thick cloud. He squints at Eli through the pall. "He wins, I get a cut. Fifteen percent."

"Five."

"Fuck you and yo' cheap ass. Twelve." Rhino passes the blunt to Eli.

Eli stares at the cherry, thinking. "Ten."

"A'ight. Ten." A glance at me. "You better fuckin' win, white boy."

Why do I keep hearing that? "I will."

He palms his knees, pushes his bulk upright. "Best hit the gym, then. See what you got." A glance at Eli. "He's fighting tonight?"

"Yeah. He's fighting Julio Moreno."

Rhino just nods. "After the stomping you just

took, that's gonna be a bitch of a fight."

"I'll be fine."

"You haven't fought Moreno, yet." A wicked grin. "You won't be fine when that's over with."

"Very inspiring."

Rhino chuckles. "You funny." He extends his hand to Eli, and they slap palms, bump shoulders. "I'll work with him. He can crash on the couch for a minute. I'll bring him to the fight tonight."

Eli nods. "Don't get in any more fights unless you're gettin' paid for it, you got it?" He points at me with his index finger, his expression serious. "I'm for real, man. You got a knack for finding trouble."

"Hear you."

Eli leaves, then, and Rhino vanishes, reappearing wearing a T-shirt with sleeves that have been ripped off. "Let's head down to the gym."

"You own the gym?" I ask, following him.

"Yeah."

The place is in darkness; the shadows of weight machines are barely visible, but I can see a boxing ring, a speed bag setup, and a heavy bag. Rhino flips a few light switches and fluorescent lights hum and flicker on. It's a small space, but all the equipment is newer and well maintained, the floors are clean and the walls have been recently painted.

He circles the ring and stops near the heavy bag. "Work the bag, lemme see what you got."

I just stand there for a second, feeling awkward. "I've never worked in a gym before. I just…got in a lot of fights."

He nods. "Which means you probably got no technique, and that's what I want to see. Just hit the bag hard as you can."

I go into a fighting stance, haul back and hit the bag with my right fist as hard as I muster. The *thwack* is loud, and the bag jumps back, wobbles and swings. My fist stings.

"Again. Just keep hitting it. Move around it."

So I hit the bag. Left, right, cross, hook, upper-cut. I throw everything I've got at it, moving in circles. I find a rhythm in it, and let myself flow. I duck, weave, bob and use my torso for momentum until I'm sweating and the bag is circling and swaying and bobbing.

"A'ight. Hold up." Rhino assumes a loose approximation of a boxer's stance. "You like this. Fists low, body facing straight on, almost standing, head up." He pivots so his body is edge-on, puts his fists closer up near his face, crouches. Chin tucked, knees bent. "Gotta get low. Give 'em less to hit, and tuck your chin in so it don't get clipped. That's the fastest way to get knocked out."

He moves closer to the bag and jabs. Just a light jab, but the bag is rocked farther back than I managed with my hardest punch. He glances at me, makes sure I'm watching him. "You're using your body, you got that much right. But you ain't using your legs. A good punch starts in your feet, way down in your mother-fuckin' toes, man. Push off with your foot, let that move in a line up through your hips, out through your arm." He moves in a sideways crab walk, ducks low as if to dodge a swing, and then brings his fist around in a whistling arc. He hits the bag so fucking hard I think for a minute he's split it open. "With a hit like that, you twist and, like I said, it's gotta come from your feet. This may sound stupid, but I try to pretend I got the whole earth pushing up with me, twisting with me when I punch. Like the power is coming up from the ground and moving through me. Know what I'm sayin'?"

I nod. "Yeah, I get it."

I crouch, twist sideways, tuck my chin in and try the jab. I push through my toes. My whole body moves forward with the punch. I feel the difference immediately, feel it in the way my body moves, in the way the punch feels, in the way the heavy bag is knocked backward. I let the bag swing, move away, circle around, duck under an imaginary punch and try to summon the power of the earth through my feet. I twist, push through my feet, push with my stomach and my shoulders and my knees and my elbow, and the impact is like a clap of thunder.

"You gettin' it." Rhino hits the bag with a flurry of punches, high and low, and cross and hook, and I realize how devastating it must be to fight a massive bruiser like him, especially with the speed and skill he's showing. "Now you just gotta practice it until that kind of motion is automatic. Second nature, na'mean? Every hit, it comes way down low. You can take a hell of a beating, and you got naturally good technique, which is prolly how you won so far. Little bitta skill, little bitta natural ability, and lotta will to just stay on your feet, am I right?"

I nod. "You're not wrong."

"Well, you want to win regular, you gotta add a lot more skill. Fighting a mothafucka like Moreno, luck ain't gonna cut it. Moreno is *good*. He's got a rep as a winner, so if you can beat him, it'll take you places. Get you big money fights. And that's what you want. Big money fights bought me this gym."

"You don't fight anymore?"

He just laughs. "Hell nah. I got my gym, don't need to fight no more."

"So you quit, then."

"I fought for four years before I quit. Saved all the money I won. Spent money on food and smoke, and that was about it. Saved it until I had enough to buy this place up with cash. You wanna get out, you gotta pay your dues. You don't get out quick." His expression is serious, hard. "You're just gettin' in, Colt. You got a lot of fighting ahead of you."

That's a sobering thought.

Six: Bad Shit

I DANCE AND BOUNCE AROUND ON THE BALLS OF MY FEET. I shake my fists and roll my shoulders and I wonder what in the ever-loving fuck I've gotten myself into. The man facing me is a predator. Lean, all sharp edges and hard muscles, cold dead eyes and a slight grin. Six feet tall, same as me, but probably ten pounds lighter. Long arms, quick feet. His fists are taped up to his forearms, and it's clear he's already fought at least once tonight, judging by the split, puffy lip and the tiny butterfly bandage over the bridge of his nose. He's wearing a pair of loose shorts and nothing else, no socks or shoes, no shirt.

Ruiz is between us, stuffing cash from the bets into the back pocket of his loose, low-hanging khakis.

He glances at each of us. "No biting, no gouging."

We're facing each other now, standing up straight, both of us taking slow, even breaths, pushing all thoughts away, summoning the coldness necessary to beat the hell out of a stranger against whom you have no grudge. Julio smirks and says something in Spanish, something insulting, if the cackles and howls of the Spanish-speakers in the crowd is any indication.

"Insults work better if the person understands them," I say.

He juts his chin at me. "You sure you wanna fight, *gringo*? Looks like somebody already wrecked you up."

There's nothing to say to that, so I just smack my fists together, knuckle on knuckle and spit on the floor. Truth is, I *don't* want to fight. I want to lie down and go to sleep and not wake up for a week. I'm hurting. My ribs ache from taking those kicks, my jaw aches, a tooth is loose and my eyes are both black and yellow.

But I never back down. Not from anyone.

So I hold my chin up, work on looking aloof and arrogant. I ignore the pounding in my chest, the thrum of adrenaline and fear in my bloodstream, the slight shake to my hands as I clench them into fists.

Ruiz steps back, drops his arm between us.

"Fight."

Moreno is like greased goddamn lightning. He's on me and hammering his fists into my gut with machine gun rapidity before I have a chance to even set my feet. And then he's dancing back and weaving, feet working him around me like a dancer. A bob, a weave, a feint, and then he's hooking a vicious right into my ribs and I'm gasping and seeing stars, and it hasn't been six seconds yet. Goddamn.

Fuck this.

I curl down, root my feet in the earth, feel the ground under me like an anchor, and feel the blood haze settle over my brain.

Moreno ducks in, expecting to land another flurry of wicked slugs, but I'm faster than he is this time. He's mid-punch, committed. I pivot, and his torso is wide open. I twist with the power of the rotating earth, grunt as I put all my force into it. I swing my arm, twist my hips, curl my torso around, haul my fist like a motherfucking freight train into Moreno's liver.

He's staggering backwards, stunned breathless by the raw, bone-crushing fury of the hit. No fucking mercy. I'm on him like a mauling bear, settling down into each punch and drawing colossal, primal vigor from the ground under my feet.

To his credit, he endures the battering I give him, and manages to deliver an elbow to my throat.

I gasp, and we're both tottering backward, taking a breath.

And that's when he changes shit on me. Instead of coming at me like I expect, fists flying, he darts forward, hops, and sends the ball of his left foot into my chest. I can't breathe, and he's spinning like a cyclone, and I can see the next kick coming but I can't get out of the way. I manage to throw up a forearm, intercepting the kick; I'll have a hell of a bruise there, that's for damn sure.

The next minute or so is a wicked, vicious blur of kicks, knees, punches, elbows, body blows and hammering hits to the face. He's bleeding and so am I. The crowd is wild, as if they can't believe the fight they're witnessing.

I have to end this.

I'm hurting so bad I can't see, can't breathe, can't think. I can barely move.

Moreno launches another flying sidekick at me, and I don't think, don't plan, just react. I catch his ankle in the crook of my elbow, pivot over him and pressure the joint hard in the wrong direction, swinging the flat of my fist down onto his knee like a jackhammer.

CRACK.

He screams.

He drops.

I stagger backward into the silenced crowd. I sag, then I'm hurled forward, and I fall on the ground beside Moreno.

I vomit and gasp.

Moreno is on the ground a foot away. Tears gleam in his eyes, and he's screaming, clutching at his knee as three Hispanic dudes rush toward him, shouting in Spanish.

"I'm sorry...I'm sorry—" I'm gasping it as I retch from exhaustion and agony.

Ruiz is in the ring. Staring down at me. "You only win if you're on your feet, Colt."

"Get up, motherfucker," Moreno snarls at me through clenched teeth. "Stand your ass up or you a dead man."

I roll to my back, gasp, spit and feel it land on my cheek, on the side of my neck. I taste blood and bile. I roll to my side and lever my feet under me, plant my palms on the cold, gritty, greasy concrete and grunt with the effort of holding my weight up.

I can't breathe. Each inflation of my lungs sends a spear of agony through me, each motion is utterly excruciating: broken ribs. I don't remember that happening.

The crowd is still and silent. Latinos stand in a protective circle around Moreno, and more than one is wielding a knife. Shit is about to go down, for real.

The tension is so thick it's like a fog in the room. No one even dares breathe. Apparently it's fine to beat a dude to a bloody pulp, but it's not okay to cripple him. Who knew?

"Winner, Colt." Ruiz shoves me unceremoniously through the crowd and outside.

The warehouse is on a wharf, water lapping gently against the pylons. The moon is full overhead, illuminating shapes in the water, evidence of a pier that had once stood here. Manhattan is a gleaming, twinkling vista across the water. We might be in New Jersey, I don't know.

"Jesus goddamn, Colt!" Rhino is there, suddenly, whacking me on the back. "You crushed his ass, man. I can't believe that shit. You fucked him *up*!"

Eli is on my other side. "That was fuckin' brutal, my man."

I keep feeling his knee crunch under my fist. I could be sick again from the memory. "I didn't mean to—"

"But you did it. Can't take that shit back, now." Rhino is standing in front of me, prodding my torso with thick fingers, nodding when I wince and groan at his touch. "Broke some ribs. You done fightin' for a minute, son. Come on."

I have to walk on my own. I refuse to lean on him, or anyone. It's a battle, though, just to make it the hundred yards up the wharf to Rhino's car, a big Escalade with shiny spinner rims and ground effects. Climbing into the smooth leather saps me of everything I've got left.

I see Eli's car ahead of us, and then he's gone and Rhino is bobbing his head to the thudding bass of the hip-hop coming from the speakers.

"Nothin' to be done for broke ribs but let 'em heal on they own," he says. "But I got some shit that'll take the edge off."

I just groan and collapse against the window. Yellow-orange lights brighten overhead and recede, and then there's the buzz of the tunnel and the occasional wash of oncoming headlights, and I have to fight for each breath.

"That was a hell of a fight," Rhino says. "You made a name for yourself with that one. The big dogs will want a piece of you, now. Big money comin' your way."

"I can't...I can't breathe..." I gasp.

Rhino just chuckles, a sound like an avalanche.

"Busted ribs'll do that. Straighten up, lean the seat back. Don't stress them fractures an' it'll feel better. Still hurts like a mo-fo, but not as bad if your torso weren't twisted."

I lever the seat backward until I feel the tugging tension lessen, and then I can suddenly breathe a little easier. The lance of agony recedes just a bit, enough that I can draw a shallow breath. Not too deep, or the pain hits likes a gunshot.

Miles and minutes pass in silence. Rhino glances at me. "I saw a guy get killed in the ring, once. Just a freak fuckin' accident. Took a hit to the skull, fell, cracked his head open. We was miles from any doctors, so he just…bled out. Twitched and bled until he wasn't breathin' no more."

"Jesus."

"It's underground fighting, dog. Bad shit is gonna happen." He twists his fist on the steering wheel. "I wrecked a few people in my time. Broke a guy's jaw so bad he needed reconstructive surgery, wires and screws and shit. Put another guy in traction for a month. Broke legs, knocked out teeth. It ain't pretty. You don't fight in those rings and not dish out pain, just like you don't fight in those rings and not take pain. You gonna hurt, and you gonna get hurt. Can't pussy out now. Just gotta deal with it."

Seven: Split; the Drive-by
Five months later

AFTER MY RIBS FINALLY HEALED, RHINO WORKED ME LIKE A fucking dog. Hours and hours and hours in the gym, to where I couldn't fucking move afterward. He forced me to choke down protein shakes and protein bars, forced me to eat fish like I'm a goddamned penguin. I'd eat two steaks at a time, half a dozen eggs every morning. He made me run five miles every morning and pushed me to lift, lift, lift, deadlifts and dips and all sorts of fancy shit all day long. No fights, no girls, just endless hours in the gym, technique lessons and hours working the bag and the speedball and sparring with Rhino. Rest on Sundays, smoke weed until I'm floating in outer space, drink a forty, listen to hip-hop, cruise the streets in Rhino's Escalade.

He introduced me to hundreds of people. He knows everyone in his neighborhood, old and young, male and female. Everyone. Kids, old folks, hard-as-fuck OGs, little babies. They all hug him, clap him on his burly shoulder and are happy to pass the time. They eye me warily at first, but eventually they accept me.

By the time the fifth month has passed, I've put on fifty pounds of solid muscle. If I was a beefcake before, I'm a fucking monster now. We never skipped leg day, either, so I'm light on my feet. There were entire days when I'd do nothing but practice footwork, hop the tires like you see on football camp news clips, do explosive jumps onto platforms three and four feet high. I'd shred my legs until I was jelly from the waist down, barely able to put one foot in front of the other.

I didn't see Eli once in that time. Rhino says he told Eli I needed time before my next fight to heal my ribs and get conditioned. In return for food and board and conditioning, Rhino has me help run his gym. I clean the machines, stack the weights at the end of the day, spot on the bench press, restock the drinks cooler, spar with training fighters in the ring. I do anything and everything, and I don't mind it. I've always relished the burn of a killer workout, but the difference between the bodyweight workouts I did in my bedroom and the targeted muscle training and bulking possible with specialized equipment is amazing. I'm not lean and muscular, now, I'm honestly ripped. Bulked out, padded with layers of muscle, low body fat. But quick, and my fists are lightning.

Rhino spars with me, late at night. As I begin to get better in the ring I notice him holding back less and less, feel his hits gain power, see him working to dodge mine and tensing to take them. I'd still never want to tangle with a beast like Rhino, but I've gained more confidence in my fighting abilities.

When I work my next fight, I'm gonna be unstoppable.

Eli shows up one Sunday and tosses a massive bag of icky-sticky on the table. Rhino pulls out a bud and breaks it up into crumbs. Eli has a cigarillo with him which he unrolls, shaking out the tobacco into the ashtray, and then hands it to Rhino, who fills the empty paper with pot, and rolls it back up into a tight thick blunt. He lights it, hands it to Eli first, his rights as the provider of the dope. Eli puffs deeply, holds it in, passes it to Rhino; there's a pecking order to these things, and I go last as the new guy.

Eli shoots a glance at me as he slowly lets the thick smoke billow out of his nose. "You beefed up, dog."

I nod. "Rhino's been kicking my ass."

"Looks good on you. You look like a straight-up killer."

"That's the point," Rhino rumbles. "He's gonna crush some mothafuckas, now."

Eli rubs his palms on his knees as I take my hit of the blunt. "I've got him a fight on Tuesday. A new guy, big and bad. Train's pick, as a come-up in case Julius don't cut it."

"How is Julius?" I ask.

Eli shrugs. "Still kickin' ass. Train put him through some Muay Thai classes with a guy named Johnny. He's been puttin' on the hurt."

I watch Rhino take a huge drag. "What's the new guy like?" I ask.

Eli shrugs again. "Like I said, big and bad. Not as big as you, now. But new. Only had one fight, and it was a close one. I don't think you'll have any trouble."

Rhino shakes his head. "He won't. I don't think many guys on the roster can touch him." A sharp glance at me. "Don't get cocky. You never know what a fighter is like until you fight him. The only fight I ever lost was to a little Filipino dude. Faster'n fuck, hit like a mothafuckin' bazooka. Jumped around so fast I couldn't get a hit in. He took me down so fast my

head was still spinning the next day. I went in thinkin'
I'd crush him like a bug, he was so damn tiny. Point
is, don't go gettin' cocky. But I don't think you'll have
any trouble."

I didn't have any trouble. I dominated that fight, and
two more that night.

And after four months of monkish celibacy,
thank god Raquel was working the fight that night.
She introduced me to her friend Lisa, and the three
of us got it on like Donkey Kong, my first time with
more than one girl, which, honestly, was a lot more
work than I thought it'd be, keeping two girls going
at once. Good thing I'm coordinated.

Three more fights the next week, and the same
the next—and now that I'd met Lisa, if Raquel wasn't
there, Lisa was, or one of their other friends. The
kinds of girls who work topless at underground
fights...they're a good time, and they all seemed to
like me. Maybe it was just because I crushed every
motherfucker put in front of me. I was a one-man
wrecking-machine. I made bank, as they say, a thousand per fight in the first month, two grand per fight
the next month, made it to five by the third month.
And I stashed it all. Every penny. Kept shredding myself in Rhino's gym, kept running the ship for him,

and trained in the ring and at the bags until my knuckles were like stone. I started taping them up, all the way up to my forearms, and fought barefoot, like Julio Moreno. A nod to him, partly, and partly because it felt right. Bare concrete under my feet, I could feel the floor, I could feel each punch twisting up like a tornado.

I saved my bank, and I fought like a wounded tiger. Fight after fight. Weeks. Months.

Sooner than I expected I'm past my nineteenth birthday, hitting on my twentieth. I haven't heard from Mom or Dad, or anyone back home. I do wonder about Kyle, how he's doing. He's thirteen, now, I think. Almost fourteen? I don't really miss home, but I do sort of miss Mom. She was cool to me, for the most part. And Kyle, too. But…I'm here now, making progress. Not much of a life, but it's mine. Better than being at fucking Harvard or wherever the fuck Dad wanted me to go. That shit sounds like hell, if you ask me.

I take beatings, of course. I go home bloody, nose broken, ribs sore. But I always win. Always.

And then I get stupid. I get cocky.

It's late, early, whatever, I don't really remember. I think it's close to three a.m., maybe near four. I've already fought once and made an easy ten grand. Beat the poor asshole six ways to Sunday. I'm feeling good, feeling unstoppable. Guys who go into the ring with me are shaking, afraid. They know what my fists can do, they've watched me wreck fighter after fighter, tearing them apart like goddamn rice paper.

Whatever. About three in the morning, Eli slides in beside me where I'm buried in the crowd, watching the fight. Bodies are sweaty and stinking around me, shouts echo in the warehouse, fists smack on flesh.

Eli elbows me. "Got a proposition for you."

I glance at him. "You know I'm up for a fight."

He shakes his head. "Naw, man. It ain't like that. It's a challenge. Two mid-level fighters want to take you on. Both of 'em at once. Never been done before, but Train and I are both willing to put money on you. Top dollar. But you gotta be sure, 'cause these two guys are good. One on one, you'd fuck 'em up no problem. But both of 'em at once? Could be trouble. Deal is, you take this challenge, we'll deal you in from what we bank on the win. You lose, you pay us. Either way, it's gonna put the hurt on you. These boys are no joke."

My chest swells. Pride—stupid, foolish hubris—fills my skull. "Fuck 'em. I'll take them both on."

Eli squints at me. "You sure, dog? You double sure? Because we're talking…a hundred G's at least.

To you, or you owe us. If you lose, you'll have to fight for free till we got our bank back."

I do have fifty grand, but that's every penny I have stashed back at Rhino's. Every damn penny. But a hundred grand…? That's a stake in an auto shop. I know a guy near Rhino's gym that has an auto shop, but he's struggling. He needs a fresh infusion of cash for new equipment, and he needs another mechanic to take clients. I've already proven my skill by disassembling and reassembling an engine for him, so it's an in. But Diego needs a hundred and fifty grand minimum stake. This one fight could get me there, whereas I'd have to fight twenty more times to make that.

Plus, I'm cocky.

"I got 'em, Eli. No sweat."

Eli smacks me on the back. "A'ight, dog. But you better fuckin' win. This is big time."

"You guys always say that to me." I roll my shoulders and glance at Eli. "When's the fight?"

Eli gestures to the ring, which has been cleared of the previous fighters, and I watch as two massive black guys swagger in, both shirtless and boasting ripped physiques, gang tats, and scars. They both have matching green bandanas tied to their belt loops, professing affiliation to a particular gang. I'm not sure which one, but I don't care. Eli wasn't joking. These boys are big, and tough looking. The only reason they're considered mid-level is because they're relatively new with less than ten fights under their belts. Plenty of blood shed for both out on the streets, no question.

I feel a twitch of doubt.

Fuck that.

I push through the crowd, and they part as they realize it's me. Once I'm in the ring, I strip off my shirt and kick off my shoes and socks. I still have my hands taped. I do some jumping jacks to get my blood pumping. I jump using only my feet and calves, then I stretch my hams and quads. The two fighters watch, smirking. They're motionless, side by side, arms crossed over their massive chests. Their knuckles are scarred. One has a cut over his eyebrow, the other a swollen lip; they've both fought tonight.

Ruiz is in the center of the ring. He's eyeing me, shaking his head. "Bad idea, *ese*. I seen these dudes fight. They nasty."

"I got it."

"Your funeral." He addresses the crowd. "We got something new tonight. A two-on-one. The one, the only…COLT! Over a hundred fights, and he remains undefeated. Trying to take him down are Irving and

Jermaine, eight fights each, no losses for either fighter. Odds? That's tricky. One on one, Colt is heavily favored. Two on one like this? His odds drop by a lot. I'd call it evenly matched at best."

Shit shit shit shit.

Now that I'm in a ring with these guys, I'm starting to feel the slightest hint of fear. This is a bad idea. A really bad idea.

Can't back down now. The only thing to do is grab on to the fear. Let it crystallize and harden inside me. Fear is what keeps you careful. Fear makes you a survivor. I'm afraid, and I'm going to win.

A hundred grand in hand. Let me get my hands on some Craftsman tools, get some grease under my nails again. Engine oil in my nostrils, the rumble of a finely tuned engine.

"Ready?" Ruiz looks at Irving and Jermaine, who simply stare impassively.

He looks at me, and I nod. I smack my fists together. The sting of bone on bone zings though me.

"Fight!" Ruiz steps back, dropping his hand between us.

Jermaine and Irving—I have no idea which is which, as they're similar enough in appearance that they very well might be brothers—split apart, circle in opposite directions so I have no way of keeping them both in front of me. Goddamn, I'm a dumbass. Fucking arrogant dumbass. I'm gonna get my ass kicked. One of them swings, a loose, lazy swipe. They have to have seen me fight; they have to know that shit won't fly. I dodge it, and that's when I, too late, recognize the tactic. I dodge…right into a hook from the guy behind me. Take it to the kidney. I grunt through it, dance backward, pivot, swing, make contact with a ribcage, plow forward and swing again. I put all my power into each hit, and now chaos is in my blood, the world is pain and suffering and punches thrown, punches taken.

Blood haze fills my vision. My eyebrow is split open. Lip cut. Gash on my ribs. I'm dishing it out, though. They're bloody, hurting, keeping their distance when they're not attacking. Tactical, those two motherfuckers. Never together, never where I can see them both. Hammer at one, the other is behind me, slamming a fist into my ribs, my back.

It's a knock-down, drag-out brawl, a brutal thrashing for all three of us. Me, mostly.

I have to end it.

I dodge one uppercut, dance and pivot, duck and weave and deliver a hammering blow to a diaphragm. The other one is behind me, battering at me mercilessly, but I call on all my will, all my determination, and gut through the pain. The diaphragm blow creates a momentary opening, a torso exposed as he gasps for breath. I rocket my fist straight in, my knuckles hit throat and he's down, gurgling, gasping and gagging, rolling away. I spin, in a clinch with the other one, long enough to catch my breath, and then shove him away and hook a fist to his gut to buy myself more time. The other one is still down, still gagging. I move for him, stand over him, meet his gaze. He's wide-eyed, terrified that he'll asphyxiate. Shakes his head, holds up a hand—*no more; I'm out.*

One on one, now.

I spit out a gobbet of bloody saliva as I face my remaining opponent. He's an enraged beast, breathing hard, one hand on his knee, drooling blood. Eyeing me with hate as he catches his breath. I stride in, straight on, chin high, chest swelling with vengeful breath. Two on one?

I fuckin' got this.

But he's fast. Faster than I thought. So fucking fast. Lunges under my swing and buries his fist in my gut, doubling me over with a hit so powerful I nearly vomit. Head-butts me, breaking my nose. Hammers three lightning punches to my liver.

I'm dizzy, reeling, sagging. He's on me, feral and frightening, brutalizing me until I'm ready to beg for him to stop, but I don't, I stay on my feet through sheer force of will. I stagger, then fall to one knee.

I'm done.

He's over me, a position I know too well, prepared to deliver the finisher, that angling downward fist of fury, to end me. Crush me.

I've got one chance left, one last burst of power, maybe.

I wait for it.

He eyes the crowd, smelling victory. I'm gagging on my snot and saliva and blood, and every fiber of my being hurts. I can barely breathe. My ribs are damn near broken again, I think, bruised from endless battering. My legs are weak and my heart is pounding from over-exertion. Vomit pools in my throat, hot and burning, acidic, bile behind my teeth. Sweat pours, blood coats my face and my chest and my fists. The crowd is screaming, they are wild, and hoping for my downfall.

He swings, a vicious arcing blow meant for my skull.

I hurl myself forward, feel the rough concrete under my shoulder shred my skin as I roll. I dive for him, catch him at the knees with my shoulder. He's barreled off his feet, and I hear his head crack on the ground. He's dazed, but not down. Taken harder knocks, I'm sure, a tough-ass motherfucker like this don't go down easy. No fucking way.

I haul myself onto him and straddle his chest, batter his face with both fists, one-two, one-two, to the shrill manic wild howling of the crowd, and then Ruiz and Eli and Rhino are pulling me away, and the moment I'm off him, I go limp.

They release me, and I sag to my knees, vomit bile and blood. I spit and cough and sob. Unable to get up, I collapse forward and feel the cold concrete smash my face, but I don't care. I can't breathe, can't move.

"Gotta be on your feet to win, Colt." Ruiz, as always. Calm.

I can't stand up. I'm drooling and there's a pool of blood under my face. I cough again, tasting bile and the metallic tang of blood. I get my knees under me, and then scramble with my palms on the gritty cement floor. It's messy and sloppy and undignified, but I'm fucking hamburger. I make it to hands and knees. Breathing hard, I struggle to get a foot planted on the floor. I have to groan and pull deep, as if I'm trying to power that last rep on the bench press. No one will help me. They can't, they won't, and I wouldn't let them. I have to stand up on my own, or it doesn't count.

Eli watches, Rhino watches. Ruiz waits. No counting, just the wait.

The crowd has quieted.

I sag back to my hands and knees. I can't fucking do it. I hurt too badly. I fucking hurt. I want to cry, it hurts so bad. I'm screaming through clenched teeth as I strain, push...

"COLT! COLT! COLT!" The crowd is chanting, pumping their fists in the air. They want this.

"Get on your fucking feet, white boy," Rhino grumbles.

"C'mon, man," Eli says. "Don't puss out on me now, dog."

"Fuck...you..." I gag, though drool and blood and sobs of effort.

One foot.

I shove myself back onto my knee with both hands, shaking, grunting as if I'm lifting the world onto my shoulders.

My second foot plants on concrete, and I'm up.

Fuck yes, hell yes, I'm up.

A hundred fucking grand, baby.

I stagger backward, bounce off Rhino, who grabs onto my bicep and holds me in place. I'm woozy, dizzy, seeing double, barely staying on my feet.

"Colt wins," Ruiz says. "Pay up, losers."

Jermaine and Irving are still on the ground. I push off Rhino and stumble over to them. Lean down and extend my hand to the one whose throat I crushed. He claps a hand to mine, and I haul him up. He doesn't say anything, and even if he could, what do you say? There was no beef between us, this is just what we do: hammer the shit out of each other for money. Crazy motherfuckers, we are. I lurch unsteadily to the other one, and he's blinking up at me through bloodshot, swelling eyes, drools through puffy, split lips. I extend my hand to him.

He hesitates. Doesn't want to take my hand or accept my help to get to his feet. There is enmity here, because you can't fight and not feel the rage burn through you. It's how you win, that rage. It's what we all have in common, a baseline rage that fuels us. But in the end, his eyes search mine. Palm slaps palm, and I haul him to his feet. He pushes me away, wraps an arm around his friend or brother, and they stagger away together. Leaning on each other, muttering to each other.

I watch their easy, familiar camaraderie with envy.

Eli and Rhino are pulling me away. They've both got stacks of rubber-banded bundles of cash in their hands. They banked huge on my win.

They leave me leaning against the front quarter panel of Rhino's black Escalade, stack their winnings on the hood and count through it, always with an eye for their surroundings. Wouldn't put it past someone to make a play for it. It's a hell of a lot of money.

"That was a close one, dog," Eli says.

And in that moment, I realize something: Eli feels zero loyalty to me. I'm a cash cow for him. He makes tens of thousands of dollars on me every fight, every week, and I'm his boy as long as I win. The moment I lose, he'll ditch me.

I see Rhino eyeing me, eyeing Eli.

He sees it, sees me realize it.

Shakes his head: *not here, not now.*

I say nothing to Eli for a few minutes, gathering my sense so I don't spit out something reckless. "But I won, though," is what I say.

"Barely." He hands me ten bundles of cash. There's at least twenty left, maybe even more. If each bundle is ten grand, he made easily two hundred grand off me, and is giving me less than half, which is a much larger percentage than normal.

I made a hundred grand off this fight, which is just my take from what Eli and Rhino netted. I've got a hundred and eighty grand banked, now. That's a hell of a lot of money; I could probably get that stake in Diego's garage, but then I'd be working for him, and that's not what I want. I need my *own* place. I'll keep banking every cent until I can afford more than a stake in someone else's shop. Not much else to do with the money, anyway.

He places his hands on the pile of cash stacks, eyes cold and hard on me. "Take a break, Colt. Coupla weeks, maybe." His eyes roam over my face, and even he winces. "Man, you are fucked up. Took some of the pretty outta you."

"Thanks." I say it drily.

Eli ignores my sarcastic jab, extends a palm to me, and I slap it with mine. No shoulder bump here. "I'm out, man." He turns to Rhino and they thug-hug. "Take care of my boy. Get him back on his feet."

"I am on my feet," I protest.

Eli just laughs. "A six-year-old could knock you down, dog."

I'm angry. At myself, at him. I wonder how much I've made him over the last two-plus years that I've been fighting for him. I'm angry that it took me so long to realize he feels no loyalty to me. Eli carries his cash to his Buick, and the engine catches with that gorgeous throaty rumble. He's gone in a cloud of exhaust and a receding trail of red taillights.

"Let's get out of here, Colt. You need some

stitches, at least." Rhino scoops up his money and tosses it carelessly onto the backseat, then hops into the driver's seat.

I'm slowly, gingerly, climbing into the passenger seat when a figure lopes out of the warehouse, heading for me. At first I think it's Raquel or one of the other girls, and in my current condition I'm not sure I can physically handle anything, as much as it pains me to admit.

"Yo, hold up." Turns out to be a black guy, maybe five-eight, five-nine, slim, lean, razor-sharp. Skin like ink, like unfiltered shadows.

"What up, Split?" Rhino says. Sounds...almost apprehensive.

"Can I get a minute with ya boy Colt?"

"Real quick."

They're trading me around like I'm a kid, or a possession. Irritating. Split walks away and stands with his back to the cinderblock wall of the warehouse, waiting for me. He establishes authority by making me come to him. I hobble over, hurt, irritated, tired, ready to crash.

"What's going on?" I ask.

Split pulls out a pre-rolled joint, lights it, and passes it to me. This is business, then. "I'm with the Five-One Bishops."

We pass the joint back and forth as we talk.

"Okay."

"You want out of the ring." It's not a question.

"I might."

"Quit playin'. I seen that shit. You won that fight by the skin of your teeth. I think there's a better use for your skills."

"Which would be what?"

"Helping me out. I need someone at my back who ain't...familiar. Push people around who ain't steppin' up the way they should."

"Enforcer, basically."

"I need a soldier." He indicates Rhino with a subtle gesture only I can see. "You quit fighting, he's gonna find someone else. No hard feelings, but it's what he does. Eli? Man, you lose once, you're done. You all alone out here. You got no friends. Rhino ain't your friend. Eli sure as hell ain't your friend."

"And you are?"

"Could be. My boys could be." I meet his gaze, finally, and what I see scares me.

He's not cold; there's a life in his eyes, but it's that of a true warrior. He's seen shit. He's known death and violence, and bloodshed, and loss. His eyes are piercing. There's a razor-sharp intelligence in his eyes, a trust-your-gut ability to assess someone with a single glance. His eyes are light, light brown, almost khaki. Fierce, piercing, penetrating.

"I ain't offerin' you a job, man. I'm offering you a *life*." He jerks a thumb backward, at the interior of the warehouse and the fights still happening within. "That ain't a life."

"Why me?"

"Cause you're a survivor. A winner. I watched that fight, man, and you was done. You was *done*. But you pulled it out. That's a quality wasted in there."

And it's not wasted running in a gang? I don't say this, but I think it. And yet… he presents a temptation.

I hate fighting. I like winning, and I like the money, but it's taking a toll. And the beating I just took…I don't know if I have it in me to do it again. It brought me money but, like Split says, I barely pulled it off. And if I hadn't, I'd be in debt to Eli and Rhino. Debt I'd never pay off. I'd never get ahead. I'm making killer bank, fighting for Eli and Rhino, but it's a losing game. Eventually someone will take me down, and I'll be done. Maybe it's time to get out of the game while I'm ahead. I could have friends, somebody to watch my back. A life where I'm not waking up in pain, with bruised ribs and bloody saliva and a broken nose. Won't make as much money, might take longer to get my shop, but I'm starting to realize that maybe there's a better way, a better life out there for me than pounding faces and getting my ass kicked week after week.

"Lemme tell you something," Split says. "You earn my loyalty, I'll have your back for life. You earn the loyalty of my boys, we got your back for life."

"How do I earn your loyalty?"

"Have our backs. Never back down. Do what you gotta do. Loyalty to the Bishops before anything. Every single time."

"I need to think about it."

"Don't think too long. Offer only stands for so long." He pinches the cherry off the quarter-inch long roach.

"How do I find you?"

"I know where you at. I'll stop by."

"All right."

Split ambles away, dropping the roach into the bottom of a pack of cigarettes. I watch him go, and when he's out of sight, I head back to Rhino's SUV. He's leaning back in the driver's seat, the flat brim of his Yankees ball cap pulled low over his eyes. When I climb in, slowly and with grunts of pain, he flicks the brim up and eyes me.

"So. Gonna run with the Bishops, huh?" He starts the truck and pulls away from the warehouse.

"Might."

"Think getting clear of the ring is hard? The Bishops'll never let you go."

"Haven't decided yet." A few minutes pass in silence. And then I risk the question. "You know Split?"

"Seen him around. The Bishops' turf is close by. As for Split? Just don't make him your enemy. All's I got to say about that."

Coming from Rhino, that says something.

The decision is made for me, a few days later. Late at night, Rhino and I are pushing weight. Just him and me in the gym. Somewhere out on the street tires squeal. I don't think anything of it. Rhino, though, hears something in the howling of burning rubber that I don't. He drops the bar into the hooks, slides off the bench far faster than a man of his size should be capable of, and grabs my two-hundred-and-fifty pound barbell in his hands, settles it, and hauls me off the bench. All this takes less than fifteen seconds. Headlights flood the street beyond the plate glass window of the gym.

There's a desk in one corner, with a big gray metal filing cabinet beside it. Rhino shoves me across the room, hard enough that I hit the wall with a thud. He tips over the desk, and then with one violent shove he knocks the filing cabinet over onto its side. He jerks me down, shoves my head down so I'm parallel with the floor, then rips open a drawer of the desk and pulls out a massive black semi-automatic pistol, a Magnum, maybe. I don't know much about guns. Big as fuck, that's all I can tell for sure.

"The hell is going on, Rhino?" I ask.

"Keep your fuckin' head down and shut the fuck up." He's behind the desk, his enormous bulk hunkered down into as small a package as possible behind the battered metal of the desk.

In that moment, as I'm about to ask again what the fuck is happening, an old four-door sedan skids to a stop out front, nondescript, tan, maybe an early '90s model Taurus or something similar. I duck down behind the filing cabinet as I realize what's about to happen. A few feet away there's a deafening blast, Rhino opening fire first. The plate glass shatters, and another thundering blast scuds through the air. And then it's a war zone. Fully automatic gunfire rattles, a shotgun rips, handguns chatter. Rhino's Magnum blasts slowly, methodically, and I hear a shout of pain, a second, a third.

I see a chunk of wall explode over my head, and then the filing cabinet is dinging and thunking from the impact of bullets. I stop breathing and can only hope the rounds don't make it through the metal. I hear a grunt from Rhino, and then three rapid-fire blasts from his pistol, a silence, then a *thud-click* as he reloads.

There's a fraught fraction of silence, and then I hear Rhino's heavy footsteps thudding across the floor, boots crunching in the glass, and he's blasting, blasting, shouting, and tires are squealing.

"Get gone, mothafuckas! Can't take me! I'll kill all y'all!"

Silence again.

I raise my head, and assess. The plaster of the wall above my head is shredded, studs showing through. A couple of the studs are blasted apart. The cabinet I hid behind is riddled with dents. The desk is, too.

Glass litters the floor and sidewalk around the window frame, and I see streetlights glinting off the glass, off the shells scattered on the pavement. Rhino is standing in the middle of the street, handgun dangling at his side. He's wearing a wife-beater tank top; blood trickles down his arm, a gash in the bicep high up, near the shoulder. I step out into the street beside him.

There's three different pools of blood on the road, gleaming black.

"Fuckin' punks. Thinkin' they can shoot my shit

up and get away with it. They just signed they's death warrants. Can't drive-by a OG, mothafuckas. I'll kill 'em all."

"You all right?" I ask.

He whirls on me, and his palm smacks against my chest, sending me stumbling backward. "NO! No, I'm not fuckin' all right. I'm shot, and my gym is fucked up. And it's all because your dumb ass couldn't turn down a fight you had no business steppin' into. Shoulda said no, stupid ass white boy. Stupid ass. Fuckin' stupid ass. Lucky those punks couldn't shoot for shit."

"That was...what were their names...Irving and Jermaine?"

"Yeah, them and the rest of the Trey-Nines come after you. Started some shit they can't finish. I'm retired from that shit, but now they done pissed me off."

"Why would they do that?"

"Get you back for embarrassin' them in the fight. You shouldn't'a won. They cain't allow that shit."

"I'm sorry—"

"You got to get outta here. They'll come back, and I'mma be gunnin' for 'em."

He stalks back toward his gym, steps through the window frame. I follow him, and when he opens a narrow closet and takes a broom, I take it from him and start sweeping up the glass.

He watches for a moment, and then stomps toward me, snatches it away. "Naw, man. My gym, I'll clean it up. Get outta here."

"Rhino—"

"I ain't mad at you, kid. But if you step up with Split and them, this is your life. It'll be you in a car like that, shootin' up somebody's house. Know that. You step up with the Bishops, that's your life."

"I don't know where else to go. What else to do."

He shrugs. "Welcome to the big leagues, dog."

I leave him sweeping up glass and plaster, head upstairs, shove my clothes and my cash savings into my backpack. I've got almost two hundred grand in that backpack, this time. It's all I've got, and it still fits in a backpack.

I unpack a stack of cash, a ten-G stack. I take it with me as I go back down to the gym, where Rhino is ripping the ruined plaster off the walls with his bare hands, tearing it down in angry jerks, hauling off huge sections of drywall and tossing it aside. I watch for a second, feeling a pang. I don't want to leave here. I liked it here, working out, eating, smoking, just chillin', safe, away from it all.

I set the cash on the desk, and Rhino sees.

"I don't want your fuckin' money, man."

"But your gym—"

"It ain't about money. I built this place with my own two hands. I put up the studs, put up the drywall. I hauled every piece of equipment in here. I built the ring. I hung the window. One stupid fuckin' drive-by, and I gotta do it all over again. I got money. It's just...it's just the fact of having to do it all over again. Na'mean?" He tosses the stack of cash back at me, and I catch it, put it in my bag.

Headlights approach, but no squealing tires. Rhino feels for the huge pistol at the back of his waistband, but doesn't seem worried. The headlights broaden until the front of a rusted 1970s Pontiac GTO slides into view. The engine rumbles nice and loud, but it's got a catch in the burble, a piston gone bad. Needs a tune-up.

The headlights stay on, the engine keeps rumbling, but the driver's door opens, and Split steps out, stretchy red do-rag tied at the back of his head. He eyes the pools of blood in the street, the window frame, the bullet holes in the desk and wall and cabinet. The passenger door opens, and another brother steps out. Shorter, stocky, black do-rag, baggy jeans hanging way low, white T-shirt hem hanging around his thighs. Walks with a deep swagger, doesn't say anything, just stands next to Split.

"Lemme guess...Trey-Nines?" Split says, stepping through the window frame.

"You got it," Rhino answers, glancing up and then returning his attention to piling the drywall in a corner.

"Think they know who they started beef with?"

Rhino shrugs. "They sure as hell gonna find out."

"Want me to take the boys for a ride?" Split asks, and the question is fraught.

"Nah. I got this. Pull the Bishops into it, we'll have us a four-way problem. Bishops, the Eighty-Eights, the Trey-Nines, and their boys the 113 Posse. Just take Colt and let me handle it."

Split nods, then looks to me. "What about it, Colt?"

I let out a breath. "That, or try the streets again on my own. I guess I'm in."

Split straightens, and faces me. "Naw, see, you got two problems. One, now that the Trey-Nines are after you, you won't last an hour out there by yourself. Two, you can't guess. You're in, or you're not."

"It was a two-on-one fight that I won! How can they be after me?"

"You weren't supposed to win. And then you went and helped them up. They gotta save face."

"And if I go with you?"

"The Trey-Nines don't dare start anything with

us. We got twice the numbers, way more turf, and way more alliances. They start beef with the Bishops, they done. We'll clean 'em up. Won't be no one left."

"And you'll take me in, just because I won that fight?"

"You gotta earn your place, but yeah."

"Hate to point out the obvious, here, but...I'm white, you're black. I'm not from here. I don't know you, or your friends. And you'd let me into a black street gang?"

"'Black street gang.'" He laughs. "You funny. You wouldn't be 'in the gang'." He emphasizes the phrase with a mocking tone of voice. "You'd be with me. Maybe in time I'd get the others to accept you, but that'd take a while."

"Why?"

He frowns at me. "Why are you questioning this?"

I shrug. "Nothing is easy. Nothing is free."

"Got that right."

"I just don't get it. I don't know much about how all this shit works, but I do know that it doesn't work like this."

"Smart. It don't, usually." He leans close. "But I got a problem, and I think you can help me solve it. In return, you'll have protection. And as a white guy in this hood, you need it."

How did I get here? What am I doing? How is this my life?

"I'm in." I don't see much choice. Rhino wants me gone. Eli'll drop me the second I lose a fight. But the sad thing is, despite the fact that I've got a good bit of cash saved, I have nowhere else to go. What would I do? Flip burgers at McDonald's? I don't know Split at all, really, but it seems like a way out of the endless cycle I've gotten myself stuck in, where I don't dare lose, don't dare mess up, don't dare trust anyone. I want to trust Split, I want to feel like I've got someone to count on. Not much to ask, I don't think.

Another pair of headlights appears, coming from the other direction. Then another, and a third set. Three black SUVs slide up, driving nose-to-tail, stopping in unison right in front of Rhino's gym, less than three feet from Split's car. Fifteen men clamber out of the SUVs, all of them dressed in black denim jackets, baggy black jeans, boots, and Yankees hats like Rhino frequently wears. They're all carrying shotguns and handguns, and a couple of them have assault rifles slung over their shoulders. They don't spare a single glance for Split or me, they don't speak a word. They push past us, into the gym. Surround Rhino, who hasn't bothered to even staunch the bleeding from the graze wound in his bicep. Low murmurs.

Rhino pushes through the crowd. "Time for y'all to go."

He's got a sawed-off, pistol-grip shotgun in his hand. His demeanor is utterly changed from the quiet, easygoing person I've come to know. Cold, hard, huge, and scary as fuck. Not someone I want to be in the way of.

Yet another pair of headlights appears, this time a box truck. It squeals to a stop, two young black guys hop out and open the back roller door. Construction equipment, buckets of drywall plaster, ladders, a huge sheet of glass secured against one wall framed off with two-by-fours, a new desk, a new filing cabinet. Brooms, trashcans, shovels, toolboxes.

Rhino doesn't wait for acknowledgment, just slides into the front passenger seat of the foremost SUV, and the rest of the armed gang members pile in after him. Within seconds, the three trucks are gone, and the two left to handle the rebuild are busily removing debris.

"Time to go," Split says. "I'll explain what I need from you on the way."

I slide in the back, a guy I don't know sits in the passenger seat beside Split.

He turns around and simply says, "T-Shawn." He

extends his fist, and we bump knuckles.

"Colt."

"Welcome to the Bishops."

Somehow, I don't think it'll be as easy as all that—a brief hey how are you welcome. You always gotta prove yourself and, in this world, that ain't always easy. But I'm about to find out.

As we drive off into the night cold reality sets in—I'm starting over.

Again.

Eight: A Girl Named India

BEING ALLIED WITH THE BISHOPS IS NOT WHAT I THOUGHT it would be. In the end it's just...living: working, eating, smoking, getting paid, the occasional tumble with one of the always-willing girls that hang around the Bishops. And, sure, there was some minor physical intimidation and bullying, fights over turf, moving bags of pot, minor shit like that. Split usually just wanted a way to get people who owed him money to pay up without having to resort to actually shooting them. Getting people to pay attention, know what I mean? So he went old school: intimidation. Rough 'em up. Show them he meant business. Which is where I came in. I was big, ripped, and willing to slug a few stomachs if that's what it took to get 'em to understand. And, for me, it meant not having to fight in the ring anymore. My main job was to scare people into paying up.

Sometimes they held out.

And that never, ever worked very well for them.

I'd be brought in; I'd throw them around. Loosen some teeth, bloody some noses, bruise a few ribs. These guys were often young thugs who thought they were hard. They'd owe Split money for drugs, or owe Split loyalty they wouldn't show. My job was to convince them otherwise without Split having to play his hand.

The first time somebody refused, Split—who normally stays back by the door and keeps quiet—stepped forward and stood in front of the stubborn asshole and just stared him down. The poor scared guy caved in a heartbeat. Clearly he knew something about Split that I didn't.

Then a few months later, somebody else decided to snitch, got one of the Bishops arrested for possession of narcotics and illegal firearms. Thing about this world is, loyalty is king. You do not *ever* talk to cops. Not ever. They tended to stay clear of our turf for the most part, except the occasional patrol, or if someone pulled out a gun and started shooting. So if someone snitches, especially to the fucking narcs, it doesn't end well.

Split told me to be rough and show no mercy. So I played hard-ass and left the snitch on the ground, a bloody mess. When it was done Split ambled over, slow, like a snake slithering through the grass toward its prey.

He knelt down and whispered something in the snitch's ear.

Immediately, I smelled urine—the snitch was pissing himself in fear.

Next day, that same guy was carried out of his house in a body bag. No one knew who killed him, but it wasn't me, and it wasn't Split. Apparently, the snitch had tried to barter with his guy on the other side of the badge for safety from Split.

Didn't work out too well for him, apparently.

A few more times, but not very often, somebody either snitched or held out. If they were just holding out, they got hurt and were convinced to pay up and play along. If they were a snitch...they vanished. Or were found dead. Messily.

I didn't care much for any of it, but what could I do? I'd allied myself to the Bishops. I had to pay attention to which side of the street I walked on, what color clothing I wore, who I spoke to. If I stepped wrong, spoke wrong, wore the wrong color, I'd end up dead or I'd start a turf war. Everybody knew I was with Split, which made me a de facto member of the Bishops.

Then one day things change.

I'm with Split and T-Shawn in Split's GTO—which I'd tuned up for him properly, of course—and we're cruising the Bishops' turf, cruising slow, slapping palms through the open car windows and exchanging greetings, waving, smoking, bass thudding low. And then, at the intersection just ahead of us, hell breaks loose in a fraction of a moment.

A young kid, new to the hood and trying to get the respect of the older G's, is just walking across the street. On his side of the turf. A car slides by, swerves hard, clips the kid with the front left quarter panel, sends him flying. His head cracks open against the curb, blood pooling out of his broken skull..

Split floors the gas pedal, and the old muscle car spools up and jolts forward in pursuit. We howl round the corner, tires screaming. The other car is a few dozen feet ahead when Split hauls out his piece from under his seat, a small black nine. He pops off a few slugs and nails the back tire and the back windshield. T-Shawn is popping off rounds as well, doing some serious damage.

I'm sitting in the back, frozen with fear; this is

new. There have been lots of rumbles and beefs before this, bats, chains, some knives drawn, and some blood spilled. But nobody has died, aside from the snitches. No guns have been hauled out and fired, not in front of me, at least. Maybe the established Bishops took care of that shit without me because, even now, I'm the outsider, the new guy, the white guy, the unknown.

The car ahead swerves, tires smoking, rims sparking on the pavement, and then spins to a stop.

Split halts the GTO, reaches in front of me and opens the glove box and hands me a pistol like his.

"Hell, no. I've never shot a gun." I shake my head.

"They killed a Bishop," T-Shawn murmurs. He doesn't say much, but when he does, you listen. "On our turf. For no fuckin' reason. Just a damn kid."

I take the piece. It's cold and heavy. It feels foreign in my hand.

Split steps out, and I follow a few seconds later, heart hammering. T-Shawn swings wide, his gun leveled. The car ahead is quiet and completely still. There's no sound. No cars anywhere.

The car is only twenty feet away at most, but it feels like a mile with that small cold heavy pistol in my hand.

My heart is in my throat, thick and bitter.

Adrenaline thunders in my veins.

Split heads toward the driver's side and gestures for me to go around to the passenger side. Gun up, held in both hands. I move forward slowly and carefully.

BANGBANGBANG!

I feel something hot and hard bite into my shoulder, and then everything goes hazy. My shoulder is hotter than hell, so hot it's numb, and I feel a throbbing ache. Pounding agony. I feel myself moving forward, see a face and a Mets logo, a sliver gun, the barrel a wide black hole. I see it buck. *BANG!* Something snaps past my face. I feel my hands jolt up involuntarily, and then I hear something crack.

Suddenly all I can see is red.

And then silence. Profound, vibrating silence.

Split is in front of me. I can't hear him but I can see his mouth moving, but I hear nothing. There's a thunder in my ears that drowns out everything. Split is pulling me toward the GTO and shoving me into the backseat, where I slump against the window.

Something wet trickles down my arm.

And it hurts like hell.

Split is silent now, and the GTO is hauling ass. He pulls out an old, blocky cell phone, flips it open and dials a number with his thumb. I hear him spitting out a few terse words to the person on the other end and then he disconnects the call. He's barreling way too fast around corners, zigzagging, squealing to slow for a corner and then hitting the gas. After a few blocks he finally slows to a normal driving speed.

T-Shawn glances at me. "You straight?"

I shake my head and twist to show him my shoulder. "I'm getting blood on your seat."

"Fuck, man," Split says. "Why didn't you say something?"

"Something?" I'm woozy, numb inside from the pain.

"Smart-ass." He spins the wheel and cuts across three lanes of traffic to make a sudden left. Split jerks his bandana off and hands it to me. "Put some pressure on that shit. Hold it tight."

"I killed him, didn't I?"

Split doesn't answer right away. "Unless that fucker can survive a hole in the face, yeah, you did."

"Goddamn it."

Split finally looks at me in the rearview mirror. "He shot first." He points to my face. "Nearly got you, too."

"He did get me."

"Naw, man. Check your shit." T-Shawn pulls open the visor, angles the mirror so I can see myself in it. There's a red line oozing blood across my temple. That last shot was millimeters from burying itself in my skull.

"Holy shit."

"You a G for real now, dog. Had our back. We won't forget that." He stops the GTO in front of an apartment building in the heart of Bishop territory.

We go in, up to the fourth floor. One of the doors flies open, and a young black woman runs out, hair in narrow braids hanging down to mid-back, gold hoops lining her ears. She's wearing skin-tight dark blue jeans and a white crop top. She jumps on Split and wraps her arms and legs around him. T-Shawn is there, but silent, as always.

"I heard," she says. "You okay?"

"I'm fine." Split gestures at me without putting her down. "He ain't fine. He needs his shoulder looked at."

"Mama's home."

Split gestures at the door, looking at me. "Come on in. You're safe here." He addresses his girlfriend. "Callie, this is my boy Colt. Colt, this is my girlfriend, Callie."

"Hi, Callie."

She smiles at me. She's short, curvy, beautiful, a vibrant white smile in a light brown face. "Heard you backed up my man today. Thanks."

"He's taken care of me, so…" I shrug, figuring the rest is self-evident.

"Split's got a good heart, he just hides it." Callie leads the way into the apartment unit.

It smells like food and cigarettes. Low ceilings, peeling paint, scuffed, scratched hardwood floor with a threadbare knitted oval rug in the middle of the floor. A twenty-year-old big-screen TV, massive speakers, a coffee table and ashtrays and cartons of Newports complete the decor. The kitchen is just off the living room, and Callie leads us there. A woman who could be Callie's twin except twenty years older stands at the stove, stirring something in a pot. A big square table takes up most of the kitchen, and my attention is immediately seized by the young woman sitting at the table.

I forget my name. I forget my wounded shoulder.

She's…stunningly beautiful. Breathtaking.

Even sitting down I can tell she's tall, maybe close to six feet, and close to my own age, early twenties. She has long curly hair hanging in tight spirals exploding in a halo around her thin, sharp-featured face. Her dark eyes are deep set between high angular cheekbones. She looks like she's part Asian, part black, all beautiful. God, so beautiful. Her eyes meet mine, and

I swear the air sparks between us.

Callie sees it and steps between us, snapping her fingers. "Oh, *hell* no. You, white boy, sit your ass down. Mama? Can you look at his shoulder?"

Callie's mother puts the wooden spoon across the top of the pot, wipes her hands on her apron, unties it and sets it on the counter. She washes her hands thoroughly, then rummages in a cabinet under the sink, pulling out a wide white ceramic dish full of boxes of medical supplies. She pulls out a chair from the table and gently pushes on my shoulders until I sit down. I can't take my eyes off the girl. I'm sucked in.

Split and T-Shawn have vanished somewhere in the apartment, leaving me alone with three women I've never met before, one of whom I can't seem to stop staring at.

"I need your shirt off," Callie's mother says. I try, but I can't get my arm over my head. Hurts too bad to even try to tough through it. She brandishes a pair of scissors. "Shirt's ruined anyway. I'll cut it off."

A couple of snips, and the bloodstained cotton is gone, and I'm naked from the waist up. The girl's eyes are immediately drawn to my upper body. Which, admittedly, is pretty beefed up. She can't look away from me, and I can't look away from her. Callie sees it, and isn't having any of it.

"Don't you have something to do, India?" Callie snaps.

India shrugs, a small, shy, sweet smile on her face. "Nope. I'm good."

Callie glares at me, and then turns back to the girl. India; god, even her name is gorgeous. Callie huffs. "He's *white*, India."

"And I'm half Korean. What's your point?"

"My point is...," she lets out a frustrated sigh. "He's *white*," she repeats, eventually.

"He could be blue as a fuckin' Smurf for all I care," India says, "he's fine as hell."

"You know I'm sitting right here?" I have to suck in a breath and try to clench my teeth around a groan of pain as Callie's mother digs in my shoulder with something sharp. "Fuck, that hurts."

"Well, if you wouldn't'a gone and got your stupid ass shot, I wouldn't have to dig the bullet out, would I? Stupid kids, shootin' each other and they selves. Over what? Drugs? Pride? All'a y'all a bunch of dumbasses."

"He was backin' me up," Split says, from the doorway of the kitchen, where he's leaning against the doorpost. T-Shawn isn't anywhere to be seen. "A car rolled up and ran into Lil B. He was just crossin' the street, and they just ran him over. Killed him. No reason. I had to take care of it."

"Lil B is dead?" Callie's mother says, her voice sad.

"Yeah."

"Who was it?" Callie asks.

"Nobody you got to worry about anymore." Split's voice is cold and hard. No regrets there. "How's it comin', Cleo?"

I'm thankful I have the pain to distract me from the knowledge of what I just did—I killed another person.

Callie's mother, Cleo, doesn't answer, leaning in close to my shoulder and squinting as she carefully withdraws the big medical tweezers—forceps maybe—out of the hole in my arm. She drops a hunk of reddened metal into a ceramic bowl and then grabs a bottle of rubbing alcohol and a thick handful of paper towels.

Cleo glances up at me as she presses the paper towels to my skin just beneath the entrance wound. "This is gonna hurt like a bitch, son."

She gets me to lean backward in the chair and I barely have time to clench my teeth and inhale before Cleo pours the alcohol into the wound.

There aren't words to describe the ripping, burning, searing agony. I'm conscious of India, watching me. I don't dare scream; pride won't let me. She's not showing the slightest hint of squeamishness, so I'm guessing this is nothing new. I try to breathe through it, only the breaths come out as grunts and groans as Cleo pours more alcohol on the wound. Finally, she puts the bottle down. Thank god. I breathe a sigh of relief.

"Don't get too excited, honey," Cleo says. "We ain't done yet. Still gotta pack the wound, and that hurts worse than cleaning it."

Fuck.

She's not kidding, either. She wads gauze into a tight ball and forces it into the wound, and I can't help a growl as she does this. Packs it in, and then more. It burns so bad. Fuck, it hurts. I want to cry it hurts so bad, but India's watching and Split is watching and Callie is watching. So I blink and breathe and curse. A bandage gets taped in a large square over the wound, and then finally Cleo stands up and washes her hands at the sink.

"You best take it easy on that shoulder for a while," Cleo says. "It's gonna take a few weeks, couple months maybe, before it's healed. Move it too much, it'll start bleeding again. You'll have to change that dressing a couple of times a day, too. Split, make sure you bring him by so I can check on him."

"A'ight," Split says. "Thanks, Cleo."

"Yep. Now ya'll git. I got to make dinner."

I rise to my feet, and stand behind Cleo. "Thank you, Cleo. For real, I—"

She spins, stares up at me, her eyes hard and angry, but there's compassion buried down deep. "Thank me by not making me do that again. Stay out of trouble."

"I'll try."

She sighs and shakes her head. "I been tellin' Split to stay out of trouble since he was knee high to a grasshopper, but fat lot of good it's done me. I lost count of the number of times I've patched up his fool ass. Same for T-Shawn. You'll be back, believe me."

Her words rattle me a bit and I sure as fuck hope she's wrong about that.

Callie, India, and Split head out the door and down to the sidewalk running in front of the apartment buildings, waiting for me. I don't know what else to say to Cleo, so I just turn and leave, taking the ruins of my shirt with me. My head is spinning, my shoulder aches like a motherfucker, and I feel sick inside. I barely make it down to the front entrance of the building and out onto the street.

Split nudges me toward his car. "Come on."

I surprise myself by saying, "Nah, man. I don't

feel so good. I just wanna go home." There's too much going on in my head, in my heart. I just shot someone, and the reality of it is hitting me hard.

Split raises his eyebrows, and I can see him wondering what my deal is. "Come on man, I got some good shit in the car. All you need is a few hits and you won't even remember what happened."

I've always manned up, no matter what the situation, but somehow this is different. This isn't just the pain of having just been shot, it's a goddamn existential crisis, is what it is.

I can see India and Callie get out of the car and head over to us. Shit, I just want to go lie down—I don't need a fuckin' audience.

India steps close to me, almost but not quite putting herself between Split and me. "Can't you see he's done in, Split? Leave him be. If he wants to go home, let him go home."

I'm not the macho sort, but having a girl stick up for me is weird. I'm dizzy, woozy. Pain is hitting me in wave after wave, making me nauseous. I'm swaying on my feet, blinking hard, trying to keep it together. But shit, I just need to sit my ass down. I can't summon the words to say any of this, though. I just sway, fighting unconsciousness.

India wraps an arm around my waist. "Come on,

you're coming with me."

I should argue, but I don't. I let her guide me back into the building, up to the fourth floor once more, past Callie and Cleo's to the unit two doors down. She digs a key out of her hip pocket, lets us in. There's no one here, the apartment is dark, silent, and has that feel of emptiness. India has to prop one hand against the opposite wall of the hallway to support my sagging weight. Through a door, into a girly bedroom, white walls with band posters and model photos and fashion magazine cutouts, a soft pink comforter on the bed, a bra hanging off the handle of the closet door, another on the back of a chair, panties and T-shirts and jeans and skirts on the floor. Messy, but lived in, smelling of femininity and softness.

I see this in a cursory glance, but then I'm feeling dizzier than ever, and the throbbing in my shoulder is so bad I can't see for the pain. India lowers me as gently as she can to the bed—not an easy task considering my size.

I flop my arm over my eyes, try to breathe through the ache. "I just need to rest a minute. I'll be out of your hair as soon as I can."

"You ain't going nowhere," India says. "My mom works at the hospital, I'm gonna see if she can get you some antibiotics. You'll need them. And some dressing so I can repack that wound."

"You don't need to help me."

"I want to."

"Why?"

"I like you. You're cute."

"Cute?"

She laughs, a musical sound. "I mean tough. And rugged. And handsome."

"That's better."

She drapes the comforter over my legs. "Relax a minute. You don't gotta be tough all the damn time."

I'm already asleep.

The next thing I know I'm waking up, still in India's bedroom, on her bed. The room is dark, the door left ajar. The bluish-white light of a TV flickers and flashes from the living room, and I can hear other nondescript sounds in the apartment, voices murmuring, dishes rattling. I lever myself to my feet, wincing at the throb in my shoulder. I try a tentative roll, but that's a no-go, the pain that shoots through me tells me I won't be using this arm any time soon. I shuffle out into the living room, find India on the couch, watching some reality show or another, a hand-made afghan on her lap. When she sees me, she lifts a corner of the blanket in invitation, a shy smile on her lips. I take a seat beside her. A little too close, maybe—thighs brushing, elbows bumping, hips touching. But India doesn't move away, even though she's got plenty of room on the other side if she wanted to. If anything, she wiggles a little closer to me.

I close my eyes, let the sounds of the TV wash over me. Everything comes flooding back; my first thought is that I killed a man. I got shot in the process, but…I shot someone. Ended his life.

"Quit thinking about it." India doesn't look at me. "What's done is done."

"I can't *not* think about it."

"Wasn't some innocent person you shot by accident," she says, offering me a smile. "He had it coming. He killed a kid. I knew Lil B. He was a nice kid. And they ran him over for no reason."

"Not sure that excuses it, but…thank you." I let my head fall back against the back of the couch, feeling dizzy all over again.

We watch TV together for a while, and I start to feel hot. Feverish, achy, tingling skin, thirsty. Faint. At some point, I think I passed out, because I start back to awareness, but now I'm horizontal on the couch, my head in India's lap, a blanket covering me. I'm sweaty, and move to push the blanket off, but immediately I'm freezing, and pull it back up. My shoulder aches, throbs, fiery and impossible to ignore.

My mouth is dry, as if I'd tried to eat a jar of cotton balls.

Everything hurts.

I pass out again.

This time, I'm woken up by India's hand on my shoulder. "Come on, Colt, you need to take this."

I don't even question her. I sit up, woozy, head thick, fever raging, shoulder on fire. She dumps a handful of pills into my palm—Tylenol, and what looks like antibiotics—and then a sweating glass of ice water. I down the pills, and then slurp the rest of the water greedily.

"Thanks."

She gestures across the room. "Thank my mom, she brought the antibiotics back from work."

India's mother is beautiful, of course, hair pulled back in a frizzy puff-ball at the back of her head, wearing green scrubs and white Keds, eating something from a takeout container.

"Thank you," I say.

"My name's Maya," she says, waving at me with her fork.

"Colt."

"You're a sick man, Colt. Cleo cleaned it out just fine, but sometimes infections are just inevitable, especially with gunshot wounds. You can stay here till you're better, but I don't want none of your gang-banger bullshit spilling into my life or my daughter's, you hear?"

"Yes ma'am."

"Oooh, an' he's even got some manners." She smiles to make it less of an insult. "Best thing you can do is rest. And take those antibiotics on schedule. India, I expect ya'll to behave. Not that he's in any shape to be causing any trouble, but I know kids ya'll's age."

"Mama!" India is mortified.

"I'm just saying. I ain't stupid."

"Don't you have to get to work now, Mama?" India says.

Another smile from Maya, this one knowing. "Sure do. I'm on a double, so I won't be back till tomorrow. Bye, India. See ya later, Colt."

I can only manage a tiny wave as Maya collects her purse and exits.

I'm in and out of it for a few days, if the brightening and fading of the light through the curtains is any indication. The fever takes a toll on me, keeping me down and out, barely lucid. I see India in fragments and flashes, her hand on my forehead, a cool compress on my face now and then, helping me take Tylenol and antibiotics, helping me drink water when I'm too out of it to even hold a cup. She's always there, whenever I wake up, smiling at me, asking me how I feel, asking if I want some water. Maya I only catch a few glimpses of, always in scrubs, hair pulled back, purse on her shoulder, keys in one hand, a can of pepper spray dangling from the keychain, a huge to-go mug of coffee in the other. She checks on me too, changes the dressing in my shoulder—which hurts like a goddamned motherfucker.

Callie, Split, and T-Shawn show up at one point. Split goes to spark up a joint, and India lays into him, which is funny, because Split is usually so scary, but somehow India has a way of putting even him in his place. It's clear I'm out of commission, and my friends leave again, with admonishments to get better.

I don't see them again after that, even though they said they'd stop by. Just as well, though, because until the fever breaks, I'm useless, barely coherent, fighting just to stay conscious, and hating it when I am. I don't think I've ever slept so much in my life as those days on India's couch.

On the fourth day, by my calculations, the fever has broken.

"I really don't want to, but I gotta go to work. I traded shifts so I could be here while you were out of it, but now that your fever has broken, I need to go in." India says this as she comes out of her room, wearing khakis and a Walgreens collared T-shirt. And she even makes that uniform look hot; I know I'm feeling better when that thought crosses my mind.

"You work at Walgreens, huh?" It's a non sequitur. I mean, obviously she does.

"Cosmetics department."

"So when will you be back?"

"I get off at seven. Not long after that. I'll bring some food back with me." She hikes her purse over a shoulder. "You still need to rest and sleep as much as possible."

I groan. "I've never spent so much time resting in my whole life. I'm going crazy."

She laughs. "It's good for you. Give you time to think."

I really don't want the time to think. I sit on the couch all that day, thinking. Reliving. Feeling the 9mm buck in my hands, seeing the red mist spray...fuck. The slamming ache of the bullet hitting my shoulder.

What's done is done.

He deserved it.

I'm a killer.

Colt Calloway, body count: one.

It's heavy, that weight. I don't remember his face. It's all a blur, except the physical sensations. I don't remember the color of the car we were chasing, how many others were in it with the guy I shot.

Just the buck of the gun, the spray of the blood, the slam of the bullet into my shoulder.

At some point, I'm beyond exhausted, both from the recently-departed fever and from the mental and emotional tax of reliving the scene over and over again, wondering what I could have done differently. I can't take any more, and I'm sick of the couch, so I move into India's room, examine her posters, a few framed photos of her and Maya across the years, a small collection of books, all of them dog-eared romance novels. An old, peeling, white wicker armchair overflowing with stuffed animals; the collection is huge, dozens of stuffed animals of all sizes and kinds. It's an odd thing, that chair full of stuffed animals. She's a twenty-something girl, not a child anymore, and, overall, her room reflects that. It's a distinctly feminine place, but it is the sanctuary of an adult, not a stuffed animal-collecting little girl.

The bed, now neatly made, has only one stuffed animal on it: a clearly special, old, faded, much-loved teddy bear. One glass bead eye, one button eye. Obvious stitch marks where it was torn, restuffed, and sewed back together. That button eye, though. It's a bright blue button, four holes, sewn on with brown thread. Blue the color of periwinkle and cornflowers, in stark and vivid contrast to the black bead eye on the other side.

I set the teddy bear on the foot end of the bed and stretch out, close my eyes.

Fade.

She wakes me up by sliding into the bed in front of me, her back to my front. She's dressed, I can make out that much. Booty shorts, a tank top. But god, all the skin I can feel, the heat of her body…it's intoxicating. I want more. But I want her to want more. I don't want this to be quick and easy, or convenient. I don't want her to be a hookup. I've had so many of those over the years I've gotten sick of it. I want more. I slide my arm across her middle, tug her closer. Breathe in her scent, relish in the tickle of her curls against my cheek.

Stifle back a groan as she wiggles her tight little ass against me, getting closer. Burrowing, nestling.

I react.

I know she feels it, and I know she knows I know. We're both awake. She's waiting for me to make a move, I think.

But, for once, I pass on the moment. I need more of her, more time to know the woman, the person, the mind, the heart, the soul of the girl, and not just the body.

So I suffer through the delirious, delicious torture of my hard cock being nestled between the globes of her ass, and I do nothing but hold her.

"Colt—" she whispers, twisting her head a little.

"Hush. Not yet."

She makes a disappointed sound in the back of her throat, but clasps a hand over my hand. I hear her snoring not long after.

It's a long time before I find sleep again, wondering what kind of fool I am to pass up such an obvious invitation. She wants me, I want her, we have mad chemistry. But I don't just want a quick fuck. I don't want a blow job in the backseat of a car, given by a girl whose name I'll never even ask. I want more. I want something meaningful with India. She's worth more. She's not a hookup kind of girl. She's not a back-alley fuck kind of girl. She's not a bent over the arm of a couch after a fight kind of girl.

She's quality. She's got potential, a future. She has dreams.

I fall asleep wondering what she wants out of life, and realizing that's why I waited, why I turned down her invitation: I want to know her dreams, I want to know what she wants, where she's going.

When I wake up, she's facing her closet, in the middle of pulling off the clothes she slept in. She still has the shorts on, and it's a good thing I couldn't see her last night, because the shorts are...not really a garment, in any sense of the word. Just a bit of cotton stretched across her hips and molded to the cheeks of her fucking incredible ass.

I realize she doesn't know I'm awake, and I also realize I'm holding my breath. She shimmies out of the shorts, baring her ass for me. I'm hard, rock hard. No panties underneath, either. Now she's naked, and she twists a little as she kicks the shorts off and toes them onto a pile of dirty laundry. The kick and twist gives me a tantalizing glimpse of her breast via sideboob, a hint of nipple, the rounded outer edge. I swallow hard as she turns to the dresser, and now I've got a full-profile vision of her. Thin, lithe, lovely. Full, heavy breasts, dark caramel skin. Wide brown areolae, flat nipples just begging to be kissed and licked. Trim hips, and a taut, muscular, bubble-shaped ass. Strong thighs, shapely calves. Hair is loose and wild, a profusion of black spirals. And god, her face, the beauty of her face in profile takes my breath away even more than her body does.

She withdraws a green thong from the drawer, and glances at me as she does so. Realizes I'm awake, and watching her. Twists to face me, giving me a front view, now. She's trimmed close, between her thighs. The shadow of the V of her thighs is taunting me, beckoning me.

I just look at her. Let my gaze move up and then down and then back up, and her eyes are warm, dark, probing. Not shying away from mine. She looks me up and down too, blatantly. Returning the gesture. I'd kicked off the blankets, apparently, so I'm in nothing but a pair of shorts, and the evidence of my desire is obvious, clearly outlined. Her gaze goes to the bulge, then to mine.

"You're beautiful." It just pops out. I feel like an idiot stating the obvious, but I've thought it every day since I've been here. And right now, her bangin' body on full display for me, I can think of nothing else.

She smiles at me, though. Ducks her head, grinning. "Thanks." A glance up at me. "So are you."

"I didn't mean to watch," I say, needing her to understand. "I just woke up and you were taking your clothes off, and—there was no way I could look away."

"I understand."

"I just wanted you to know, I'm not, like, a creeper or anything."

She takes a step closer. "It's fine, Colt. I wouldn't have risked getting undressed with you in the room if

I was worried about it." Another step.

She's less than a foot away now, and my every sense is on high-alert, attuned to her. I could reach out and touch her, take her in my arms and pull her down to me. Do a million dirty, wonderful things to her.

"About last night," I start.

"You don't have to explain," she cuts in.

"No, I do. I wanted you so bad. Right now, I want you." I sit up. Clench my fists on my knees.

Her eyes go to my erection, still raging, still visible as a bulge in my shorts. "I felt it last night, and I can see it now." Her eyes flick to mine. "So why aren't you moving on it?"

"Because…I want more than that with you. I've never had a real girlfriend before, India. Not someone I cared about. But you…you're different."

"How am I different?" She still has the green thong dangling from her fingers. She's still naked, inches from me, testing me to my limits.

"Jesus, India, you've got to put on clothes." I mutter this, because the majority of me doesn't want her to. "You're not a girl I'd just hook up with. And that's all I've ever really done, is hook up. You're better than that. More than that. And I want that with you."

"So you're saying you want to wait to have sex

because you want to get to know me?"

I sigh. "Yes, that's what I'm saying."

She laughs. "I think that's a dream come true for most girls, to hear a guy she likes say that. But you know how frustrated I am, right now? This is the second time I've all but thrown myself at you and been shot down."

"I'm not shooting you down, India."

She furrows her brow. "Yeah, you kind of are. Sweetly, and for a really great reason. But Colt...I *want* you. I want you to touch me. I want to reach into your shorts and..." She shakes her head, cutting off. "And you're just sitting there, got that big ol' hard-on going, me naked in front you, flat out telling you I want you, I want this. And you're not making a move."

"You think this shit is easy?" I shake my head. "It's the hardest thing I've ever done, keeping my hands to myself."

A moment, then. Her eyes searching mine. Mine searching hers. "You for real? You want something long-term with me?"

"Hell yeah."

"And you for real want to *get to know me*—" That phrase is heavily emphasized, almost sarcastic, "before we sleep together."

"Yes."

"You're crazy." But her smile is bright, brilliant, and hopeful. "But I'll play your game."

"It's not a game, India."

"I know. I guess I don't see why we can't get to know each other *and* get it on."

"Because once I get a taste of you, I won't be thinking of anything except getting more of you. Not for a long-ass time."

I'm not sure that helped, judging by the excitement that lights up her features.

"Oh," she breathes. "It's like that?"

"It's like that."

"So I'd better cover up, huh?"

"Before I come in my pants just looking at you, yeah."

"I could help you out with that."

"Don't tempt me, woman. I'm trying to be the good guy, here."

"Oooh, the bad boy is trying to be good." She's teasing me, on so many levels.

She tags a robe off the top of a laundry basket full of clean clothes, shrugs into it, sadly but prudently covering her glorious body.

"So, I've been wondering. Why doesn't Callie want this to happen?" I gesture between us. "What's she got against white people?

Another smile and my heart flutters. "It ain't because you're white. Not really. It's more because you're part of the Bishops. She's worried about me," she says, sitting on the bed beside me.

"I'm not exactly part of the gang."

"You're Split's friend. That's all that really counts to her. She's just protecting me."

"That's what friends do, I guess."

She nods. "She's afraid I'll get attached to one of Split's boys, and then—" India shrugs, waves a hand. She doesn't really need to finish the thought.

I nod. "I know what she means. After what I experienced, it makes sense."

"There's history behind it, though." India returns her attention to me. "Callie had a brother, Isaac. Split grew up next door to Callie, and me on the other side. Split and Isaac were like brothers—closer than brothers, really. The three of them started the Bishops together. Split's mom is…not a good person, so he was at Callie's most of the time. Cleo is like a mom to him, only one he's ever really had. Him and Callie have been together forever, their whole lives. Never was much of a question about that." She blinks back tears. "And Isaac and me…" The way she trails off says everything that needs to be said.

I don't like where this is going. "What happened?"

She nods. Her tight spiral curls bounce. "They were out with the other guys. Some kind of beef with some other gang, the usual shit. Split and T-Shawn came home carrying Isaac and they were all bleeding. Shot up bad. Isaac died in his own living room. Cleo tried her best, and Mama too, but they knew, they both knew it was too late, even for an ambulance. Split blames himself, even though he's never really said what happened. Can't forgive himself for letting Isaac die." A long, shuddering breath. "They carried him two miles to get back home, even though they were both shot too."

"Were you—there?"

She nods again. "Yeah. I was…I had Isaac's head on my lap. I watched him…I watched him—"

"Fuck. I'm sorry, I—"

She shakes her head, tries to smile, blinks hard. "It's just a sensitive subject. For all of us, but for Split most of all."

"Are you worried?" I wonder where the question came from, but now that I've asked it, I can't take it back.

"About?"

"What Callie is worried about."

"Oh." She bobs her head side to side. "Yes, and

no. I'm an optimist. I try to believe the best. I want to get out of the 'hood. I want to make something of myself. I want to find a man who ain't like the others in the Bishops. Nothing wrong with them, necessarily, but…that's all they know. That's all they'll ever know."

"And you want more."

She nods. "I want more."

"Me too." I hear myself say it, even though I hadn't even dared think it to myself until now.

"You do?" Once again, she sounds surprised.

I laugh, a little self-deprecatingly, a little sarcastically. "Yeah, I mean I never thought I'd be…doing what I'm doing. I'm not exactly sure what it is I *do* want. But I want more. I'm from the white suburbs outside Detroit. My dad is a senator. It's not like I moved to New York and went, 'Hmmm, I sure do want to join an inner-city gang.'"

India eyes me. "A senator? Like in the Senate in D.C.?"

I shrug. "Yeah. Don't get too excited, though. I refused to go to college and he disowned me."

There's more to it, of course, but I really don't want to get into all that shit. Not now, anyway.

But she persists. "You got disowned for not going to college?" she asks, compassion and confusion in her voice.

I nod. "I mean, it's a complicated situation. Even my mom, a career stay-at-home mother, has a college degree. But I'm just—I'm not cut out for college. Never have been, never will be. My dad couldn't accept that, and one thing led to another, and…here I am." I shrug.

"So what *do* you want?"

I think about her question, and look at her out of the corner of my eye. Her long legs are tucked under one thigh, and her hair is loose and wild and incredible, a massive explosion of thick black spiral curls around her face and shoulders and hanging to mid-spine.

What do I want? Besides India, that is?

The answer emerges on its own. As I speak it, I find the truth rupturing up through me and into my consciousness. "I want to be a mechanic. I want to own my own garage. I want to custom-tune hot rods and rebuild classics."

"You can do that?"

I nod. "Yeah. I'm good with cars. I can take apart an engine blindfolded and put it back together so it works better than it ever did."

"Really?"

"Sure. It's what I was good at. It was more than

just a hobby. It was really all I had."

India twists to face me. I turn as well, and our knees brush. She pulls herself closer to me and her gaze is dark and serious.

"You're gonna get that garage." Long, thin, elegant fingers toy with the knot of her robe.

The edges have fallen loose a bit, giving me a tantalizing glimpse of her fucking amazing tits, and I find myself hardening, glancing at the hint of cleavage, trying mentally to justify a way to let myself have her despite what I said.

"I hope so," I say.

She shakes her head, curls bouncing. "No, Colt. You're *gonna*. You're too good for that shit." She points at my shoulder.

While I had been talking with India I'd almost forgotten about the pain in my shoulder—she's just that distractingly beautiful.

"What do *you* want, India?"

She ducks her head, lifts one delicate shoulder. "It's silly."

"No, it's not."

"You don't even know what I was gonna say!" she protests, laughing.

"It doesn't matter. It won't be silly."

"A model." She whispers it. "I want to be a

model."

"You totally could be. You're so gorgeous, I swear magazines would be tripping over each other to sign you up."

She laughs, and it's a sweet sound. "That ain't how it works. You sign up with an agency, go to calls and hope for a call back. But I think I could do it. I'm tall and naturally thin. I've got exotic features, or so I've always been told."

"So why don't you try it?" I ask.

She tries to pull away, but I feel a rush of daring, and grab her, locking her close to me. She doesn't pull away. The robe, the fucking robe isn't staying closed, and she doesn't seem to mind.

"I'm scared," she whispers, resting her head against my chest. "What if they say no?"

"Don't let them say no. Keep trying until they say yes."

"It's just a dream." She says this like it's an excuse. Or a reason.

"That's why you gotta work to make it real."

Her head tilts up, her gaze finds mine. "Which is what you're doing, huh?" Her voice is sharp.

"I'm just saying." I smile in a pathetic attempt to defuse the sudden tension.

"Well, I'm just saying too." Her smile in response

is soft, a little sensual and no longer sharp.

"So how about we make each other a promise that we'll both work as hard as we can to make our dreams a reality?" I suggest.

"So what are you gonna do to get that garage?" she asks.

"Save money. Getting a space is the biggest step. I need a hell of a lot of money to buy or rent a space. I've got some, enough for a space, but then I still have to get all the tools and equipment, and that takes more than I have. And then I gotta get the clientele. So, all the shit I've been through, all the money I've saved up, and I'm still only *maybe* halfway there."

I have my back to the wall, and India is between the side wall and me, her head against my shoulder, curled in against me. Her head is tipped up so she can look at me, one small warm hand on my bare chest. I have one hand on her hip, almost casually, yet my heart thunders. Something about this girl has me mixed up; girls don't make my pulse thunder, they don't make my thoughts go wobbly, they don't make my crotch throb with just a look. But India? She's different. She does all that and more.

"What's your plan in terms of becoming a model?" I ask her.

She lets out a breath. "I'm thinking cosmetology school. I like everything to do with make-up, and maybe someday I can go into the city and go to a call or something. I've got my job at Walgreens and I'm trying to save money for school, but it's gonna take a long time. You know?"

I nod. "Me too. Kickin' it with Split and T-Shawn hasn't all been bad, and I owe him for getting me clear of some…well, some unpleasant shit. I owe him. I keep thinking I've got enough, because I've been stashing away as much as I can, but I sometimes go looking at garages and whatever, checking out spaces, pricing out the equipment, and it always adds up to more than I've got. And being young, no credit cards or credit history, I've got zero chance of a loan, so cash is my only option. And no matter how much I save, it's never enough."

A silence falls between us. I'm thinking about the future, and I think India is, too.

Abruptly, India lifts up, leans in close, Her arms go around my neck and she's pulling me toward her. She's being gentle because of my shoulder, but I can feel urgency in her actions. Strong and demanding, her hands are soft and warm in the hair at the back of my head, guiding me inexorably to her. Warm wet soft lips mash against mine, and her tongue slides between my lips. She's not holding back.

God in heaven, kissing her is like finding a whole new universe, it's like drifting away into bliss. I lose myself in the kiss. Her breasts squish soft against my chest, and her hips are now wedged between my thighs, hipbones hard against mine. She knows what she wants. And, holy shit, so do I.

"Damn," she breathes, barely breaking away far enough to move her lips. "You kiss good."

I just breathe a laugh and kiss her again. Harder. Showing her what a kiss really is. I bury myself into the sensation of her arms around me, of her hands sliding under my shirt to feather against my skin.

My fingers find the edge of her robe, sneak under the cotton, find bare skin. Explore, seek, hunt. She's moaning into the kiss, lifting up to get closer, begging for more. I'm lost. There's no way I can stop now, no way to go back, now.

I need this.

Jesus, I need this.

But then the front door opens. "Hello!" It's Maya. "I brought dinner. Thai from down the street. I hope you like pad thai."

India pulls away reluctantly, sitting up, fixing her hair, pulling her robe closed. Sliding off the bed, ducking out of the room with a quick backward glance at me, a secret smile just for me, because we both know we've started something big, something hot and real and intense.

Nine: The Last Night There'll Ever Be

A COUPLE WEEKS LATER, I'M FEELING PRETTY MUCH recovered. My shoulder is weak and stiff and aches, but the fevers and the sweats have disappeared—Maya said I was damned lucky in more ways than one. India works a lot during the day, so I'm at home—India and Maya's apartment is home now, somehow—alone a lot, listening to music, watching TV, and doing a lot of thinking.

What I keep coming up to is that the longer I stay away from the streets, the more I know I don't want to go back.

The best part of my life, though, is India. She's tightly threaded all throughout my world. We've al-

ways got something to talk about, and we discuss
hopes and dreams and fears, things I've never talked
to anyone about.

But we never get any time alone. People are stopping by to visit or India's mom is home. One way or
another, we never end up getting any time to follow
up on that one kiss we shared. Sure, we steal a kiss or
two when no one is looking, but it's not enough. It's
never enough.

It's not until we decide to go to a party at a Bishop's dingy, nasty pad that we finally get time alone.
The party is a rager, lots of Bishops and their non-
gang friends, lots of girls, lots of booze, pot, and other shit I don't touch; India isn't interested in it either.
She sticks with her girls, Callie and some others, and
I stay with Split and T-Shawn, since I'm not close
with any of the others. I like T-Shawn, though. He's
quiet and he keeps to himself, but he's wise. When
he speaks, he's worth listening to. He does what he's
gotta do. Unlike the others, he accepts me in his own
way, without a word about it, and I can tell he feels
comfortable around me. I sense he's a guy who is way
more interesting than he lets on, and I'd like to get to
know him better. When the others talk shit to me, all
he has to do to shut it down is stand by my side and
glare at them. They shut up and move on. He has a

very unassuming manner about him, and with that comes a sense of don't-fuck-with-me. He's got a low tolerance for assholes and he'll wreck you if you don't have the sense to back off when he gives the hint.

The party rages on. More people arrive, then scatter and vanish. Split and Callie find each other eventually, and as the hours pass, they get more and more wasted. They're all over each other and pretty soon they're groping each other, going at it hot and heavy, until someone shouts at them to get a room. Which they do, noisily.

It is getting late and I'm dizzy and hot and my shoulder aches. I find the fire escape and climb out and sit on a step, breathing in the cool night air. I hear the door open, glance up to see India, and I can't help but smile at her.

She's wearing short shorts that cup her tight round ass, and a shiny, slinky top that just barely covers all the important bits. She sits down beside me, wedging herself between me and the railing. And then she leans against me, and my heart almost bursts.

"Hot in there," she remarks.

"Yeah, it is."

We exchange comments about the party and the people, the idle chatter of two people utterly comfortable with each other.

And then she turns it serious. "You said you didn't grow up in this life. How *did* you grow up?"

We've talked about a lot things, but never about my life growing up, beyond that first admission. Which is how I find myself with her on that fire escape until dawn, telling her about my childhood, my dad, the fights with him about school and just about every other thing. But I leave out the fact that I can't read very well because, hell, that's fuckin' embarrassing. I just give her the impression that I hate school and leave it at that. And that's true enough—no lie there. She tells me about Isaac, and about how losing him messed her up for so long. She admits that she's still not really over him, but figures she's as over him as she'll ever get.

Then she looks up at me with those big brown eyes and tells me she's ready to move on.

"Yeah?" I ask, not missing her meaning, but wanting to be clear. "You mean move on with someone else?"

"Don't play, Colt. We can't put this off any longer. You know what I'm saying." A pause, as a thought occurs to her. "But Callie's gonna kick your ass, when she finds out about us."

"Because of Split?"

She shakes her head. "He won't care. I'm his

girl's friend, not his. But he won't step in if Callie goes after you."

"It'd be worth it."

"It would?"

My fingers find hers, and our palms touch, our fingers tangle. "Hell, yeah. You're totally worth letting Callie kick my ass."

"You think so?" A note of wonder, a note of doubt.

I breathe a sigh of disbelief. "India. I want you so bad it hurts. I haven't been able to think of anything else since I walked into Callie's house that day and saw you sitting at the kitchen table."

She lets me see the vulnerability in her eyes. "Don't play me, Colt."

"I like you, India. A *lot*."

She smirks. "What are we, in third grade now?"

"I guess so, yes."

This gets me a laugh, as she stands up, offering me her hand. "Let's go."

"Where?"

"There's an empty bedroom upstairs." She climbs up the fire escape to the next floor up, and I follow her.

She pulls up the window, peers in, and makes sure the room is empty. It is, and she climbs in. I go in next. It's a dump—I've been in some shitty places, but this place is one of the worst. The air smells stale, and an old mattress and box spring sit in the middle of the room. There's a tattered, hand-stitched quilt folded up on the bed, and one pillow so old it's almost flat. An ancient dresser stands in one corner, scratched and battered, the finish peeling, and a desk is jammed against the wall.

The place is well and truly a shithole.

But it's private.

India shuts the window and checks the lock on the door.

Then she turns to me, and somehow I'm standing right up close to her, and she's gazing up at me. We both know what this is, and we both know we've wanted it to happen for a long time. She waits for me, blinking, wanting it, just waiting.

My hand floats up to touch her hip, the other cups her face. I brush her hair out of the way and nudge her chin up. She smiles, leans closer, breasts flattening against my chest. She tilts her mouth up closer to mine.

I kiss her. It's not a sweet kiss. It's sudden and short and almost brutal in its rough passion. I don't know what this is between us. I've been with a bunch of girls, but it's never been like this. Never been this sense of…desperation. Like if I don't get more of her, closer to her, I'll combust. She seems to feel it too, and the way she pulls away from the kiss to stare at me and gasp for breath tells me it's as surprising to her as it is to me.

But I stop myself. We're in a dark, stinking room in a strange house.

"I want our first time together to be better than this, India."

"I don't care where it happens, Colt," India breathes. "I just want you. I can't wait any longer."

"But this is one of the nastiest shitholes I've ever been in. You deserve better." I can't help but snatch another kiss. "*We* deserve better."

A pause, a moment, a breath. And then India makes my world complete. "Mama's on the early shift, and she's working a double again. Won't be home till tonight."

"Then what are we doing here?" I pull her back to the window, out onto the fire escape. "Let's go home."

We run home—the party is only a couple blocks from the apartment complex. By the time we get there, we're both laughing and out of breath. India is fumbling with the key and the lock, and I'm sliding my hands all over her, kissing the back of her neck, digging my hands down the front of her shorts, cupping her ass, groping her breasts, nipping at her earlobe, grinding my raging erection into her ass.

Finally—fucking *finally* she gets the lock and shoves the door open. We fall through, and she locks the door behind us once more.

Turns to me. Grabs my shirt. Rips it off, and then pushes me aggressively toward her room. I grab her by the front of her shirt, pull her with me as I walk backward to her room. We're kissing, fumbling at each other. I take her hands and press her palms to my stomach, urge them downward, but she pushes my hands away, palms my cheek, her face close to mine, her eyes wide, liquid brown, eager, blazing with need. Then she pushes again, and I topple backward to fall onto the bed and she's all over me, sitting on my thighs and wrapping her arms around my neck and kissing me as if this is the last night there'll ever be.

And then, god…and then she leans back and strips off her shirt. If I was hard before, I go diamond at the sight of her in her bra. It's red lace, pushing up a pair of gorgeous, chocolate brown C-cup tits. I slide my palms over them, but she bats at my hands.

"Not yet."

"No?"

She shakes her head. "Mmm-mm."

She reaches up behind her back and unhooks her bra, tossing it aside. She bares herself to me. She has the most beautiful tits I've ever laid eyes on. "Now," she says.

Fuck, I want them, I want to taste them, feel them, lick them, fuck them. Leaning forward, I close my mouth over the small pert nipples. I flick my tongue over them, tasting her delicious skin. I lean back and look some more. Full, round, taut with large dark areolae surrounding the nipples. Heavy. I lift them in my palms. Soft, so fucking soft. I let my tongue roam, areolae, nipple, the underside. She gasps when I run my tongue in quick circles, flick, flick, flick. She arches her back, thrusting those goddamned perfect tits into my mouth.

I cup one, lift it to my mouth, frame her lower spine with my palm and pull her closer. Her legs close around my waist, her hair hangs down her back, her throat is a slender column angled toward my jaw. I kiss up her body, between her tits, her throat, her chin. I gently caress her breasts and slide my palm up her spine and into her hair. I take a handful of that thick curly mass and tug her face to mine, demanding a kiss.

And holy hell, does she deliver. Kisses me delirious, leaving me breathless and faint.

And then India slides off me, moves to her feet, stepping backward, her tits bouncing beautifully. She unbuttons her jeans and shimmies out of them, and that shimmy makes me even harder, so hard it hurts. The move sends her tits shaking and jiggling as she works the tight denim down her thighs, kicks them off. Underneath she's wearing a red thong, just a triangle of silk over her core—and goddamn if that little scrap of material isn't dark with the dampness of her desire.

"Get over here," I growl, reaching for her.

She dances backward. "Uh-uh! You gotta take off your clothes too, Colt-baby. You get this—" she gestures at her lush body, "—when I get that—" gesturing at me.

At my crotch.

I stand up. Maybe flex a little, but not obviously. Just tense my abs and pecs a little. Make a show of going slow, unzipping, unbuttoning, shucking the denim off to reveal tight black boxer briefs, and you'd better believe I'm bulging out of that shit, harder than I've ever been in my life, staring at the sexiest girl in the world, watching her watch me, desire in her eyes, greed in her gaze.

She wants *me*.

Hell, yeah. And I want her, I want her more than

any woman I've ever met.

I take a step toward her, slow and predatory. "Take it off, India," I say, pointing at her thong. It's a command. Not sure where this is coming from, but it feels good. The rough command, the ballsy directness. And damn, she digs it.

Her eyes blaze and spark, and she lifts her chin. "Make me."

My first instinct is just to rip them off. But I don't. The challenge was to make *her* take them off, not for me to take them off for her. So I sidle closer, so close the tips of her tits brush my chest. I stare down into her eyes, our noses not quite touching, both of us breathing hard with restrained need. I reach down and gently scrape my finger over the wet fabric. I feel the outline of her pussy inside the thong. I trace my finger across each lip, and the slit between. She inhales sharply, but remains motionless. She's staring up at me, resolute. Determined. Which of us will be the one to rip her thong off first?

She will, damn it; I'm gonna make her.

I hook an index finger in the elastic against her inner thigh and pull the triangle aside, slip the index finger of my other hand into her. Oh, fuck. It slides in so smooth, slips easily into her warm wetness, and she moans. Her knees tremble. I withdraw and let the underwear snap back into place, then trace her opening over the fabric. I tease and push my finger in, through the silk. India grinds against my touch, seeking more. Angling for my finger inside her. I trace her seam again, then slide my finger under the elastic. I run my finger over her bare opening, but not quite going in.

"Colt." It's almost a plea.

I give her what she wants and I slide my finger in, smearing her juices all over her opening and over her clit. I tease that hard little nub until she's gyrating and grinding against my finger. And then I pull it away, and this time she whimpers.

But she plays dirty, too. She digs her hand into my underwear and grips me, stroking me. God, the way she touches me, so hungry, yet somehow so sweet. Deliberate and delightful. God, it takes all my control to hold back. Shit, I'm close, and we haven't even started. I'm seriously about to come in my drawers like a damn virgin.

I drop to my knees, and out of her reach. And that little moan again, that little murmur of protest: *Mmmm-mmmmmmmmm!* As if to say *what are you doing? Give it back!*

She wants it, and I love that she wants it. I want her to have it.

I wish she could touch me forever, but I've got a challenge to win. I tug her thong down just enough to bare the top of her slit, and I work my tongue into that tiny opening, just the upper swell, the slight gap where her tight sweet little pussy starts. And then I hear a full-on groan. God, yes. She really wants that. So I pull aside the triangle and give her one good probing lick with my tongue, and goddamn if she doesn't taste as sweet as fucking sugar. I can't resist tasting her again. And again. And again. And then suddenly I'm devouring her, eating her clit as if it's my last meal.

"Fuck—Colt...please..." she murmurs.

"Take 'em off, India."

"Uh-uh." She grinds against my mouth even as she denies me.

"*Now*, India." I put a whip in my voice, and her eyes fly open, finding mine.

I let the underwear slide back into place and sink back onto my haunches. Teasing her. I press my lips over her opening and breathe a hot breath onto her.

"Damn you," she snarls, and pulls the red thong off. She throws it at me. I let it fall onto my face, inhaling her scent on it. Which earns me a laugh. "You nasty."

"Hell yeah." I grab the backs of her thighs and pull her closer. I bury my face against her pussy. "Let me feel you come."

"Colt-baby…?"

"Hmmm?"

"Shut up and eat my pussy." She pulls my face against herself, greedily arching her back and writhing her hips, grinding her slit against my lips.

I devour her. I ravage her clit with my tongue and slide my fingers in and out of her opening until she's grinding and gasping, holding onto my shoulders for balance and riding my face. I lift a thigh up and onto my shoulder, opening her up even more. Then I lift her up so she is sitting on my shoulders. I stand up, and she grabs onto the lintel of the door with both hands, grinding against my face. I palm her tight, juicy ass and lift her core closer to my face, lap at her clit in circles, up and down, side to side, eagerly and faster and faster until she's writhing non-stop, using the lintel to lift herself up and down onto my mouth, riding me.

She comes with a scream, and I taste her essence. Lap it up, lick until she's breathless. Until she jerks and groans and comes again.

"Down, down, let me down." She wriggles, widens her thighs and pushes backward and slides down my body.

She holds onto my sides for balance as she wobbles on unsteady legs, but she wastes no time divesting me of my underwear. Then she goes to her knees and takes me in her mouth.

God, that mouth. Those lips, wrapped around me, is hotter than I had ever imagined. Her eyes go wide as she takes more and more, looking up at me. I ache to let go. Throb with the need to move, to thrust between those beautiful lips. But I don't. I hold still and let her do her thing. Which...shit, it takes all I have and something extra to keep it back, to hold on, to not come down her throat.

I have to pull away, gritting my teeth and flexing every muscle in my body with the effort of holding back.

"You close?" India is there, on her knees in front of me, watching me.

"Fuck...yeah, so close."

"Give it to me." She moves in, but I stay out of reach.

"No, not like this."

I lift India to her feet.

I can't help it: I bury my fist in her hair, that fucking amazing hair. Gently but firmly I yank her head back and kiss her with all I've got. Until we're both breathless. And that's when I bend at the knees, nudge her opening. Beautiful, willing creature that she is, India doesn't hesitate, just reaches between us and fits me into her, goes up on her toes and when I'm nestled just inside her tight wet slit, she sinks down and I thrust up.

We groan in unison, and our mouths collide. Our teeth click and lips mash, and I feel her clamping around me. I lift her up, both hands on her ass as I lift and lower her. She grinds, and we're kissing, gasping, exchanging breath, moving and writhing together.

"Bed—" India gasps. "Lay me down."

I take two short steps and then lower her gently onto the bed. She's got her heels around my spine and she's moving, and I forget about everything. The strain on my shoulder, a throbbing ache, fades into the background and all I can do is stare down at her and move with her.

I take over then, and she goes still as I control the pace. Slow, shallow. Letting the urge to orgasm recede a little, and then ramp it up. Faster, deeper, harder. She reaches between us and her fingers go to her clit. I adjust my position on top of her, leaning back until I'm upright and my cock is stretching away, and I'm thrusting deep, and she's madly vigorously desperately stroking her sweet little clit, and god I love that, the way she takes control of her pleasure.

She arches her back and I feel her coming, feel

the tightening around me and watch the way sweat beads on her lip and on her forehead and dots her breasts. She thrusts crazily, and her eyes fly open.

"Now, Colt-baby. Now, come now."

Who can disobey an order like that? Not me. I let go. Thunder hammers in my veins and I let myself thrust hard and wild. And India, bold and perfect, takes each pounding thrust with a whimpering encouraging grunt, still touching herself. Shit, she's coming again. The girl has a hair trigger. Her pussy tightening around my throbbing cock as she comes is all it takes.

I lean over her and bury one hand in her curls and shamelessly pull, mash my mouth to hers as I come with an explosive shout.

She moans long and high, as if the sensation of me coming inside her like this gives her sexual pleasure. Moaning with me, writhing with me, milking it out of me. Taking all I have and demanding more.

Both of us spent, she pushes on my chest until I'm lying down, and she curls up almost entirely on top of me. Her hair tickles my nose. It makes me grin like an idiot, for some reason.

A long, long, comfortable silence. We're both drowsy.

No words are necessary; we both fall asleep.

"Colt?" Her voice is small, hesitant. "What happened? With Lil B. Tell me what happened."

We're awake, still naked, still in her bed, still tangled up together.

I let out a breath. This is not what I was expecting her to say, but I decide that being open and honest with her is more important than anything else. "It's not pretty. Do you really want to hear this?"

"Just tell me."

"The kid was just crossing the street. Right at the edge of Bishop turf. This car just…sped up, swerved, and nailed him. Sent him flying. He was dead the second his head hit the curb, head split open like a fuckin' melon. So Split guns it, takes off after the fuckers, you know? We caught 'em no problem. Split got lucky, popped off a few shots and hit their back tires. Then he pulled out another gun and gave it to me. I—I didn't want it. But I couldn't back down. I'd never shot a pistol before. It felt so heavy, for something so small. It all happened in a blur, after that. I remember guns going off, I remember a Mets hat, someone shooting at me. I remember being hit in the shoulder and almost being hit in the face." I touch the healing scar along my temple. "My gun went off and I—I shot him. It was over before I knew what happened. I remember—blood. Blood everywhere. The car was red with it—the hood where they hit Lil B, the windshield, the seats, the dashboard. And then I realized I had just shot someone."

I'm finally dealing with what happened, and I don't like it. But, in another way, it feels good to talk about it.

"But they shot you first."

"Yeah. But I still killed someone." I choke. I hold back the panic, the freak-out building inside me.

But she knows, though, India knows what I'm feeling. Her face is on my chest, her hands move in gentle circles, touching my scar, my face, brushing my hair away. "You had to. You had no choice."

I can't speak. I try. But I can't. I can't breathe.

"Colt?"

I shake my head and try to push her away, physically and metaphorically. I try to sit up but she's not having it. "No way, Colt." She pushes me back down to the bed. She's *strong*. She sits on me. Her hair is wild around her shoulders and her eyes are wet with tears. "I'm here. It's okay. I get it. It's not okay, but it's okay."

"India—"

"It's okay not to be okay. When Isaac died, Cleo told me the same thing. It's okay not to be okay."

"Guilt sucks."

"Yeah." She rests her palms on my chest, staring into the middle distance. I can tell she's dealing with her own memories of the past and then she speaks, almost to herself. "Isaac, he was mad at me. When him and Split went out that day we was arguing about him getting in trouble. Getting hurt. Us girls, we know all we can do is accept you men as you are. You're gonna do what you gotta do to stay alive, and we get it, but it don't mean we like it. It's why I didn't want to get involved with any more Bishops, or anyone else from a gang. I want more. I don't want to have to worry. And I don't want to fight with my man about worrying, neither. I keep thinking that if I'd just…said something different, kept him at home, somehow. I don't know. Maybe—he'd still be here."

"No, India, you can't—"

She cuts me off with a violent gesture. "I know, okay? I know! But I still think about it. So I get the guilt, a little. Not the same, but…yeah, guilt sucks."

"I'm a part of the Bishops, sort of. Not a full member, but still…"

She laughs, and it's rueful. "I know. That ain't slipped my notice. But I'm involved, now."

"I'm sorry."

She shakes her head. I love that, how her hair flies when she shakes her head. "Boy, you shut up with that 'sorry' mess. I knew what I was getting myself into. I knew. But you're different. You can be more. I believe that. You're *gonna* be more, Colt."

"So will you. It'll be different. I'll be different."

"I know."

The moment is fraught with meaning: *Be more. Do more. Be different.*

Don't end up dead. Like Isaac. Like Lil B. Like I almost was.

India rummages around in the bedside table and comes up with a tiny pinner joint in a Zip-Loc baggie. She lights it, takes a deep drag, leans close to me, kiss-close, and shotguns the smoke into my mouth. We kiss and breathe and taste the THC as it runs through us. Another drag, and this time she inhales and holds it. Then she hands me the joint, and then lifts my flaccid cock to her mouth, taking it in. Mouths it. Exhales through her nose while working me erect with her soft warm mouth. She takes the joint again and tokes while stroking me with her hand, eyes on me, a smile teasing the corners of her mouth.

It doesn't take long before I'm rock hard and aching. She keeps the smoke in her mouth and takes me deep into her throat, smoke trickling from her nostrils. She backs away and exhales the rest, goes back down to my cock. I smoke and watch her, watch her hair move, groan with the bliss of her mouth on me.

"India, enough—"

She sits up, snatches the joint from me, takes a hard drag, her eyes on me as she works her way back down. She pushes against me, so I'm laying down, making it clear how this is going to go. She blows smoke out through her mouth and nose, smoke curling around her face and my erection, and then there's only her mouth on me, sliding up and down. Fist twisting around my base, pumping and stroking and cupping my balls, no slowing now, no mercy, only her tongue sliding against the side of my shaft, her lips on the glans, sucking hard.

I can't hold back; I don't dare.

I grab a fistful of that fucking gorgeous hair, and she moans an affirmative, glances up at me as she bobs up and down, up and down. She puts her hand over mine and shows me that she wants me to pull. God, this girl. I pull hard. Jerk at her hair, thrust gently at first and then harder and harder, pulling at her hair, her head.

She moans encouraging noises—*mmmhhhm- mmm, mmmmm, mmmmm, mmmhhhmmmm*—as I lose control. I fuck. It's an unstoppable force within me, and she's taking it and acting like she loves it.

I tug twice, then, short sharp tugs to tell her I'm

close. She backs away until her lips are around the thick head, just in time. I unleash with a shout, and she takes it. All of it, milking it out of me until I'm faint and limp and breathless.

And then she flops down beside me, takes the still-smoldering joint from my fingers, and finishes it.

It's a few seconds before I can formulate a thought. "Jesus, India."

"Yeah? Good?"

"Good? Honey…if I wasn't in love already, I sure as hell am now."

She stills suddenly. "You—what?"

I realize what I said. It just sort of popped out on its own. But it's true and it's irrevocable.

"I—um."

She relaxes. "You can take it back. Heat of the moment and all that."

I roll onto my elbow and fix my eyes on hers. "No. You can't take words back. And I don't."

Tears prick her eyes. "Don't, Colt. Don't play me."

"I'm not." I thumb a tear. "It's crazy…but I don't take it back."

"It was just a blow job. I'll suck that fine-ass cock of yours anytime you want. You don't have to tell me you love me for that."

"I'll totally take you up on the blow jobs. That was fucking incredible. But..." I trail off, start over. "I never believed in love at first sight. Until I met you."

She laughs and rolls into me. Kisses my chest. "Boy, you stole that line from a movie."

"Sure did. Don't know which one, but I did. It's a good line and has the additional benefit of being true."

"Smooth," she says, laughing.

The laughter turns to moaning, though, as I kiss my way down her body, laving at her nipples until they're hard, and then down, nipping at her thighs, licking the crease of her slit, licking harder and harder until my tongue-tip prods through those lower lips. Lick until she's writhing, slide a finger into her, alternating curling and licking. Smear juices, lap them up. And when she's desperate with the need to come, I give it to her, hard and fast and unrelenting. Lick and flick and thrust fingers in and out until she just about tears my hair out with the wild force of her orgasm. I suck her clit between my teeth and then let it go, flick and flick and flick it until she comes a second time.

Again and again. I lose track, and I'm sure she does too. There is no limit, it seems. And she's more gorgeous every single time.

"Stop, Colt-baby, stop. I can't take any more."

She pulls me up, pulls my face to her breasts and holds me there.

The day goes by as we sleep, curled around each other.

Ten: Body Count

I DON'T KNOW WHY OR HOW, BUT BEING WITH INDIA GETS better every single day. We've been together for six months now, and I love her more than ever. We're hot and heavy all the time and it makes some people sick to death, but we just can't stop. Callie did indeed kick my ass. I let her, but I also made sure she knows I'll never give up on India.

She's worth it, and more.

Callie came to accept us, and me.

India and I talk a lot about the future, and we start to make plans, real plans. She's applying to go to cosmetology school next semester and she's really excited about it, which makes me happy. She doesn't know it, but I have a plan I haven't told her about: I want us to get a place together, our own place. I start looking…outside the hood. We do talk about moving in to our own place, but it hasn't happened so far and I want to keep it like that, so when I find the right place, she'll get the surprise of her life.

I can't wait.

In order to make enough money that I can afford the new apartment while still saving toward a down payment on a garage, I return to what I know: I run with Split and the Bishops, and we work a pretty lucrative pot trade. I'm not real proud of the fact that I'm still on the street, or about how I'm making my money, but it's cash and it'll buy me what I want. Split knows my goal—about the garage anyway—and he knows my plan is to leave the gang eventually. Funnily enough, he supports the idea, and I think I even see a bit of envy in his eyes the few times we talk about it. Split doesn't have that option, not really. As a side business, and to start building a clientele base, I've been making extra cash helping people with their cars, fixing, tuning, customizing.

I'm still staying with India, at her mom's place, and I pitch in with food and rent. We honestly have a decent amount of privacy, as her mom is always either gone or sleeping because she works a lot of late and double shifts. We've talked a few times, but she keeps to herself. Old hurt bleeds in her eyes, and something about me makes it worse. Something about India's father, probably. I've only heard bits and pieces of that story—a love between a black woman and a Korean immigrant here on a temporary visa, in a time when such things were still fairly taboo. Shit, it still is, to some people. India was just a kid when his visa ran out; he had no choice but to leave, and they never saw him again. India never knew him. She grew up half-Korean in an all-black neighborhood, and learned to be tougher than everyone else because of it. Girls can be ten times more cruel than boys, is all India will say on the subject.

Good things never last forever.

Not for me, at least.

Starts out like any old day. I'm over at the basketball court with a few of the Bishops I'm closest to, playing some pick-up ball. I'm bricking shot after shot, because I suck at basketball, but it's what you do on a lazy Sunday afternoon in the hood. I'm about to *finally* nail a shot when Split tenses, straightens. Everybody goes hyper-alert. Then T-Shawn ambles over to the bench, slips on his shirt and, not-so-surreptitiously, shoves his piece into his jeans. Split is like a live wire, humming with restrained violence. Mo, tall, skinny, always unpredictable, is looking around and I can see the tension in his eyes. Lil Shady, a small, aggressive, angry brother with a wild hair up his ass, ready to rumble at all times, stands with his head up, watching, waiting. He's always accusing me of trying to steal his girl, despite the fact that I've got my own, not to mention I don't even *like* his girl. Red is there, too, big, wide, slow, always dropping rhymes and talking about 'making it'.

Six guys come swaggering onto the court. They spread out, hands in pockets, heads tipped back, eyes glittering in the sun. They're new, think they're tough. But they don't know who they're fucking with.

I wait beside Split as they trade insults, spit venom, the usual shit-talking that leads up to beef. Except, in this case, it's an excuse to start a turf war. I stay out of it, like I usually do in these circumstances. My job is to be backup. Jump in if I'm needed. I'm the exception; still an outsider, and anyone not in the inner core of the Bishops doesn't really accept me. Members of other gangs certainly don't. They'd shoot me on sight, just for being who I am, and for being here.

Shit goes south in an instant—a knife blade flashes, and suddenly this turf war is real.

I can only watch it happen. Everyone is paired off, fighting, one-to-one. We're winning, too.

And then the fucker T-Shawn is pounding on rolls away, digs in his pocket, flicks open a black three-inch blade and shoves it into T-Shawn's throat…twice.

Blood sprays.

T-Shawn falls onto his back, and I hear the most fucking awful sound: gurgling, wet bubbling gasping for breath.

I toss aside the little punk who came over to scrap with me, level him with an elbow. I'm across the court in an instant, and I've got the fucker in my hands.

I shove him to the ground, sit astride him—I can feel myself doing this, but somehow it's not me. It's just happening, my body on autopilot. I know as it happens I'll never wash this blood off my hands. I'm smashing his head against the concrete, over and over and over, until my hands are red and my face is wet and sticky, and hands are pulling me away.

The rest of the enemy fuckers are gone, they ran off, leaving their dead friend on the court with us.

Colt Calloway, body count: two.

T is on the ground. I grab him, pulling him into my arms. He's bleeding everywhere, and the gasping gurgling is fading, and I can tell he's slipping away.

"T…" I rasp. "Come on, man."

Split is impassive, but I see the cracks in his expression. No one says a damn thing, we all just watch as T-Shawn bleeds out, and goes silent. It all happened in a few seconds—there was nothing anyone could do.

Except prepare for the next time because, sure as shit, there will be a next time.

And, sure enough, a week later it's Lil Shady. Bad shit. Him and me had just smoked a blunt at his place, and then we left to go our own ways. Then, an hour later, the door slams open at the pad of the guy I'm doing some mechanic work for. Mo and Split have Shady, carrying him. He's gone already. Limp, head lolling, blood dripping nasty from a hole in his skull.

Who'll be next? Me? Split? Mo? Red?

T-Shawn is gone, and now Shady?

Fuck.

India and I talk that night for a long time. Then we go to bed and it's rough and hard, and then it's sweet, and she holds me, like she did after T died. Like she does every night, but she holds me especially tight that night.

Before sleep claims me, I decide to wrap things up with Split tomorrow.

India and I are getting the hell out of here.

The next day I get up early, and when India wakes up

I tell her to pack her things, that I'll be back around lunchtime to collect her. I'm going to go see Split and then India and I are heading over to Brooklyn. I've got enough saved; we'll find a place.

It's time to start over.

I see India's face light up when she hears my plan—she's as ready for this as I am.

I'm passing the basketball court, and I see a rumble in progress—it's the same fucking rival gang. They're using bats, chains, and fists. It's wild and gnarly for a few minutes, but then it breaks up on its own. Sort of. Some guys scatter, others go after them. Split and me are left alone, and there are still a good half dozen of the other guys piling out of cars, coming for us, pulling pieces as they swagger toward us.

"Shit." Split pushes me. "Go, dog. Go! Run, motherfucker!"

If Split says run, you know it's bad. We run. Like dogs, we run. The six guys chase us down alleys and side streets. Something cracks behind us, and the windshield of a parked car shatters. Bullets thunk into quarter panels and into the asphalt. The road dead-ends at a chain link fence around a vacant lot. Split—lighter, smaller, more nimble—scrambles up and over it like a goddamn monkey. I make it halfway up when I feel something tug at my sleeve, and then hear an angry buzz past my ear, followed by a *snap*. Too damn close. Pistols crack a split second later.

Split is torn, about to climb back over to help me.

I jump back off the fence. "Go! Get the fuck outta here. I'll go through the yards."

"Meet back at the court." He says this as he turns and runs. Then Split is gone. Boy can run like a goddamn cheetah when he needs to.

I risk a glance as I peel off through the backyards of the neighborhood. I'm slower than Split—speed and agility aren't my strong suit. I have a piece, of course, but I'm reluctant to use it, always have been, since the shit with Lil B; I had planned to return it to Split today, but now I don't think I have much choice. I pull it out, check the load of the clip as I hide behind a crumbling partial wall. I trip over scooters and Big Wheels and fire trucks as I twist down a side street, juke down another. They follow me, just a few yards behind me and gaining. Occasional shots ring out. A round stings my thigh; another rips the hat off my head.

Run, motherfucker.

I turn at random, circle back, and hop fences when I can, trying to lose them. Run, run, run! I go a mile, maybe more, through old run-down neighborhoods, past ramshackle houses, shotgun houses, all built close together with the paint now fading and bars on the windows and doors, surrounded by chain link fences and yellow strips of grass and cracked sidewalks.

Finally, the shouts fade; I lose them by running right through somebody's house, an old black couple watching *Jerry Springer*. They aren't fazed in the slightest. They just curse me out from the couch and demand that I at least close the goddamn front door behind me.

I slow to a walk, listening, my senses hyper-alert. I'm gasping for breath. The sweat is pouring down my face, my lungs are aching and my legs are burning.

Just as I go through an intersection, I hear a shout. "There he is!"

They smell blood.

I take off again but they're right behind me, all six of them. They're less than twenty yards behind me, and they're gaining fast. All of them have guns. One lifts his piece, cracks off a shot, which goes wide and plunks into a car. Then another shot is fired, missing as well. A third round goes high and smashes into a house. Someone shouts, screams.

Goddamnit. They're gonna hit someone innocent.

I pivot, take careful aim, slowing down to do

so, and crack off a round. Blood spills, and he topples over, holding his gut. I fire again, and a second one goes down, clutching his chest and I can see him choke back vomit. The third is quick to fire back, and a round hits my bicep, tearing a gash along the outside. I take off again as a hail of careless rounds fire behind me. Fuck, fuck. Fear hounds my every step.

This is it. This has to be it.

I just shot two more people. Fuck, fuck.

I scrabble around a corner, gasping in agony at what I've done, barely aware of the searing pain in my leg.

Colt Calloway, body count: four.

He's right behind me. I'm tripping over my own feet. I cut through a yard, hop a fence, run pell-mell down a street that looks exactly like all the others, but it's familiar somehow. I've been on this street before; I've partied at a house here—it's a frequent hangout spot for anyone associated with the Bishops.

Then, at the house, some thirty feet away, I see a face and wild black hair.

India.

What the hell is she doing here? There's a bunch of other people sitting on the porch with her. They see me hauling ass toward them, and they all scatter or drop down onto the ground. The guys on the porch haul iron and pop off shots, scattering my pursuers.

"Get down!" I shout so loud my voice goes hoarse.

India sees it's me, and ducks behind the porch, out of sight.

I see Split in the distance, with Red and Easy, driving this way. I shout for them, but they're too far away and they can't do anything from where they are.

Guns pop and crack around me, and I turn behind to see they've mostly all scattered. All except for one.

He stops, almost uncaring, and petulantly fires off a round. It misses me and goes over my shoulder and makes a hole in the thin wood slats of the porch.

I hear a wet *thunk*.

There's no scream.

"Oh, shit." I hear him say it.

He knows.

I know.

I stumble to a stop, willing India to be okay.

Willing the truth to not be reality.

I forget the other guy, I forget everything.

Run.

Slip in the grass, fall, and scramble around the corner.

No.

No.

No.

Blood, India's blood stains the grass.

There is no screaming, no pain, no crying.

No sounds.

I pull her to me and scream her name.

My thighs are wet with her warm blood.

Her eyes are open. Staring at me. Unseeing.

Hands pull at me. Voices shout. Sirens howl.

Someone pulls me, pushes me, gets me to my feet and into a car.

Where is India?

And then I remember. I see her blind stare—and the hole between her eyes. Her beautiful brown eyes.

Split is driving. He's crying silently.

Sun glints on the water as we cross over a bridge. I am aware of the sound of tires humming on the metal bridge deck.

"It ain't your fault," he murmurs. "It was a accident."

"She's dead."

And those are the last words I speak for a very long time.

Eleven: A Seedling Sprouts

"COLT. C'MON, MAN. TALK TO ME, BROTHER." SPLIT SQUATS in front of me.

He's been there for…I don't know…a long time. Pleading. Begging. Getting angry. He's trying to elicit a response from me. But he's not getting one.

I'm empty. Except for the pain, I'm empty.

I just stare right through him. Not seeing him. The only thing that fills my vision is India, the hole in her skull, the vacant eyes.

"You're gonna starve to death. You ain't eaten in a week."

Good. Starving to death would be a fitting punishment, and death would feel a fuck of a lot better than this.

"You gotta get up. You gotta let her go, man. She's gone. I'm sorry, but she's gone. You giving up ain't gonna bring her back. I miss her, too. Callie misses her. Maya misses her. And none of us blame you. Okay? You might, but I don't. Callie don't. Nobody blames you. It wasn't your fault. It was an accident."

Something acidic boils down deep in my gut; thick, hot, angry, bitter gall. Rage.

I've got rage boiling in the pits of my black, unfeeling soul. I choke it down. I blink and shake my head. It *is* my fault. I led them to her. The bullet missed me and hit her instead. It should have been me. Should have been me. I ran, instead of staying and fighting. I ran, led them to her, and got her killed.

No matter what anyone says, it's my fault that India is dead.

Split rises to his feet, hissing in frustration, scrubbing a palm over his unkempt scruff of hair. He hasn't shaved his face or his head since India died. I haven't either. I haven't showered. I haven't eaten. I haven't moved. I'm on India's bed. I keep trying to call up the feel of her in my arms. Try to summon the beauty of her nude body beside mine. The way she kissed me. The light in her eyes first thing in the morning, when she saw me.

Split leaves without a backward glance. Good.

Go. Stay away. I don't deserve friends. And I sure as fuck don't deserve their forgiveness or pity.

Shadows shift as the hours fade one into another. I see only memories, only images of India. I'm consumed by the thoughts of what we could have had, what we nearly had, and I hate myself even more.

The door to the bedroom opens, and I expect Callie or Split, but it's not. It's India's mother, Maya. She looks haggard. Bags under her eyes. Shadows within shadows in her gaze; India was her only child, her only family.

She sits near my feet and stares into nothingness, not speaking for a long time. Finally, slowly, her gaze shifts to mine. "Cain't stay here, son. Not no more."

I expected this. I nod, and—stiff and sore and aching from being immobile for so long —I sit up. I get to my feet, feeling wobbly and dizzy. I move toward the door.

"I wasn't finished. Sit down, Colt, and listen to me."

I turn, stumble and take a seat beside her. I owe her this, at least. I have to listen as she tells me she hates me. That I killed her daughter. She stares at the carpet under her feet, hair bound back for work as it always is—I don't think I've ever seen her with her hair down. She's wearing hospital scrubs, as always.

She reaches out and takes my hand. "Look at me, boy." I look up, but it's hard to do, hard to meet her gaze. Hardest thing I've ever done, looking this woman in the eyes. "I forgive you."

I shake my head; deny the hot salt stinging my eyes. I deny the ache in my heart. I shake my head so hard it hurts.

"Yes. I do." She grips my hand with fierce strength. Her palms and fingers are callused and strong. "My India, she was all I had. Now she gone. And...I ain't gonna sugarcoat it. It's because of you that she's gone. If she hadn't gotten mixed up with you, she'd still be alive. I told her not to hang out with no more of them Bishop boys. They bad news. Bad, bad news. She knew it. I knew it. After Isaac...I didn't think she would ever go back to being with a Bishop. But she told me, 'He's different, Mama. He ain't like the others.' And I believed her. I let you be here when you wanted to be here, and do what you want. Ya'll are adults, gonna make your own decisions. And... you loved her. I saw that. I saw it in her. She was hurt so bad when Isaac died. And you brought her to life in a new way. She was getting that cosmetology degree. Gonna be a model in the city. But now...she gone."

I can't help a choked-back sob.

Maya takes a long breath and grabs my other

hand, holding them so tight the bones grate together. She fixes her eyes on mine. "I forgive you. And you… you got to go. You stay here; you'll waste away on that bed. I can't let you do that. She wouldn't have wanted you to lie there, giving up, letting yourself go. I forgive you. And for her sake, I'm gonna make you go. If you wanna give up, it ain't gonna happen here. And…honestly, you got to go, for me, too. I need to learn to be alone now. And you remind me of her. So you got to go. For you, for her, and for me."

I nod. It's all I can manage. She's right. I know she is. But…it doesn't matter. Nothing matters. I can't feel anything but the pain. So I stand up, turn and face Maya. She sees the *I'm sorry* in my eyes.

I can see there is something else she wants to tell me. "What, Maya? Just say it."

She shakes her head. "I can't—I just can't."

I stare at her for a long time, but she remains silent. "Thank you. For…everything."

"Goodbye, Colt." It's final. She puts a hand on my shoulder, and then she's gone, and and I'm alone.

It only takes a few minutes to pack my things. I've got my saved cash, clothes, extra pair of shoes, that's about it. That is all I've got. And the gun. I hold it in my hands, staring at it. Stuff it in the back of my pants, because I don't want it in my bag. Got to get rid of it.

I'm done. Done with the Bishops. Done with everything.

I'm at the front door, bag on my shoulder, taking one last look at the living room where India and I spent so much time together. That couch…god, we made love on that couch so many times, under that ivory afghan, watching TV.

Maya stops me. She's carrying one of India's teddy bears, the one with the blue button eye. Wordlessly she hands it me. For a moment that feels like an eternity, I hold the teddy bear in my hands, smelling India on it, feeling her on it. I swallow hard, blink harder. With tears in my eyes, I leave India's apartment. Don't look back.

Down the stairs at the front of the building, turn right, and start walking.

This is familiar. The walking.

I make it a few miles before Split catches up to me. He stops his GTO in front me and gets out. He looks hard at me. "You're gonna leave, just like that? Fuck you, Colt. I thought you had more guts than this."

I shake my head; I don't.

He pushes up against me, chest to chest, nose to nose. "Fuck that, man. I ain't letting you walk away like this. I know you're hurting. I know you hate your-self. But you don't get to walk away. We're in this to-gether."

In answer, I pull out the 9mm, eject the clip, pull the slide to eject the shell in the chamber, hand it all to him. I push past him.

He grabs my arm, spins me around, shoves me backward, and then decks me with a wicked right hook. It levels me. I topple backward to the ground, blood dribbling from the corner of my lip. I stay on the ground, shocked. Split tosses the gun, clip, and shell onto the backseat of his car, and moves to kneel in front of me.

He grabs the front of my shirt. "I've had it, Colt. You can't puss out on me. I ain't gonna let you." He stands up, hauling me to my feet.

He lunges at me, hits me again. I let him. I take it on the cheekbone. He hits me yet again, a right to the gut. I double over, then straighten up. I deserve this. Again, and again, he punches me, and I do nothing but take it.

"Fight back, goddamn it!"

I can't. I won't.

He stops, breathing hard, staring at me in fury. "You gonna give up like this, then…you didn't de-serve her. You never deserved her."

That cuts. Deep.

I stagger from the pain of his words. It's a real, physical agony, the knowledge that I don't deserve her. That I never did. And the pain from Split's hard, accurate punches makes it all the more real.

I like the pain. It's something to hold on to.

"Thought you were my boy, my brother." Split is cracking. Anger and agony are a maelstrom in his eyes. He shoves me, hard. "You ain't. You ain't nothin'."

I can't argue with that.

But the slicing pain of knowing he's right drops me to my knees. And Split is there, grabbing me by the hair. "Get angry, Colt. At me. At yourself. At the assholes who caused all this. I took care'a them, you know? Made sure they paid. They *paid*. Now, you gotta get up and show who you are. India wouldn't love a pussy. A pathetic piece of shit who would just give up like this. Just walk away. From me, from Callie, from Maya, from Cleo, from the Bishops. That ain't you. You gotta find you again, Colt."

He hauls me to my feet by my hair. Shoves me. Watches for a moment, waiting for a reaction. I say nothing, do nothing. I have nothing, I am nothing. I'm not the man India loved. He died when she did.

Split spits on the ground at my feet, gets in his car

and drives away. But he only goes a few yards before screeching to a halt. Stalks angrily toward me, grabs me by the shirt and hauls me to his car. Shoves me in, closes the door after me. Gets in and starts driving. I don't ask where. It doesn't matter.

Split drives a few blocks, to the hospital, and parks in the general parking lot. "C'mon. Mo's in here, got hurt bad in all that bullshit. You owe it to him to at least pay him a visit."

Fuck, I gotta visit Mo. He's a good dude, a little crazy, but good. So I haul my ass up to the ninth floor and check on Mo. He took one to the chest and made it to the doctors in time to get patched up. He's hooked up to all sorts of machines and monitors, looking pale and pissed. Bored. I'm there, and that's all that's necessary. He doesn't say anything to me about India, and I don't say anything at all.

Eventually, I have to get out of the room. I'm halfway to the elevator when I'm stopped by a pretty young girl with her hair in cornrows, wearing nurse's scrubs.

"Hey, you Colt?" she asks.

I nod.

"I was friends with India." She ducks her head, seems hesitant. Afraid. "Not sure if Maya's mom told you, but…um. India—she…when she died, she was—

" A long, long pause, then. A tear trickles down her face. She finally looks up at me, eyes wet. "She was pregnant."

I think I collapse. I only remember cold tile under my face, and feeling cold inside. Then I become aware of hands lifting me, carrying me. I might have been crying, I don't know. It's all a blur, a haze, darkness.

I'm on a couch at some point and realize I am at Split and Callie's apartment.

I feel hunger, and thirst, but I ignore it.

Split forces me to eat, and I do it just to get him off my back. I'm empty, for I don't even know how long.

I'm on Split's couch.

I'm seeing India.

I'm seeing her bleed onto my legs and onto the grass.

I'm hearing Maya tell me it's my fault but that she forgives me.

I don't forgive me; all I deserve is pain.

The only thought I have is that I need to feel pain.

Late one night, something—I don't know what—propels me to get up off the couch and tiptoe into the kitchen. I open a drawer and pull out a steak knife. I don't know what drives me to stand over the sink and drag the blade across my wrist. It stings, but not enough. I'm shirtless, and something dark and black and thirsty whispers to me, telling me to pull the blade across my chest. Directly under my left nipple, a long slow slice.

The pain is sharp and sweet. While I bleed, I can breathe. But it fades all too soon. So I pull the blade across my chest on the other side. I press hard so the blade cuts deep. I flex and the blood flows. I breathe, sucking in a breath.

But when the pain dulls, the anchor pressing on my chest is back.

I'm about to cut my chest again when the door to Split and Callie's bedroom opens. Callie comes out, wearing one of Split's shirts and looking sleepy. She doesn't see me at first as she grabs a glass from the cabinet and moves to the sink to fill it with water. Then she sees me.

"Shit, sorry, didn't see you." She blinks up at me, still bleary-eyed. And then her gaze fixes on my chest; the thin trickles of blood trailing down my chest. She sees the long deep slices in my skin, in the muscle. Sees the knife in my hand, the blade red. "Colt? What the fuck are you doing?"

I just stand there. I have no words, no explanation.

She shakes her head in disgust. "Man, you need help. That's fucked up." She gets her water and goes back to bed.

I hear her talking to Split in low murmurs, and after a minute he comes out, wearing a pair of low-riding shorts. His gaze rakes across my cuts, then goes to the knife.

"I gotta worry about finding you dead in my kitchen?" he demands.

I have to think about that. Eventually, I can shake my head in the negative. It's not about seeking death. It's about finding pain so I can breathe. Even if I could speak, I couldn't explain it.

Split takes the knife from me. "Don't be an idiot, man. This ain't the way." He washes the knife carefully, dries it, and puts it away. I just watch. When he's done, he faces me. "Colt, I don't need this shit. You want to cut yourself to pieces, do it somewhere else. Not in my house. Not around my woman. She's been through enough. I know you're hurt, but doing that ain't gonna fix it. I won't sit by and watch you do that shit."

He's right. She's right. They're both right. It's fucked up and it doesn't fix anything.

But I can breathe when I bleed. I can breathe when the pain is sharp and fresh. I can't breathe without India and I don't deserve to.

So I cut, but I do it when I'm alone, where they can't see, and I don't ever let them know.

I find a razor blade and keep it in my wallet. I walk the streets at night when the streetlights buzz and hum and the streets are empty and the playgrounds are still. Sometimes I sit on the swings and think of India, and think about flirting, living, falling in love with a girl.

I lift my shirt and slide the razor across my chest, then down my bicep. I watch the blood and breathe while it flows.

Split knows I'm still doing this, but I keep my promise, and I never cut around him, or Callie.

I never thought I'd be a cutter.

Just like I never thought I'd be homeless, or a member of a gang, or an underground fighter.

I'm all those things, and none of them are worth a damn.

A couple months later, I go back to fighting. Every night there's a fight, and I fight as many times as Ruiz will let me. The fights are the only times I feel alive. I fight like a wounded tiger. Night after night, week after week. My face takes a battering. My nose is permanently crooked. I bank my money, save it all. I don't even bother to count it, I just stuff it into a duffel bag and stash it at Split's place.

I fight.

I cut.

And I walk.

I barely sleep.

I try, but I can't.

When I'm alone in the apartment I listen to music and I sing to myself. It started out as nonsense, but it turns into…something. I write a song to sing to myself and, in the process, find a way to push away the emptiness, to push away the need to cut:

Quiet your crying voice, lost child.

Let no plea for comfort pass your lips.

You're okay, now.

You're okay, now.

Don't cry anymore, dry your eyes.

Roll the pain away, put it down on the ground and leave it for the birds.

Suffer no more, lost child.

Stand and take the road, move on and seal the hurt behind the miles.

It's not all right, it's not okay.

I know, I know.

The night is long, it's dark and cruel.

I know, I know.

You're not alone. You're not alone.
You are loved. You are held.
Quiet your crying voice, lost child.
You're okay, now.
You're okay, now.
Just hold on, one more day.
Just hold on, one more hour.
Someone will come for you.
Someone will hold you close.
I know, I know.
It's not okay, it's not all right.
But if you just hold on,
One more day, one more hour.
It will be. It will be.

The song is for me. It's for India. It's for the little life she had inside. And I think, in sadness, maybe she didn't even know about it herself. I hum to myself, my little tune, with its childish-lullaby words. I sing to myself, under my breath, and finally I can sleep.

One day, after hours of aimless walking, I find myself walking past a garage. I glance inside at the bays and see cars up on lifts, mechanics in coveralls underneath, tinkering and doing oil changes and whatever else. I can't help but stop and watch. This simple scene has fired my imagination like nothing else for the past few weeks. I light a smoke and lean against a wall that offers a good view. A scruffy kid in too-big coveralls is working on a pickup truck jacked upon a hydraulic lift, and I can tell from here that the kid is fucking up some poor dude's exhaust system. The kid has no idea what he's doing, and no one is supervising him.

Whether it's frustration, or the simple fact that I can't bear to watch him struggle any longer, I walk over to the service bay, shove the kid aside and take the wrench from him.

"Hey, man, what the hell?" he protests and tries to push me out of the way, at the same time trying to take the wrench back.

One glare from me has him backing down. "You're fucking it up. Let me help before you fuck it up so bad it can't be fixed."

He steps back, watches as I undo his mistakes, paying attention as I dismantle the entire exhaust system, go over it piece by piece and put it back together the right way.

When I'm done, my hands are covered in grease, and there's something alive in my chest. The load weighing me down has lifted, a little bit.

A burly guy in coveralls with the upper half tied around his waist approaches me and the kid, and the late-model Ram 1500 I just fixed. "What's going on, Ricky?" he asks, coffee in hand.

The kid, Ricky, gestures at me. "I don't know, Carl. He just showed up. Took the wrench, redid everything I was working on."

"And you just let him?"

Ricky gestures at me again. "You see him?"

Carl, obviously the owner of the garage, examines the exhaust system. "It's good work. What's your name?"

I've barely spoken in the last few months but suddenly...I feel alive again. Maybe with a bit of grease under my nails and a wrench in my hand, I can find a way to breathe other than cutting.

So I clear my throat. "Colt."

"You know cars, Colt?"

I nod. "Yeah, I do."

Carl points at a Camry up on a lift. "Have a look at that one."

I toss the wrench back to Ricky and duck under the Camry. The brakes need replacing, and there's oil leaking from somewhere. The leak is probably why it was brought in here in the first place. I sniff out the cause of the leak in a few minutes.

"Found the leak," I say, emerging from underneath the car.

Carl nods at me and then glances at Ricky, "Sorry kid. You've just been replaced."

"Aw, c'mon, Carl. I just started! And Aunt Linda said—"

"My sister doesn't run my shop. You don't know shit about cars and I don't have time to teach you. You can work the counter."

"This is bullshit," Ricky says, but it's under his breath and he's already heading into the front of the shop.

Carl extends his hand. "I need full-time. I got work orders coming out my asshole, and my one skilled employee quit on me last month."

"I'll work till I drop. You won't be disappointed." I shake his hand.

"Start you at fifteen an hour. Keep your nose clean and don't fuck anything up, and I'll add to it."

"Sounds good."

And just like that, I have a job. A real job. A legitimate, legal job doing the one thing I've ever gotten any enjoyment from. It feels odd, filling out W2 information, and signing my name. I realize I'll need a bank account to deposit my pay checks. I smile wryly to myself—going legit means no more cash, it means putting money in the bank like everybody else. Somehow this thought makes me feel good.

I step into a pair of coveralls, zip them up and get to work.

It feels like the barren, fallow soil of my soul has suddenly sprouted a seedling.

Perhaps hope has somewhere to grow.

I start work that day, right then. I work on the Camry and fix the leak and replace the brakes. The next challenge is an old as fuck Volvo, which I manage to breathe enough life into to see the owner through another summer. After a lunch break, I change the oil and fix a faulty starter on a Focus. I forget everything as I work. Everything. Time, myself, India, Split, the past, everything. Nothing exists but the tool in my hand and the mechanical problem that needs fixing.

I've got my head under the hood of a sweet-ass restored Charger, tinkering with the spark plugs. I'm aware of a presence behind me and then feel a tap on the shoulder. Instinct has me spinning around, and lunging forward. Tool in hand, I raise my arm, ready to strike. Suddenly I come to my senses. I realize I've got Carl by the throat and I'm about to bash his head in.

Immediately I let him go and drop the tool onto the engine block. "Shit. Shit. Sorry." I back up. Blink hard, wipe at my face. "Sorry. I'm sorry."

Carl swallows, straightens. "Jumpy much? Jesus."

"I don't do well being snuck up on."

"No shit." He rubs his throat. "Do I gotta worry about you?"

I shrug. "Nobody's gonna come after me."

"Not what I mean. You gonna snap? You almost brained me just now, and all I did was walk up behind you."

"Just...I was just surprised is all. I didn't hear you."

He nods, and then pauses before he says, "Okay. Just...keep that shit in check, man. Customers will sue me if you pull that shit on them." He taps his wrist. "It's after ten at night, time to knock off."

I gesture at the Charger. "I'm almost done here. I don't mind staying to finish up."

Carl shakes his head. "I'm going home. And, no offense meant, but I don't trust you here by yourself just yet. So. Time to knock off."

"Got it."

"How do you spell your name? I wanna make sure your name tag is right."

"C-O-L-T."

He locks up, turns the lights off, and closes the bay doors. We stand in a bright pool of light from a floodlight on a wire overhead. Cars pass in ones and twos in both directions.

"I'll have your name tag for you tomorrow. My wife does embroidery. Be here at nine." He extends his hand to me.

Tentatively, hesitantly, I shake it. I have a boss, and he's a decent guy, it seems. Not everyone would be willing to overlook my jumpy, street-attuned instincts. "See you tomorrow, Carl."

I walk back to Split and Callie's place. They're on the couch together, Callie is watching Split play Xbox and they're sharing a bottle of booze, her head resting on his lap. They're comfortable together. It's easy and quiet and peaceful for them.

Split hears me come in and pauses his game. "Where you been, dog?" Not expecting a reply. But then he turns to look at me, sees the coveralls, the grease on my hands. "No shit! You got a job?"

I risk a very rusty smile, and I shrug. "Yeah."

Split claps a hand to his heart, a comedically overdramatic gesture. "He speaks! Lawd be praised!"

"Shut up." I duck my head, embarrassed. Mainly because I feel like a person again. It's odd and painful and refreshing.

"For real, though. I'm happy for you, Colt. Where at?"

"Carl's Auto Garage. Few miles north of here."

"You done fighting?" It's a loaded question. He's

also asking if I'm done cutting.

I shrug. "I think so. I'm going to try."

I sit on the far side of the couch, Callie's feet on my knees, watching Split shoot zombies. It feels good to sit down. I take a drink from the bottle and pass it back.

The past is still there. The misery. The grief. The guilt.

But…

But I realize it's not all there is, somehow. If I can work on cars, I might survive this. It's what India would have wanted.

"India would be proud of you," Callie says.

"That's what I was just thinking," I tell her.

It's hard to look at her because she's always glancing at my chest, looking for blood where it sticks to my shirt after I've cut. She's always looking at me as if she sees India.

But now, I look at Callie, and she just sees *me*. We share a smile full of meaning.

I just might survive this.

Twelve: Learning to Play

TIME HEALS. THAT'S WHAT THEY SAY ANYWAY. I'VE GOT THE healed scars on my chest to prove it. Inside I still hurt, still hate myself for what happened. I haven't been able to forgive myself yet, but I'm getting there.

My life has become pretty simple: I work for Carl, fixing cars. I save my money, keep my head down, my nose clean, and try to just make it, one day at a time. I don't fight anymore and I have to admit that feels good.

One day, not long after I started working for Carl, Split and I are sitting on the steps outside their apartment building, smoking a joint.

He hands it to me, blows out the smoke and then glances at me. "I ain't trying to kick you out, but…

you ever think of getting your own place?"

"Yeah. Funny you mention it, because I've been thinking about it."

"You know you're welcome for as long as you want to be here. But it could be good for you to be on your own."

I've lived with Split and Callie ever since India died. They deserve their own space and it's time for me to give it to them.

Split is right. He didn't say it in so many words, but in a way I'm using them as a crutch: when I'm alone, the temptation to cope with the loneliness via a razor blade is far too strong. But I have to face that demon the same way I faced opponents in the boxing ring—I've gotta man up and commit myself.

I hand him the joint. As the smoke floats above our heads I say, "I'll find somewhere."

"Colt, you know I'm not—"

"I can't live with you guys forever." I slap him on the back. "I'm good. It'll be good."

Which is how I find myself in a crazy scenario: subletting a bedroom from an old woman. I found the place in a classified ad, and called her up on a whim. She wanted to have a face-to-face meeting and, for reasons I still do not understand, agreed to sublet a room to me. It's cheap, and it's close to the garage.

The landlady's name is Tilda. She's white, eighty-seven, spry, sweet, and strict. No women past midnight. No smoking anything in or around the house. No loud music. Shitty rules for most guys my age, but in my situation…it's perfect. And impossible. There is no way now to avoid my demons, no way to avoid having to cope.

More often than not, I go to work, and then come home, and have to face being alone with my thoughts, with my memories. With my demons.

I can't smoke in my room, and too much booze only heightens the loneliness. When I'm drunk, I cut—the temptation is overwhelming. It's too much.

And then something truly odd happens. It is something totally ordinary but it completely changes me, completely alters my outlook on life.

One evening, Tilda puts a record on her old stereo—it's an ancient old thing with a fancy wood cabinet. The music compels me out of my room and into the living room.

It's an actual vinyl record, and the sound is incredible. Soft, slow, old music. A woman singing.

God, what a sight she is, all dressed up in her fanciest dress, hair done in a white perm. She's dancing alone, a big smile on her face as she twists and sways slowly in place, clearly seeing something from decades long past.

"It's Nina Simone, Colt." She stops dancing, and somehow those old eyes see things they shouldn't. She extends a wrinkled, papery hand. "Dance with me."

I listen to the words; the singer is singing about a new dawn…what would a new dawn feel like, I wonder?

I take Tilda's frail hand in mine, put a hand on her waist, and we dance slowly, swaying to Nina Simone. The song ends and another one comes on. We keep dancing.

"Frank and I used to dance like this." She speaks into my shoulder. She's tiny and seems fragile, but her voice is strong. "We both loved Nina. Frank used to sing for me. We'd dance, and he'd sing."

"Well…just don't expect *me* to sing," I say.

"You ever try?"

I shake my head. "Not really." Except for the little song I still sing sometimes to myself, when I can't sleep, but I'd never tell anyone about that.

She pulls away from me, adjusts the record, puts the needle down, and "Feeling Good" comes on again. "Sing it. I know you know the words. Everybody knows this song."

So I sing—you can't say no to an old woman like

Tilda. It's odd at first. Foreign. Awkward. But the music is like a drug, a new kind of drug. I feel it in my veins, burning, coruscating, effervescent and wild. So I sing.

I sing.

When the song is over, I feel something powerful inside. Tilda is staring up at me. "Why, Colt, you have a beautiful voice! Absolutely lovely. My Frank, he couldn't sing for nothing. But he was so earnest about it, so I never told him. He only sang for me, anyway. But you, Colt, you should sing more."

She lets me go after one more dance. But later, alone, I sing that Nina Simone song over and over, under my breath. And it helps me get to sleep.

When I wake the next morning there's a guitar case outside my bedroom door with a note on it in Tilda's looping cursive: *This was Frank's. He played about as well as he sang, but he sure loved trying. You should too.*

I don't even know where to start. I've never held a guitar, much less played one.

I take the guitar out of the case and just stare at it. It's old. It could be worth a lot, or maybe nothing at all—what do I know? I strum the strings. Eeesh, even I know it is out of tune.

I put it back in the case and forget about it while I am at work that day.

I come home from work that night and there's a teenage girl sitting on the couch next to Tilda, watching TV. When I walk in, the girl's eyes go wide and she cringes into the corner, panicking, even lets out a little scream of fear.

I stop halfway inside the doorway, confused.

"Oh hush, you," Tilda scolds the girl. "It's just Colt. He lives in my spare room."

The girl stares at Tilda like she's grown a second head. "Are you crazy? He's the scariest looking person I've ever seen!"

She's right, though. My other coping mechanism has become exercise. Tilda's basement is empty and unfinished, so she let me bring some exercise equipment down. I work out like a madman every day, now, and I'm beefed up bigger than I've ever been. Add in the tats, the shaggy uncut hair, weeks worth of scruff, the greasy hands...even I know I look like the thug I am.

"I'm sorry to bother you." I avoid their eyes and move toward my bedroom.

"Wait, Colt." Tilda's voice brooks no argument. I stop in the hallway and turn around. "Frankie, I'm ashamed of you. You don't know anything about this young man. You think I would bring him into my home if I was worried about what he might do? You owe him an apology."

"It's fine, Tilda. She's got a point," I say.

"No, Colt. She's judging by appearances, and I *know* I taught my daughter better than that. I would have hoped she'd passed that lesson along to my granddaughter as well." Tilda looks upset.

And so does Frankie. She's near tears, in fact. "Grandma, I—"

"No, Frankie. Stand up, go over to Colt, and apologize. Or you can go back home right now."

Frankie stands up slowly and shuffles over to me. She sniffs, then risks a glance up at me. I try to look... softer. More approachable. But it doesn't seem to work, the poor girl is shaking like a leaf.

"I'm sorry," she mumbles, almost inaudible.

"It's cool." I should say something else. Something reassuring. "I'd never let anything happen to Tilda. She's a badass."

This earns me a slight smile from both of them.

"Sit down, Colt." Tilda pats the couch. "Watch *So You Think You Can Dance* with us. You might like it."

Frankie snorts, and I nearly do, too. Sounds dumb. But like I said, you don't say no to Tilda. So I sit down and watch a bunch of skinny shits prance around on a stage.

The whole time Tilda is eyeing her granddaughter, a light of speculation in her eyes. When the show is over, Tilda clicks the TV off. "Frankie, you still do your music, right?"

Frankie shrugs. "Yup. I go to the conservatory for lessons. You know that, Grandma."

"Which instruments do you play?"

Frankie is confused by the sudden questions, and looks at her grandmother like she should know the answers. But she responds anyway. "Guitar, piano, harp. And I sing."

Tilda nods. Stands up. "It's settled then. You're staying the night, and in the morning, you're going to give Colt guitar lessons."

"I what?" Frankie stands up, in a panic all over again. "I can't. I don't—Grandma, come *on.*"

"I have to work, Tilda." I stand up too. This is a bad idea.

Tilda shakes her head. "You owe him more than a paltry 'I'm sorry' for your unkind reaction. And he's interested in learning to play the guitar and sing. Aren't you, Colt?"

"Um." I waffle, but deep inside...yeah, shit yeah I want to learn to play. But I'd never admit it. And this chick is fifteen at most. What could she teach me?

Tilda swats at me. "You're too big, bad, and manly to admit it, but you do want to learn. And my

Frankie is talented. She could teach you a thing or two. I've heard her play. She's amazing. You can spare an hour or two in the morning."

I just blink. "I—um. Okay, I guess."

"Grandma—"

"Frankie, swallow your pride." Tilda doesn't take any shit.

A shrug. "Fine."

"Very good." Tilda waves her hands, scattering us. "Now. Everyone get to bed."

In the morning, Tilda is gone. She left me a note: I've gone to bridge club. Colt, maybe you can pay Frankie for the lesson? Not much, just a little something. And be nice to her. She's sweet.

Frankie is at the kitchen table, eating cereal, ear buds in her ears, cell phone in hand, thumb flying crazily, sending a text message.

She sees me, sends the message, turns off the phone and yanks out the ear buds. "You really want me to teach you guitar?"

I shrug. "Yeah, if you don't mind."

"You know *anything* about music?"

I shake my head. "Nope."

A sigh. "Super."

"I'll pay you for the lesson. So you'll get something out of it, even if I suck."

"Oh, you're gonna suck. The point of a lesson is learn how to suck less." She stands up, rinses her bowl in the sink, and takes a seat on the couch. "Where's your guitar?"

"Um. In my room."

She waves. "Well? Go get it. Can't learn without it."

This is so weird, taking orders from a teenage girl. But I'm game. I get the guitar case and bring it out, open it up and take out the instrument. But then I notice Frankie is staring at me.

"What?" I ask.

"That's...it's Grandpa's guitar."

I nod. "Yeah. Your grandma gave it to me."

Frankie is still, tense. Eventually she whispers, "Grandpa got me interested in music because of that guitar. I'm named after him. Grandma...she *gave* it to you?"

Shit. This is awkward. "I mean, she just said I should try to play. I guess."

Frankie shakes her head. "No, she did. She gave it to you. You're a shitty liar."

"No, she didn't expressly give it to me. She left it outside my room. I just assumed. You can take it."

Frankie shakes her head. "You don't go around

Grandma. I just…I always thought she'd give it to me someday."

"I'm sorry, Frankie. I didn't know."

A shrug. "It's fine." She takes it from me, strums it. "Oh my god. *Way* out of tune." She plucks the strings one by one, twisting the pegs until they sound right to her ear. Strums it again. "There. That's better."

She hands it to me.

"Just strum it—that's an open chord."

She follows this with a fast and technical rundown of the various chords, finger positions, rhythms, a breakdown of the use of frets…it's dizzying. She sees I'm not following so she takes the guitar from me.

"Just watch, okay?"

I nod, and watch in fascination as she launches into a shockingly impressive piece of music. It sounds classical, like Mozart played on a guitar. She's bent over the guitar, eyes closed, frowning, concentrating, fingers flying on the fret board, on the strings.

When she's done, she grins at me. She just showed off, I realize. To show me her credentials. And then she plays "Mary Had a Little Lamb" slowly and carefully. Hands it to me. I try to mimic what I saw her do, and she corrects me.

An hour passes, and at the end I can almost play

the song correctly.

The next week, Frankie comes over and gives me another lesson.

This becomes a regular thing. She's a sweet girl, talented as hell. We never talk about anything but music, but we develop a rapport through it. She's not afraid of me anymore. In fact, I would say we're kinda friends. Which is weird, but cool.

Within two months, it's clear I have a little bit of natural talent, at least. I'm picking it up faster and faster. Learning more and more complicated songs. Chord work, actual technique.

It's fun. It's another positive coping mechanism. I can express myself. Lose myself in the music as easily as I do at work.

At night, alone, I sit in the backyard and quietly strum the guitar, and sing along. For no one but the crickets and the stars, but it's better than cutting.

Frankie becomes like a little sister. She reminds me of my own brother, Kyle, back in Michigan. I wonder what he's doing? If he's still friends with that one girl...Nell. The neighbor girl. Cute little thing, sweet, smart, just as perfect as Kyle. Those two were always inseparable, the golden boy and golden girl. I left and never looked back. But Frankie, she's young and sweet, and she reminds me of Kyle.

The landline rings at three in the morning on a weekend. Tilda's landline never rings. I didn't even know she had one, to be honest. But I wake up from a dead sleep, a ringing noise coming from the kitchen.

Tilda sleeps like the dead; she takes out her hearing aid at night so she won't be disturbed.

I stumble out, answer it. "Hello?"

"Colt?" The voice on the other end is tiny, timid, afraid. Quiet, as if afraid of being overheard.

"Who is it?"

"It's Frankie."

"It's three in the morning, Frankie. Where are you—what's wrong?"

"I—" There's a shout on the other end, cutting her off.

"Frankie? Talk to me."

"I'm at a party. It's getting crazy, and I don't know how to get home, and I don't have any money, and the guy I came with is—he's not right. I'm scared."

"Where are you?"

"I don't know!"

"Can you see outside? Can you see the buildings near you, or the cross streets, an address, anything?"

She fumbles. "Hold on." The line goes silent, and I hear noises in the background. Long minutes pass before she returns. "There's just apartments and condos everywhere. I don't know. I got the address, though." She names an address on a street, way in uptown Manhattan, an expensive part of town.

"Okay. Hide somewhere. Don't drink any more. Stay away from everyone. I'll be there as soon as I can."

"You will?"

"Damn straight. Just sit tight and stay safe."

"I'm scared."

"I'm coming, Frankie. You'll be fine. I promise."

"Okay. Just…hurry."

Tilda has an old Cadillac and she leaves the keys on a hook in the kitchen. She told me if I ever needed to that I could borrow it, as long as I fill up the tank and return it safe. So I borrow it, and haul ass over the bridge into Manhattan, head way, way uptown. I find the address, some swank highrise condo building. The kind with an awning and a revolving door and doormen in fancy uniforms.

I'm visiting a friend, I say. Clearly, the night doorman is used to parties like this, with all sorts of questionable characters coming and going. Not very secure if you ask me; shit, *I* wouldn't let me in. But he does, so I go up to the fourteenth floor.

Music pounds from behind the door, which is

propped open by the lock bar. I push it open and go in. There are bodies everywhere. It's a rich kid rager, bottles of expensive booze all over the place, lines of coke on antique tables. Girls in skimpy designer dresses grinding on punks with the collars of their polos flipped up like the little douche-canoes they are. No one pays me any attention. There's a couple fucking on a couch. Another couple fucking in a corner.

Jesus, what a mess. No one supervises these kids? None of them are over eighteen.

I hear noises from behind a closed door. Not good sounds: grunts, muffled, high-pitched whimpers. A belt buckle jingling. A slap. I don't care who's behind that door, I'm going in.

I kick in the door, one solid crack of my Timberland just under the knob. It splinters open, and I see a skinny, white-ass little punk with his pants around his ankles, about to rape Frankie.

Oh *hell* no.

I grab him by the hair and haul him off. Hold him. He gets scared when he sees me; he should be, because I'm seeing red. Frankie's wearing a nothing little skirt which has been shoved up past her hips, her shirt pushed up, her bra half off, pale small breasts bared. Her cheek is scarlet where the little shit hit her.

My rage is like an inferno.

"Frankie. Out." My voice is low, a growl that promises blood.

"Colt?"

"Out. Now. Wait outside." I don't want her to see what I'm about to do.

She hurries out, hears the warning in my voice. Straightens her clothes as she goes.

When she's out of sight...blood flies. Without a word, I turn the little fucker into hamburger.

When I'm finished with him, I leave the room and find Frankie huddled against the wall, a crowd around her, shouting questions at her. They saw me, saw what I did.

I shove them aside, grabbing Frankie. "Come on. I got you."

"What...what did you do to Heath?"

"I taught him a lesson." I drag her out of the party to the elevator; ignore her questions until we're in the Caddy.

She's trying to stifle sobs. "I'm—I'm sorry."

I halt at a red light. "Sorry? Fuck, you got nothing to be sorry for. You okay?"

She nods. "Yeah."

I ignore the green light, sit at the intersection, turn to look at her. "Give me the truth, Frankie. Did he rape you?"

She shakes her head. "No. No. You got there before he could. He—he would have, though. He was about to." She shivers. Starts to cry. "He—he told me I was...that I'd asked for it. We've gone to parties together before, and he's been trying to push things with me, physically. I always shut him down, told him I wasn't ready for that yet. He just...he was always so pushy about it. He'd grab me. Touch me. Always acted like it was a joke. But then tonight, he cornered me in that room after I called you. I thought I'd locked the door, but he—I don't know. He got in. Dress like a slut, he said, and you...you get what you ask for."

"Jesus. What a prick."

"I know my skirt is a little short but—"

"Stop." My voice cracks like a whip, and she looks up at me. "No. Just...fucking *no*. Listen to me, Frankie: that's complete horseshit. It doesn't matter what you wear—consent is all that matters. No one ever gets to touch you without your permission. You dress however you want, it doesn't make you a slut. Doesn't mean you asked for anything. You didn't deserve it. You didn't ask for it."

She shudders, tries to shake it off, but she can't. She breaks. "He made me feel like I did." Sobs.

I tentatively touch her shoulder. I don't know much about comforting people, certainly not a young girl like Frankie, and certainly not the platonic, sibling-like relationship I've got with her. Do I hug her? I don't know. She might not want that.

"You *didn't*. It's his fault, Frankie. The only mistake you made was spending time with a piece of shit like him in the first place."

"He's popular at school, and I'm—I'm not."

"I don't know shit about high school politics or whatever—I've always been a loner. But you ask me, it ain't worth it. Those assholes, the popular ones, they won't matter in a few years. Being popular in high school, it ain't worth shit. Just be you. Do what you do, and be the best at that. Fuck everyone else, fuck all the drama bullshit." I sigh. "Point is, it doesn't matter who he is. What he said, how cool or popular he is, what you wore or didn't wear. He showed his colors the first time he put his hands on you in a way you didn't like."

She nods, and she's quiet for a long time. "It…it sounded like you hurt him pretty bad."

I don't know how to answer. "I did," I say, eventually, because the truth is usually best. "I'm a rough guy, Frankie. I'm not nice. And pieces of shit like him, there's only one way to handle 'em. But Frankie, please…just know this: I'd never, *ever* hurt you. Don't gotta be afraid of me. You're my friend, and *nobody* fucks with my friends. So someone hurts you, threatens you, yeah, I'll fuck 'em up. Send 'em out in an ambulance."

Once upon a time, Heath might have been hauled out of that party in a body bag, but I've gentled a bit, lately.

"You *are* kinda scary." She glances at me, at my knuckles, which still have the asshole's blood on them. "But I'm not afraid of you."

"Don't ever date anyone like me. I'm no good. Find someone good, someone who'll treat you right."

She leans her head back against the headrest, glancing sidelong at me. "I don't know. Someone like you seems better than someone like Heath."

"Maybe. But there are guys out there better than both of us. Find one'a them."

It's quiet again, until I'm pulling up to Tilda's house and turning off the engine.

She puts her hand on my wrist. "Thank you, Colt."

I just nod. "You ever need me, I'll be there."

We both get out, but before we go in Frankie touches my arm. "Colt? Don't tell Grandma. She'll tell Mom, and I'll get in trouble, and—"

"Frankie," I interrupt. "I won't say anything. I think they deserve to know, but it's your call. I won't lie, though, if anyone asks."

She nods. "Thanks."

I walk her in, make sure she's safe on the couch, and go into my room.

…And promptly have an anxiety attack.

I don't know why. I got there in time. She's not even any relation to me. Just my landlady's grand-daughter.

But Tilda is more than a landlady to me, and Frankie is my friend. They've taught me a lot, between the two of them.

And through it all, for one of the first times since I came to New York, I'm thinking of home—of Michigan.

Fuck if I know why.

Seven a.m. rolls around, and I'm awake, tired, sluggish, and thinking of my family. Mom. Kyle. Kyle, mostly.

Some strange impulse has me dialing a phone number I've never forgotten, the little-used landline in the house I grew up in.

Mom answers. "Hello?"

Panic hits, but I have to say something. "Um. Hi."

"Who—who is this?"

"It's…it's me, Mom."

"Colton?"

"Yeah."

"Oh my god. I wasn't sure—I wasn't sure I'd ever hear from you again."

"I didn't think you would, either. I don't even know why I'm calling."

"I—a few months ago, I flew to New York. By myself. Your dad doesn't know I went. He was in Washington, of course, and—well, I...I looked for you. I spent the entire weekend walking around, looking for you."

"You did?"

"Yeah."

"That's crazy, Ma. How could you expect to find one person in all of New York?" A pause. "How did you even know I was *in* New York? I could be any-where."

She's quiet. "I know, but you mentioned it, the day you left, you mentioned you might try there, and I—I don't know what I thought I'd accomplish. I just...I had to do *something*. But...I should never have let you go. It was wrong. Your dad was wrong. And for what it's worth...I'm sorry, so sorry." I hear her sniffle. She sounds so heartbroken. "You were right, you know. I look back, and—I regret letting him treat you the way he did."

"Thanks. I guess."

"Will you ever come back?" She dares to actually sound hopeful.

I hate this. I don't know why I fucking called. "No, Mom. I've got nothing there to go back for. I've got a life here."

"Have you—have you been okay?"

I laugh. "I'm fine." There's no way I could ever tell her even a quarter of what I've been through.

"You're a bad liar, Colton."

I laugh again. "So I'm told." A non-answer is the only answer.

A long silence and then she asks, "Can I call this number? If I have to get hold of you?"

"I guess. But I'm gone a lot. You won't get me most of the time. So…"

"So what you are saying is don't call unless it's really important?"

"Pretty much."

"I'm sorry things have turned out this way, but I am so glad you called, Colton."

It's weird to be called that: no one ever calls me Colton. I don't think most people even know Colt is short for anything. "I need to go now. Bye, Mom."

"Bye, son. I love you."

"Yeah, uh—you too."

Do I? Do I love her? I don't know. I honestly don't

know anymore. She let a lot of things slide when I was growing up and she let some things just happen. Do I love her in spite of that?

Just before we disconnect I realize I never even asked about Kyle, and he was the reason I called in the first place. "Mom, wait. How—how is Kyle?"

"Kyle?" She sounds surprised to hear me even say his name. "Um. He's eighteen, and...he's about to graduate high school. He was named valedictorian, and he accepted a football scholarship to Stanford. He and Nell Hawthorne have been dating for a while now. You remember her, I'm sure. They're pretty serious, I guess. Why do you ask?"

"I...something happened today that made me think of him. I don't know. It's what made me call in the first place. Sounds like he's still the golden boy, huh?" That sounded bitter as fuck.

"Colton—"

"Never mind, Mom. Sorry. I'm glad he's doing well."

The call ends, then. I hang up first. A little abruptly, because I don't know what else to say. I don't even know why I called. I just stirred up old memories, things I don't want to think about.

Work that day is weird, busy but strange. I'm full of odd thoughts, a desire to not just...subsist anymore. I'm thinking about wanting to live the way India and I talked about—normal and ordinary, reaching for dreams.

Thirteen: Another Kind of Grief

YOU DON'T KNOW THE MEANING OF TERROR UNTIL YOU SIT on a bench outside Central Park in Manhattan, playing music for complete strangers. Frankie dared me to busk—to play music in public for tips.

I never back down from a dare, so I'm trying it.

And I suck.

But it's exhilarating. So I come back week after week, every Saturday and Sunday, all day. I sit on the bench, the same bench every week, case at my feet, a few bucks on the red velvet for bait, and I play, and I sing. I get better. People actually stop and listen after awhile, and eventually some even put a few bucks in the case, although I'm guessing they do it as much for the spectacle of a huge, muscle-bound, tattooed thug doing Nina Simone, Ella Fitzgerald, and Billie Holiday as for the actual music. But it's something, and it makes me feel good.

I grow to love it—almost as much as I love my work at the garage.

As promised, Carl gives me more and more responsibility, lets me take on clients myself, do some restoration work as well as the boring-ass repairs that really pay the rent. He pays me well, and lets me use the space on the weekends for my restoration work when he's closed.

I've got a shitload of money saved in a bank account. Tilda helped me get my duffel bag full of cash deposited and earning interest, and now I've almost got enough to think about finding my own garage. I've even got a few leads.

I've almost forgotten my bizarre, one-off call to Mom. And then, early on a Monday morning, as I'm getting ready for work, the landline rings. Tilda, who is frying eggs for the both of us, just stares at it.

"Who could be calling this early, and on that phone?" Tilda asks, puzzled.

"Dunno. I'll get it," I say. "Hello?"

A sniff. "Colton?" Another sniff. "It's…it's Mom."

"Hey. So, um…What's up?" I don't want to sound rude, but it's weird that she'd be calling at all, much less at seven thirty on a Monday morning.

"I—something happened, Colton." Mom sounds…broken.

My heart sinks. This isn't good.

"Mom—what happened? Talk to me."

"I—" She sniffs again, breathes out shakily, as if barely holding back the sobs. "It's Kyle. There was an accident, and Kyle—he's…he's dead."

I'm so stunned that for a moment I can't speak. "Are you shitting me?"

"Colton, no. He was up north with Nell and…it was a freak accident. There was a big windstorm and a tree fell on him. He's gone. He's gone. My baby—my baby is gone…" She's sobbing now. Hysterical.

"Jesus…no way." I let the phone slide out of my hands. It dangles by the cord, and I slump into a chair. Tilda takes the phone, speaks briefly to my mom, and then hangs up.

"Colt?" She puts a hand on me. "I'm so sorry."

"I barely knew him. He was a lot younger than me, and I—I've always had problems with my family. My dad, mainly. My own brother, and I—never even knew him. Not really. I—I was so…and now he's dead. Jesus. I don't even know what to think."

"Your mom said the funeral is in two days. I wrote down the address for you." She rubs my back.

"Is there anything I can do?"

I shrug. "I don't know. I barely even knew Kyle."

Even as I say those words he's all I can think about. I hated being around him when we were growing up because he was always the golden boy and he set a standard I could never measure up to. So I stayed away from him. Kept to myself. Especially since Dad always seemed worried my stupidity would, like, infect him or something. I don't know. So I never really knew him, but he was my brother, after all, and I must have cared more than I wanted to remember, or I never would have called home in the first place.

I ran away to New York, and never looked back. Barely spared him a thought.

And now he's gone.

I don't know what I feel.

I just know that I have to go to the funeral. I don't really want to, but I have to. I have to do it for Kyle—it may be the only positive thing I can ever do for him.

I call Carl right away and explain the situation. That I need few days off. He offers me the use of his truck, which I didn't even know he owned; he always takes the bus to work. But, whatever, I have to get to Michigan and he's offering the perfect solution. So I take the truck and make the long drive back home.

It's fucking weird as hell to be back in Michigan. I never thought I'd come back here. I drove straight through, eleven hours without stopping. I'm at home—well, what used to be home. New York is home, now. This is just my parents' house, the house I grew up in. Last night I crashed on the couch in my old room and tried not to think too much. My old room is a man cave now with a big flat-screen TV, surround sound, thick leather couches, a pool table, mini-bar, the works. Nice. They probably changed it the day I left. But now they're letting me sleep on the couch in there. They don't pester me, at least not until the next day.

But the next morning, it's awkward. I'm in jeans and a tank top, and both Mom and Dad are staring at me like they've never met me. They don't hide the fact that they're blatantly examining all my new ink, and the various scars I've got on my arms and shoulders. They're staring at me like I'm an alien, is what they're doing. Mom is haggard, red-eyed, broken. Dad is just…tired. As if Kyle's death has sapped him of all his energy. It's so tense. So much is unsaid between us.

"Colton," Dad starts. "Now that you're back—"

I cut him off. "I'm not back. I'm not here to talk about old bullshit. I'm here for Kyle's funeral, and that's it. So you can take whatever you were going to say and shove it up your ass. I don't want to hear it."

"Colton, at least hear him out," Mom says.

I shake my head. "Fuck that."

I walk out. Take Carl's big, tricked-out F-250 and cruise the old neighborhood. I stop at a liquor store and buy a twelve-pack of beer, a bottle of Jameson, and some smokes. I don't know how else to mourn Kyle, how else to cope with being back here.

I stopped cutting months ago, ever since I've been living with Tilda. Don't even smoke pot anymore, now that I'm not around Split and Callie quite as much. It's just too hard to be around them—reminds all of us of too much bad shit, I think.

My only vice left is booze and, even then, I don't use it that much.

I remember, as I'm headed back to the house, that I don't own a suit. Can't very well show up to a funeral in jeans and a wife-beater, can I? So I hit a Men's Wearhouse and buy a suit. It is a little tight in the shoulders and biceps, and too long at the heels, but whatever. I'll never wear it again, most likely.

He's fucking dead, so it's not like Kyle gives a shit what I wear to his funeral.

Jesus.

It hits me every time I think about it. What a shitty brother I was. I mean, really, I wasn't a brother

at all. He might as well have not even *had* a brother. He was, what, eleven when I left? Something like
that. Just a damn kid. Not even in junior high. Been
what...? Six, seven years or more since I left? He's
eighteen, or was when he died. And that makes me
twenty-three, going on twenty-four. Damn. Time
went quick. I hate that I abandoned my kid brother.
But I wouldn't have done him any good, even if I'd
been around. I'm nothing like he was. He was smart,
good, talented. Full ride to fuckin' Stanford University for football, damn near perfect grades. Had a girl
he loved, a good girl, from what I hear. I remember
Nell Hawthorne being a sweet, skinny little thing in
red-blond pigtails with these freckles across her nose.
Skinny legs flashing in the sun as she and Kyle ran
around in the backyard while I studied.

Me? I mean, I'm getting there. Making something of myself. Out of the gang, out of the ring,
working an honest job, living with a sweet little old
lady. Shit, I'm even becoming something of a musi-
cian. Who'd'a thought?

Not like Kyle, though. Kid could have *been* something. Owned a company like Mr. Hawthorne, or a
senator like Dad. President. Football player in the
goddamn NFL. Who knows?

But he won't be anything now, all because of a

freak accident.

And I don't know the first fucking thing about him. His favorite color, favorite band, favorite food. Was he funny? Serious? Shit, I don't even know what he *looked* like. Haven't seen a photo of him since I've been back. There are some on the mantel at Mom and Dad's, but I haven't been able to bring myself to look at them too closely. I just have an impression of a tall, dark-haired, good-looking kid.

Dusk comes and I'm rumbling down dirt track roads somewhere far from anything. It is a beautiful summer night, warm, the air is soft and the stars are out. I pull Carl's crazy, big-ass truck over, just lie in the bed and stare up at the stars for a long, long time. You don't see stars like this, back in New York.

It's damned peaceful and I could almost forget why I'm back here.

Almost.

When I get back to the house, sometime well past midnight, all the houses on the street are dark. There are no lights on except one at the Hawthorne house. The blinds are drawn, but a dull yellow glow lights up a patch of perfectly manicured grass between our house and theirs. The window must be open, because I hear music. Mumford and Sons.

And someone is crying.

'Crying' is not the right word—shit, that word isn't even close to the reality.

Someone is sobbing.

Gut-wrenching, soul-wracking sobs.

A grief that could rip the world apart.

It's the most god-awful tragic sound I've ever heard in my entire life.

And I know exactly how she feels.

I still feel that grief, every day, for India. It never goes away. The razor edge of grief is always sharp, but time has a way of making you numb to the agony of it.

I want to climb up the side of the Hawthornes' house and pull that poor girl into my arms and let her cry, comfort her somehow. Do *something*. But I don't know her.

And it's not my place.

Besides, I'd probably just scare the shit out of her.

So I go inside, sit on Dad's fancy leather couch that costs more than I make in a month, and drink whiskey and chase it with beer until I'm dizzy and numb enough to sleep.

Fourteen: A Dock, a Kiss, a Mistake; a Beginning

DAD STANDS IN FRONT OF KYLE'S CASKET AND CLEARS HIS throat. "Kyle—*ahem*. God, this is so hard. Kyle—" Dad has to blink, stare at the ceiling then clear his throat again. He starts over. "Kyle was my son. He was—he had so much *potential*. Not just in terms of athletics, you know? I mean, he was great at football. So talented. Such a natural leader. But…in who he was as a person, he had such great potential. Smart, charismatic, compassionate. Such a great kid. So much potential, cut short way too soon. I'll miss him."

And then he has to sit down, pinching the bridge of his nose, his shoulders shaking.

I'm standing in the back of the church. I don't

dare sit with everyone else. I've been gone so long, they'll all probably wonder who the hell I am. I'm better off back here.

Some kid goes up to say a few words. He's on the shorter end of medium height, stocky, blond, good-looking. "I'm Jason Dorsey. I had the exceptional privilege of being Kyle's best friend. And I do mean privilege. He was the best friend anybody could ask for. He'd do anything for you. He'd be there, no matter what you needed. He was funny, but never at the expense of others. He was just...*cool*. I know that sounds stupid or whatever, but he was. He was truly just a cool guy. Everyone wanted to be around him, wanted to be his friend. He'd light up a room, you know?" The kid pauses, breathes deeply, composes himself admirably. I don't know this this kid, but I like him. "And I got to be his best friend. I'll always be grateful for the time I had with him. I'll mourn him. But also, he'd want us to celebrate how awesome he was in life. At least, that's what I'm going to do."

A long pause, then.

Silence. Throats clearing, sniffles.

And then a young woman in a long black dress takes the podium. Her hair is...I don't know how to describe it. Burnished copper? Red-gold. Strawberry blond. It's down, loose, a few pins holding it away from her face, which I can't see, because she's got her head ducked. One arm is in a cast. She grips the side of the podium for dear life, holding on so hard I can see her knuckles going white.

She turns her face up, and I'm struck dumb.

She's an angel. Lovely, perfect, exquisite. Gorgeous. Wide, vibrant gray-green eyes that stun from across the room. Pale, flawless skin. That spatter of freckles across her nose.

Nell Hawthorne.

I have to shake myself, because I'm staring.

She's not looking at the crowd, at me, or at anyone. She simply looks up for a moment and then turns her gaze back down to the podium. Then she takes a shaky breath.

"I loved Kyle." Another breath. Her voice wavers, shakes. "I loved him so much. I still do, but...he's gone. I don't know what else to say." She slides a slender gold band off her finger, a tiny diamond glinting at the center. "He asked me to marry him. I told him we were too young. I told him...I told him I would go to California with him. He was going to go to Stanford to play football. But I said no, not yet...and now he's gone." She slides the ring back on her finger.

Then, choking on sobs, she runs on three-inch heels out of the church, right past me without seeing me, without seeing anything or anyone. I catch a glimpse of her face as she passes me; gray-green eyes wet with tears.

I don't know why, but I follow her. Instead of going out the front doors, she rounds a corner and leaves via the back door. Once she's outside, she starts to run, kicking off her shoes and just running. Flat out, sprinting. Her long dress is flying out behind her, and her long hair is whipping around her shoulders.

The sky is gray, heavy, and leaden with rain. A few seconds later the sky opens up and thick slow drops of rain begin to fall.

There's a huge old oak tree behind the church, a lone sentry in acres of rolling green grass. She runs right for it. Collapses against it, shuddering, shaking.

I'm pulled across the grass toward her. I don't know why, I don't understand the compulsion to go to her. But I am. I'm compelled, forced by some un-stoppable need to be near her, to offer her whatever comfort I possess.

So, out into the rain I go. As I get near her, I hear a...a keening. That's the only word for it. Not sobs, not crying, more a sound as if she's holding in some volcanic spew of grief, and it's boiling over. Her shoulders are shaking with it. Her dress is thin black silk and it's sticking to her wet skin, revealing a goddess body, all killer curves and slender, athletic lines that I can't help but notice. I also notice that her skin is goose bumped with cold, and that she's shivering.

She's clawing at the bark of the tree with her fingers, her forehead smashed against the trunk. Keening, keening, keening, trying to hold back a tidal wave of grief.

I slip off my suit coat and settle it onto her shoulders.

She looks up at me. Eyes striated with shades of moss and stone gaze up at me, tears shimmering but not falling, eyes piercing, vulnerable, yet fierce somehow.

I'm changed in that moment. Something about her calls to me. A siren song weaving sorcery into my veins.

I don't know what to do, what to say. So I don't say anything. Just lean against the tree next to her and let the silence well up. She just looks at me, but I notice she's backed away from the edge of shattering, so that's something.

I don't know what to say, so I reach into the inside pocket of my suit coat, pull out my Zippo and a pack of smokes. The cigarettes are a once in a while thing, for moments of stress and for breaks at work. It's not an addiction, but something I still do every once in a while.

I pull one out and light up. Inhale, savor the rush. Her eyes communicate her disgust at smoking in general. Her nose scrunches up, her brows lower, mouth turns down. It's a cute expression. Shouldn't be, but it is.

"I know, I know," I say, going for nonchalance. "These things'll kill me."

"I didn't say anything." Her voice sounds hoarse.

"You didn't have to."

There's something here, something between us. As if I know her. I don't, but she feels...familiar. Her presence, her proximity. It feels not like someone I just met, but rather...someone I've always known. It makes no sense. But it feels right.

Yet so wrong, all things considered. I shouldn't be here, with her. My dead kid brother's girlfriend. Her grief is that of a widow. She loved him, and here I am chatting her up.

"I can see it in your eyes. You disapprove." I take another drag.

"I guess. Smoking is bad. Maybe it's an inherited dislike." She shrugs. "I've never known anyone who smokes."

"Now you do," I say. "I don't smoke much. Socially, usually. Or when I'm stressed."

"This counts as stress, I think."

"The death of my baby brother? Yeah. This is a chain-smoking occasion." I hate how casual that sounds, like I don't give a shit. Like it's any old thing. I wish I knew how to express my emotions, but I don't. I don't even understand how I feel.

Silence again, as I smoke. The cigarette is almost done.

"Can I try?" Her voice is small, hesitant. As if she's daring to do something forbidden, venturing a thought she'd normally never voice.

I shouldn't, but I hand it to her, cherry up, filter down. Our fingertips touch, and it's like lightning striking me. Her fingers are small, delicate, clean. Mine are thick, rough, and permanently dirty, the lines and whorls of my fingerprints etched with grease, the underneath of my fingernails forever blackened.

She takes a drag. She takes too much, too soon. Especially for a virgin smoker. She coughs, and I can tell the rush hits her like a ton of bricks. I grab her elbow to steady her, and that touch, my hand around her arm—it's as if I can feel every particle of her being through that innocent contact, as if I can read the nuclear fusion of grief coursing through her, as if I can feel the life and the sadness and the beauty and the pain.

Once I know she's steady, I let go.

That was a fluke, that feeling. It don't mean a thing; besides, I'm going back to New York tomorrow.

Back to my life.

Away from her, away from this place.

Somehow, the thought of leaving her doesn't sit well with me.

I glance away, and see Mrs. Hawthorne standing in the open back door of the church. Looking at me, looking at Nell.

"Shit. Guess it's time to go." I gesture at her, and Nell nods.

She sighs. Glances at me. Eyes wide and pleading. "Can I ride with you?"

I don't understand the question, even though it's obvious and simple. She messes with my head. "Ride with me?"

"To the cemetery. They'll…want to talk. Ask me questions. I can't…I just can't." She's shaking again. Eyeing her mother as if she's the last person on earth she wants to be around. As if the thought of a car ride with her mother is just too much.

I pinch off the cherry of the cigarette, stamp it out, pocket the butt—these are beautiful grounds, no reason to litter. "Sure." I shrug. "Come on."

I open the passenger door for her; hold her soft

small hand to help her climb up onto the chrome step and into the truck. It's a massive beast, Carl's truck. Knobby off-road tires, jacked-up suspension, diesel exhaust pipes sticking up behind the cab. It's got mad torque, a wicked diesel snarl to it. Not my thing, but still pretty badass. And Nell looks sexy as hell in her wet dress, climbing up into it.

What the hell am I thinking? Jesus, I'm an asshole. Such a fucking dick. I let go of her hand as soon as I can, wipe my hand on my leg to smear away the sensation of her hand in mine.

It felt too right, and that's *way* too wrong.

I turn over the ignition, setting the gargantuan engine to rumbling. "Barton Hollow" comes on, by The Civil Wars, kicking in where it cut off when I stopped the truck. It's a damn good song, so I leave it on. Maybe she'll like it. I don't know. I don't expect the reaction I see in her as I back out, though. It's a visceral reaction, like she's been hit in the gut. I start the song over, and drive in silence. Let the playlist from my USB stick take over. They're all songs I'm learning to play, and I use them when I busk. Good folksy songs that have meaningful lyrics, and melodies that translate well to acoustic covers.

I can tell Nell is caught up in the music, so I leave her to it. Let her ride the music, because sometimes you just have to get swept away, let it give you a moment of not feeling, not thinking, a moment when all that matters is the music.

We're at the cemetery all too soon. I hop out and come around to help her down. We stand there, in the gravel parking lot of the rural cemetery, in the rain, our eyes locked. I can't look away. I try, but I can't look away. I give myself a moment to just look at her, to memorize what perfection looks like, because this is the closest to it I'll ever get.

I realize we're still holding hands.

I let go. Let out a sigh. "Let's do this." Reminding both her and myself why we're here.

She looks like she's about to bolt. This, burying Kyle, she'd rather die than do this. The church, that was just a service. Meaningless in the face of this kind of grief. But seeing that casket sink into the soil, watching dirt cover it, knowing the possessor of your love lies in the box, knowing it's really real…that they're really gone? That's impossible to do, but you have to do it anyway.

I walk in front of her to the awning covering the casket and the burial plot. I feel her behind me. Maybe following me will help her do what she needs to do.

The casket is closed, now. I never saw him in it. Didn't want to. Couldn't. It's better to remember him as the kid out in the yard, tossing the football up in the air and catching it himself, floppy black hair in his eyes. Smiling, happy, alive. Carefree. He'd be a stranger in that box, if I saw him.

I stop, off to one side as Nell goes up to the casket. All eyes are on her. She tries to turn away from the casket, as if it's too much, as if she just can't do it. Which I totally get. I almost didn't make it up to India's grave, that day. Split had to prop me up, push me, carry me. The spike of Nell's heel catches in the grass, and she stumbles. I catch her, right her, let go.

Even that brief touch is irrevocably electric.

There's a basket of blood-red roses near the grave.

A minister in black with a white collar stands up and performs the burial service. He quotes the Bible, talks about loss and finding comfort in Jesus.

I wonder if anyone is actually listening to him.

Certainly not Nell. She's gone—she's lost in thought. She stares at the casket, barely containing her tears. She's riding a fresh wave of grief, holding back the crest.

When the pastor finishes, there's a long silence. Everyone is waiting for Nell to throw the first flower on the casket. You'd think it'd be Mom or Dad, but they wait for her. The love, the loss, the grief, everyone just instinctively gives way to Nell, to the massive presence of her pain.

She stumbles up to the casket, takes a rose in trembling fingers as the casket is lowered into the ground. She's breathing hard, as if it is physically exhausting just to be alive without him, to survive the loss, to contain the grief she clearly won't let herself express. It's heart-rending.

She has to let it out or it'll kill her; I know this personally to be true.

She tosses in the rose and whispers something meant only for Kyle. Then she turns, trips, kicks off her shoes and leaves them in the grass. Then she runs, sprints barefoot, wild and desperate.

For a moment, no one knows what to do. Everyone just watches her go.

"Let her go," Nell's dad says. "She knows the way home. She needs time alone."

No one goes after her, which is just…fucking stupid.

I toss my flower in, stare in mental and physical silence at the casket, not even knowing how to say goodbye to the brother I never really knew.

And then I jog after Nell.

Her parents are fighting, her mom clearly demanding that her father go after Nell. He should, and he does. He gets in his fancy-ass Mercedes SUV and drives after her.

I don't bother with the truck—I'd rather run. The rain feels good. And something tells me Nell needs to run. After a mile or so, I catch up to Nell, who's running crazily. Her arm is bound in a thick cast, which can't feel good; the jostling and jouncing has to hurt that broken arm like a bitch. I see her dad cruising beside her; see him leaning out the open window, pleading with her. Hear his voice, and her mom's. Nell just shakes her head and keeps running. Barefoot on a dirt road. Tripping on rocks.

They pull away. Clearly, they're just gonna let her run.

Another car pulls past me and slows next to Nell. It's that kid, Jason.

Eventually, he drives away, too.

I'm not a runner, but I keep pace with her. When it's clear no one else is going after her, I pick up my pace and run just behind her. She knows I'm here.

She ignores me and that's just fine. As long as she knows I'm here.

We're not quite a mile from our street when she steps on a big rock and rolls her ankle.

I catch her. Lift her in my arms. I'm gasping for breath, and I've got a charley-horse in my thigh, but

I carry her.

"I can walk," she insists, so I let her down.

Except she can't, her ankle gives out and she has to hop for balance. She's tough, determined. She continues to hop, not putting any weight on that ankle.

"Let me carry you, Nell," I say. My voice is gruff, rough. I want her in my arms. She belongs there. But that is not going to happen. It's stupid, it's wrong, it's fucking horrible of me to even think it. But it's also true.

"No." Her voice is so full of determination it makes me shake my head in wonder.

And then she puts her weight on that ankle, walks normally, as if she didn't just sprain her ankle. Damned impossible. Shouldn't be walking. Should be limping. But she doesn't. The pain has to be unbearable. But she pushes through it. All I can do is follow her, letting her make her own way. I want to scoop her up, but she'd hate me for that. So I follow her, amazed at her pain tolerance, her toughness, and her fortitude.

She's crying. Her hair is loose from the pins, and it's falling around the front of her face, obscuring her features. Although I can't see them, I can just tell... tears are trickling down her face, mingling with the rain.

I ache for her.

I walk her home; make sure she gets into her house, where her parents can look after her.

They offer me their condolences, and I leave. I head back to my house and stalk past my parents up to my old room. I leave them to their grief. They don't need me here to witness it, they don't even want me here. I'm a stranger, an intruder.

Somehow, the rest of the day passes, and I sleep a little. I wake up at three in the morning, thinking of India, thinking of Kyle, missing India, hating myself, aching inside. I grab my guitar, Frank's old acoustic Taylor that Frankie insisted I keep. I grab the liquor and the beer and my smokes and head out to the deck. I sit in the old wooden Adirondack chair, watch the moon ripple on the water, and drink whiskey, chase it with beer, pluck at the guitar. Hum under my breath.

At some point, I realize Nell is on the deck with me. Barefoot. Wearing a big hoodie that must have been Kyle's, judging by the fit and by the way she huddles into it, as if hoping he'll speak to her through the soft old cotton.

We drink, smoke, and chat. It's idle chatter, but I'm watching her. I know she's still holding it in. The grief, the ache, the pain.

"You can't hold it in forever," I tell her, at one point.

She doesn't blink, doesn't falter. She knows exactly what I mean.

Her answer is immediate. "Yes, I can."

"You'll go crazy. It'll come out, one way or another." I know that from experience. I held it in, about India. I bled it out, cut it out of me. Eventually, I just had to face it, feel it, own it, and move on.

I'm still feeling it. Still healing. Still learning to live without her.

"Better crazy than broken," she says.

I can't argue with that.

So we drink, and I play. Sing. It's all I know how to do, the only thing I have to offer. I play Mumford, Simon & Garfunkel, Iron & Wine, City and Colour. Everything I know, I play. Eventually, there's nothing left, just the need to keep putting what I feel into music. It's the only way I know to grieve, I think.

So I play for Kyle.

There are no words, it's not really a song, just notes that come out of the guitar on their own, as if I'm just a vessel. It's a goodbye for my kid brother.

And something about that song just...fucking breaks her.

She lunges off the chair; hobbling on her fucked-up ankle, arm in a cast awkwardly waving for balance as she hobbles off the deck. I don't even know where she's going, and I don't think she does either. She's choking on sobs, still trying to keep it in. She stumbles off the deck and collapses into the sand at the water's edge.

I put the guitar down and crouch beside her, not daring to touch her.

"Leave me alone," she snarls.

She doesn't want comfort, doesn't want to hear what I have to say.

"Let go, Nell," I tell her. "Just let it out."

"I *can't*." It's a broken whisper.

"No one will know," I tell her. I know the embarrassment of grief. "It'll be our little secret." That sounds so paltry, but I'm no good with this shit, with being sensitive and comforting.

She just shakes her head.

She's got sand on her lips. I want to brush it away, but I don't.

Her breathing goes ragged, sucking oxygen past the grief, losing the battle against the pain.

The first sob is the worst. It's like the whole world is grieving through her vocal chords. I can't not touch her. I put my hand on her back, her shoulder, an innocent touch just so she knows I'm here. She writhes away, but I know she needs the reminder that she's not alone. She'll get lost in it, if she doesn't have that grounding.

I know that from experience too.

There's nothing to say, so I say nothing. Just sit beside her as she cries.

She tries to stuff it back down, of course. Tries to stand up, and can't. So I lift her to her feet. Her ankle gives out, she cries out with pain, and she falls into me.

I catch her, hold her. Inhale her scent. The smell of woman, shampoo and soap and a bit of perfume.

I let myself hold her. I pretend, just for a single instant in time, that this is okay. That this is allowed. It's not, but I pretend anyway. I try to tell myself that I'm doing what anyone would do in my position—I'm comforting my dead brother's girlfriend. But I know it's so much more than that, and I feel guilty as shit for it.

But I don't stop.

I don't know how it happens. One second the top of her head is under my chin, and I'm smelling the shampoo in her silken copper hair, holding her body against mine, pretending this isn't wrong on so many levels. And then, the next moment, she's staring up at me, and the universe is in her eyes, those goddamned mesmerizing gray-green eyes that seem to know me better than I know myself.

She's falling into me; I'm falling into her.

Her lips touch mine. God, I can't stop it. It's magnetic. Tidal. Galaxies are colliding. Her lips are soft, sweet, tasting of Jameson.

Warmth, a kiss like no other.

It's perfection, a haunting familiarity, as if this kiss was meant to be, from the beginning of time. The first kiss of a lifetime of kisses.

Lies, such lies. Such sweet, tempting, beautiful lies.

She's not mine. Never will be.

But...*fuck*, that kiss. I drown in it. Revel in it.

And then she's ripping herself away. "What am I doing?" Her voice is full of hate and confusion. "What am I doing? What the *fuck* am I doing?"

I move in front of her, stop her, grab her. "Wait, Nell. Wait. Just wait."

"Don't *touch* me," she hisses. "That...that was wrong. So wrong. I'm sorry...so sorry."

"No, Nell. It just happened. I'm sorry, too. It just happened. It's okay." It's not okay. But I have to try to absolve her somehow. It's my fault.

"It's not okay! How can I kiss you when he's dead?" She's yelling. Her voice is venomous with desperation and self-loathing. "When the man I love is gone? How can I kiss you when...when I—when Kyle—"

"It's not your fault. I let it happen, too. It's not your fault. It just happened." I have to cling to that. It's all I have.

"Stop *saying* that! You don't *know*! You weren't *there*! He's dead and I—" Her teeth click together, she cuts herself off so suddenly.

And just like that, the conversation has shifted.

"We're not talking about the kiss anymore, are we?" I ask.

"I can't—I can't—I can't..." She turns, stumbles, shaken, blasted.

I want to go after her, but I can't.

I'm shaken, too.

I feel the guilt, too.

For Kyle, for kissing his girlfriend when he's only been in the ground a few hours.

But also for India. For feeling such shattering potency in a single kiss, such intensity in that kiss. For feeling like that single, accidental kiss was somehow...

more—

Than anything I ever shared with India. Whom I loved, so much. Whom I got killed.

That guilt wrecks me.

I take my stuff inside and drink the rest of the bottle of Jameson until I'm wasted, dizzy, fighting a maelstrom of emotions that being drunk only confuses and worsens, but in drunkenness at least I can keep drinking until I forget, until I pass out.

The next day I wake up past noon, my head throbbing, my mouth so dry it hurts. My stomach is roiling. I swallow some Tylenol with the dregs from the whiskey bottle, grab a couple bottles of water, and carry my guitar and backpack the couple of miles over to the cemetery, where the truck is still parked. I toss my gear on the rear seat.

I walk to Kyle's grave.

I stand over it, staring down at the fresh soil.

"I'm sorry, brother. For—everything. For not being there for you. For what happened last night on the dock. For never knowing you." I feel the grief for the first time, for him. It's a low throb, a thickness in my throat. "I probably won't ever come back here. But you're my brother, my family, and...fuck. I don't know, man. I'm sorry."

I set a guitar pick on top of the headstone, the only memento I have to leave.

"Bye, Kyle."

I get in the truck, and not quite twelve hours later, including a stop for gas and lunch at a greasy spoon to sop up the booze, I'm back in New York.

As soon as I walk in the door, I wish I'd either not gone, or not come back.

Frankie is on the couch, flipping through a photo album.

Kleenex in one hand. Eyes red. An older version of Frankie, a younger version of Tilda, is sitting beside her.

Frankie looks up at me and bursts into tears. She leaps up and runs over to me. She hugs me, much to my surprise. "Oh god, Colt. I'm sorry, I'm so sorry."

Fifteen: The Will

"FRANKIE?" MY VOICE IS A LOW BASS MURMUR. I DON'T DARE think it.

"I didn't have a phone number for you. I didn't know how to get a hold of you."

"Where's Tilda?"

She shakes her head against my chest. "Gone. She—it was so fast. She fell, broke a hip. After that, she just...I don't know. It happened so fast."

"Goddamn it." My eyes sting. I loved that old woman. "I was only gone three days! How can—how can she be gone?"

"I'm so sorry, Colt."

"I'm so fucking sick of people fucking *dying* all the goddamn time!" The sentiment rips out of me.

Inappropriate, inconsiderate, foul, and true.

Frankie's mom inhales sharply in surprise. Frankie just looks at me, not judging.

I wipe at my face. "I'm sorry. I'm sorry, I just—I'm sorry."

Tilda's daughter, Frankie's mom—I don't even know her name—clears her throat. "Tilda spoke of you a lot. She really cared about you."

"She was a great old lady and I have a lot to thank her for. I really liked your mom." I hem, haw. Scuff my foot on the hardwood of the foyer. "I—she was like family to me."

Saying *I love you,* or anything like that, is impossible. I told India I loved her, and I got her killed. Maybe it's superstition, but I just can't say it again.

"I don't mean to sound—inconsiderate, or anything. But...my family, *her* family will be arriving soon. We have to go through her effects, things like that. And we'll have to sell this house, as part of liquidating her estate." Frankie's mom sounds matter-of-fact, but I can tell she's uncomfortable, delivering this news to a guy like me in a situation like this. "So—I'm sorry, but—"

"What Mom is trying to say is that she's kicking you out, because you aren't actually family." Only Frankie could say something like that and still have it sound compassionate, somehow.

"Frankie!"

Frankie shrugs. "What? It's true. No point in beating around the bush about it. Just fucking say what you gotta say, Mom. Jesus."

"Language, young lady!"

Frankie glares at her mom. "I can say what I want. I'm not a kid." She glances at me. "Colt knows what I mean."

I move past her, ruffle her hair. "I sure do, kid. Say what you mean, and mean what you say. Shoot straight or shut the fuck up."

I gather up my clothes, trying not to be angry, and failing. First I lose my kid brother, then I fuck up and kiss his girlfriend, only to come home and find out one of my only friends has just died. Not only that, but I'm losing my home, too.

Life sucks.

Homeless again.

I pack quickly, setting my bags in the foyer, then turn to address Tilda's daughter. "This is most of my stuff. I've got some weight machines in the basement, but I'll come by for them later, once I've figured out where I'm gonna land. Or you can just sell them with the estate. I don't give a shit."

Frankie stands up and shuffles awkwardly to

stand in front of me. "Where will you go, Colt?"

I shrug. "Dunno. I'll be fine, babe. Don't worry about me." I give her a one-arm hug. "Ain't the first time I haven't had a roof over my head."

"I'm sorry, Mr. Calloway—"

I cut her off. "It's fine. You gotta do what you gotta do, right? No hard feelings." I lift my bags again. "When's the funeral?"

A beat. "Thursday, but—"

"Listen, lady." I give her a hard, steely stare. "You sell the house, kick me out the same day I find out Tilda is dead, as soon as I get back from my brother's funeral. It sucks, but I get it. No problem. Gotta settle her estate. But you're *not* telling me I can't go to the funeral. Fuck you. She was my *friend*. I know I'm just some thug, but I cared about her, and I deserve to be there." She says nothing, so I just wave at Frankie. "I'll see ya around, kid. Stay out of trouble, huh?"

"Bye, Colt."

And just like that, I'm homeless again, friendless again.

Except for Split, of course, but he and Callie are better off with me not all up in their business.

So I walk.

Think.

Dream.

Tilda's funeral is…how do you describe a funeral without sounding trite? 'It was a lovely service.' You hear shit like that all the time. But that's meaningless. You lost someone you loved—it doesn't matter if there's some nice flower arrangements or some eloquent words. It's a funeral. It's shitty. It sucks.

Tilda's funeral is shitty, and it sucks.

I fight the urge to cry the whole time, standing in the back, watching them lower the casket into the ground. I wait my turn, wait till everyone else has tossed in their rose, and then I stand there over the hole, staring down at the casket, once again not knowing what to say.

So I sing "Feeling Good" *a capella*, just for Tilda. People stop, listen. No one expects a big, rough-looking fuck like me to be able to sing the way I do, but in this case, I really don't give a shit. I'm singing for Tilda.

Frankie leans into me, wraps a skinny arm around my waist and sings with me.

When the song is over, she looks up at me. "This sucks."

I blink and sniffle and try in vain to smile at her. "Yeah, kid, it does."

That's really all there is to say:

This sucks.

I'm walking the streets one day after work, back to my old habits—I haven't told Carl I'm homeless. I just walk around after work, crashing in a no-tell-motel. Maybe sleep on the couch in the garage office, get up and leave early, come back and pretend I didn't sleep the night there.

I'm walking around Queens, somewhere. Not real sure, don't really give a fuck. Just walking, missing Tilda and...I hear jazz. A Nina Simone tune is coming from a window. I glance up and see an open window, and I can see an old woman who reminds me of Tilda, sitting at a window seat, drinking tea and staring into memory. I stop and watch for a minute.

God, I miss Tilda.

And then I glance across the street, and see a building for sale. Old, run-down, but sturdy looking. It has roll-up bay doors, and a little apartment above. It's an old garage, not a bad area, but not great. I could probably get it for a decent price. I jog across the street and peer in the windows. It's fucking perfect. Three hydraulic lifts, an oil change bay, counters lining the walls, a tiny office, lots of space. Needs a shitload of cleaning, scraping, painting, refinishing. The floors need to be stripped and re-coated, and the windows probably need to be replaced, as well. There's lots of work to do, but it could be *mine*. I've got enough clientele now that I could hang out my own shingle easily, doing restoration and custom work.

Back at the shop, I call the phone number for the agent and ask about the listing price.

"I'm sorry," the agent tells me. "That property has already been sold, I just haven't had a chance to take down the signage. I'm sorry for the confusion."

"Can I make a counter offer or something?"

"No, I'm sorry, the deal is already done."

"Well, thanks anway." I give the agent my phone number. "Call me if anything changes?"

"Sure will."

I hang up, press the phone against my forehead.

Well fuck.

There goes that dream. I try not to be bitter, but it's hard. I *really* wanted that place. It just...felt right.

I make my way back to Carl's, try to deal with my disappointment by cranking wrenches underneath a rusty old Fairlane. I see a pair of shiny shoes approach across the open bay, too expensive for this neighborhood. I roll out from underneath the car, wipe my hands on my coveralls, and examine the visitor: lawyer type, three-piece suit, Bluetooth earpiece, fancy shoes, gold and leather watch.

"Help you?"

"Are you Colton Calloway?" he asks.

"Yeah. What can I do for you?"

"My name is Gregory Hall. I'm with the firm Hall, Pryor, and Williams. I represent the estate of Mathilda Irene Stafford."

"Who?"

He frowns at my ignorance. "Your former land-lady?"

"Oh, Tilda? Okay…what's this about?"

He pulls out an envelope. "She's named you in her will. You can drop by our offices tomorrow morning for the reading of the will, then we can get a few signatures and share the particulars with you."

"What's that mean in plain English?"

He lets out a tiny breath. It is obvious he is not happy to be here, talking to a guy like me. "It means she's left you something from her estate. A memento of some kind, most likely. As I said, the reading of the will take place in our firm's offices in Manhattan to-morrow morning at nine. Since you're named in the will, you are entitled to be present for the reading."

"Okay, thanks." Not sure what else to say.

"Have a nice day." He hands me a business card and then leaves.

So next day I'm on a train into Manhattan, staring

up at the towers like a tourist, then taking a gold-plated elevator up to the eighteenth floor of an office tower. I'm in my suit. I don't know what the protocol is, but better to be over-dressed than under-dressed, I figure. I locate the firm's office, follow the cute little receptionist through a maze of offices to a conference room.

Tilda's daughter is there, Frankie as well, and six or seven others. Nephews, nieces, a brother maybe, I don't know. The proceeding is boring as hell. Gregory Hall reads the will in a monotone, everyone else shifting in impatience.

I'm not sure why I am here, and I don't hear anything that is of concern to me: the meeting entails a lot of explanations, dividing up Tilda's possessions, the money liquidated from her savings and bonds and the sale of the house, and a lot of other stuff I don't even know about. I quit paying attention until I hear my name.

The guitar. This all about the guitar. I stifle a sigh, and tune in.

"...And as pertains to Colton Calloway, my very good friend, I bequeath to him my beloved husband Frank's guitar. I'm sorry, Frankie, I know you wanted it, but Colt needs it more. Furthermore, from the liquid assets of my estate I bequeath to him a sum of one hundred and fifty thousand dollars. Less than he deserves, surely, but more than my family will appreciate. Not that I care. They have what they need, and my money is mine to bestow as I wish. I love you all.

"Written in my own hand, in good mental health, and with witnesses present, signed…Mathilda Irene Stafford."

Jesus.

What?

There's an uproar. Shouting. I remember other dollar amounts being named. All less that what Tilda left me. The crazy old woman left me a hundred and fifty grand? Why?

Frankie is sitting next to me and she leans in close. "I told her what happened. What you did. How you rescued me." She giggles. "I didn't know she'd do this, though. Mom and Uncle Larry are *pissed*. You got more than them."

There are glares. Tears.

I don't know what to do. The lawyer is in front of me, handing me a stapled packet of papers, asking me to sign. I stare up at him, shocked. "Can I—I don't know, refuse it?"

He shrugs. "You could. It would delay the execution of her will a good bit, because we'd have to renegotiate with everyone else."

Frankie speaks up. "He'll sign. Just a second." She leans close to me, whispers in my ear. "It's what she wanted. She'd be mad if you didn't take it. She's giving it to you so you can buy your garage." Her voice is small, but earnest. "Take it, Colt. Don't worry about them."

"It's not fair."

"No. But what is fair in this life?" Wise words from someone so young.

I hear Tilda's voice: *Don't you second-guess me, young man. I know my own mind.*

I grin at the thought of what she'd say if she were here. I take the pen, sign where the little pink sticky tabs indicate. I tune out the instructions from the lawyer. I'll call him later, figure it out then.

I make my way back to Carl's garage in a daze. I sit on a stool at the workbench, silently thanking Tilda.

A few weeks later, my phone rings.

"Hello?"

"Hi, Mr. Calloway? This is Rachel McKenna. I'm a real estate agent, we spoke a few weeks ago regarding the auto garage in Queens?"

"Hi, Rachel. How can I help you?"

"I won't waste any time, Mr Calloway: are you

still interested in purchasing the garage?"

"Absolutely, yeah. But I thought the deal was done?"

"It turns out the buyer wasn't able to secure the financing." There's a pause. "Pardon me for saying so, but...you sound rather young. Are you able to finance the purchase, Mr. Calloway?"

"What's the number?"

She hesitates. Names a number, way, *way* lower than I'd thought it would be.

I hide my excitement, try to sound like I'm waffling. "I don't know, Miss McKenna, that place needs a lot of work."

Another hesitation. "What were you thinking?"

I counter with a number a full two hundred grand less, not expecting her to bite. But she does. Must be desperate to unload the place.

"I can do that," she says. "Not a penny lower, though."

"You've got yourself a deal, Miss McKenna." I'm giddy, wary, hopeful.

Rachel McKenna names an office building, an address in lower Manhattan, and we arrange a meeting for the next week, since it's currently late afternoon on a Friday.

With Tilda's money, I'm able to front a sizeable

enough down payment that my bank grants me a loan for the remainder. I spend an entire day signing documents, but then, at three o'clock on a Tuesday afternoon, Rachel McKenna hands me the keys to my very own auto garage.

It's run-down.

It needs a fuckload of work to make it presentable.

There are probably going to be unforeseen problems.

I now owe a sizeable mortgage payment every month.

But it's *mine*.

I stand in the empty bay, breathing in the thick odor of grease, old oil, and dust.

I worked my ass off, and I made my dream come true.

I did it, India.

I did it.

Sixteen: We Weren't Done Talking
One year later

I'M SITTING ON A PARK BENCH ON THE EDGE OF CENTRAL Park, busking. I've got my case on the ground next to my feet, a few bucks inside as seed money bright green against the maroon velvet.

I haven't busked in months; the shop has been too busy, too many orders, too many rebuilds and custom jobs.

But this, the open air and the lack of expectations, this is where I live. Where my soul flies. Like my weekly gig at Kelly's bar, it's not about the money, although I usually make a decent chunk of change.

It's about letting the music flow out of my blood and into the guitar, letting it seep through my vocal chords.

I'm adjusting a string, tweaking the tuning for my next song. My head is down, tilted to the side, listening for the perfect pitch. I get it, bobbing my head in approval.

I start in on "I and Love and You" by the Avett Brothers. This is a song that always draws a crowd. It's the song more than me, really. It's such brilliant piece of music. So much meaning stuffed into the lyrics. I look up after the first verse and scan the sidewalk in front of me. An older man in a business suit, a phone against his ear, another clipped to his expensive leather belt; a young woman with bottle-blond hair in a messy bun, a sticky-faced boy-child gripping her hand, both stopped and listening; a gay couple, young men holding hands, flamboyant, bouffant hair and colorful scarves; three teen girls, giggling, whispering to each other behind cupped hands, thinking I'm cute.

And her.

Nell.

I could write a song, and her name would be the music. I could sing, strum a guitar, and her body would be the melody. She's standing behind the rest of the crowd, partially obscured, leaning against a parking meter, a patchwork-fabric purse slung over one shoulder, pale green dress brushing her knees

and hugging her curves, strawberry blond hair twisted into a casual braid and hanging over one shoulder. Pale skin like ivory, flawless and begging to be
caressed. Kissed.

I'm no saint. I've hooked up with other girls since
I last saw her, but they've never been enough. Never
been right. They've never stuck around for long.

Now, here she is. Why? I tried so hard to forget
her, but still her face, her lips, her body, glimpsed beneath a wet black dress...she haunts me.

She's biting her lip, worrying it between her
teeth, gray-green eyes pinning me to the bench. Shit.
For some reason I can't fathom, that habit, the biting her lip...I can't take it. I want to throw down the
guitar and go over to her and take that perfect plump
lower lip into my mouth and not let go.

I almost falter at that first meeting of our eyes,
but I don't. I meet her gaze, and continue the song.

I'm singing it to her, as I reach the final chorus.
"I...and love...and you."

She knows. She sees it in my eyes. It's utter mad-
ness to sing this song to her, but I can't stop now. I
watch her lips move, mouthing the words. Her eyes
are pained, haunted.

The person standing in front of her moves, and I
see a guitar case resting against her thigh, the round

bottom planted on the sidewalk, her palm stabilizing the narrow top. I didn't know she played.

The song ends and the crowd moves away, a few people tossing in ones and fives. The businessman—still on the phone—tosses in a fifty and a business card announcing himself as a record label producer. I nod at him, and he makes the universal "call me" gesture with his free hand. I might call him. I might not. Music is expression, not business.

She approaches, bending at the knees and lifting her guitar case, slides onto the bench next to me. Her eyes never leave mine as she sits, zips open her case, withdraws a beautiful Taylor classical acoustic. She bites her lip again, then plucks a few strings, strums, begins "Barton Hollow."

I laugh softly, and see that the pain has never left her. She's carried it all this time. I weave my part in around hers, and then I'm singing. The words fall from my lips easily, but I'm barely hearing myself. She plays easily and well, but it's clear she hasn't been playing for too long. She still glances at her fingers on the fretboard as she switches chords, and she gets a few notes wrong. But her voice...it's pure magic, dulcet and silver and crystalline and so sweet.

We draw a crazy crowd together. Dozens of people. The street beyond is blocked from view by the bodies, and I can tell she's uncomfortable with the attention. She crosses her leg over her knee, bounces with the rhythm, and ducks her head as if wishing her hair was loose so she could hide behind it. She slips up on a chord, loses the rhythm. I twist on the bench to meet her eyes, we lock eyes and I nod at her, slow down and accentuate the strumming rhythm. She breathes deep, her breasts swelling behind her Taylor, and finds the rhythm with me.

The song ends all too soon. I half expect her to rise and put away the guitar and float away again, without a word exchanged, just gone again as mysteriously as she appeared. She doesn't, though. Thank god for that. She glances around at the crowd, chews her lip, glances at me. I wait, palm flat on the strings.

She takes a deep breath, plucks a few strings, idly, as if deciding, then nods to herself, a quick bob of the head as if to say, "Yeah, I'm gonna do it." Then she begins to strum a tune I know I know, but can't place. Then she sings. And again, her admittedly mediocre guitar playing fades away, replaced by the shocking beauty of her voice. She's singing "Make You Feel My Love" by Adele. The original is simple and powerful, just the piano and Adele's unique voice. When Nell sings it, she takes it and twists it, makes it haunting and sad and almost country-sounding. She sings it low in her register, almost whispering the words.

And she sings it to me.

Which makes no sense whatsoever. But still, she watches me as she sings, and I can see the years of pain and guilt in her gaze.

She still blames herself. I always knew she did, and hoped time would cure her of that, but I can see, without having even spoken to her, that she still carries the weight. There's darkness in this girl now. I almost don't want to get involved. She'll hurt me. I know this. I can see it, I can feel it coming. She's got so much pain, so many cracks and shards and jags in her soul, and I'm going to get cut by her if I'm not careful.

I can't fix her. I know this, too. I'm not going to try. I've had too many goody-goody girls hook up with me, thinking they can fix me.

I also know I'm not going to stay away. I'm going to grab onto her and let myself get cut. I'm good at pain. I'm good at bleeding, emotionally and physically.

I let her sing. I don't join in; I just give her the moment, let her own it. The crowd whistles and claps and tosses dollars into her open guitar case.

Now she waits, watches. My turn. I know I have to choose my song carefully. We're establishing a dialogue here. We're having a conversation in music, a discussion in guitar chords and sung notes and song titles. I strum nonsense and hum, thinking. Then it comes to me:

"Can't Break Her Fall" by Matt Kearney. It speaks to me, and it's unique, a song people will remember. And I know she'll hear me, hear what I'm not saying when I sing it. Half-sung, half-rapped. The verses tell such a strong, vivid story, and suddenly I can see her and me in the lyrics.

She listens carefully. Her gray-green gaze hardens, and her teeth snag her lip and bite down hard. Oh yeah. She heard me. I catch the tremble in her hand when she sets her guitar in the case, zips it closed, and tries not to stumble as she runs from me. Her braid trails behind her, bouncing between her shoulder blades, and her calves flash pale white in the New York sunlight. I let her go, finish the song, and then I click the guitar case closed and jog after her.

I walk across the street, Yellow Cabs honking impatiently, through the city noise, and then down to a subway. I see her swipe a card and struggle with the turnstile, guitar case held awkwardly by the handle. She swipes the card again, but the turnstile won't budge and she's cursing under her breath. People are lining up behind us, but she's oblivious to them, or to me standing mere inches away. She tosses her head, stops struggling and takes a deep breath. At that moment, I reach past her, swipe my own card and gently push her through the gate. She complies as if in a daze, lets me take her guitar from her and I slip the straps over my shoulder, holding my own hard case by the handle. The palm of my free hand cups her lower back, prompting her onto the waiting subway car. She doesn't look at me, doesn't question that it's even me. She just knows. She's breathing deeply still, gathering herself. I let her breathe, let the silence stretch. She won't turn in place to look at me, but she leans back, just slightly, her back brushing my front. She doesn't put her weight against me, merely allows a hint of contact.

She gets off after a few stops, and I follow her. She catches another line, and we continue in silence. She hasn't met my eyes since she ran from the Central Park bench. I've stayed behind her, just following. I follow her to an apartment building in Tribeca, follow her up the echoing stairwell, trying not to stare at her ass swaying as she ascends the stairs. It's hard not to, though. It's such a fine ass, round and taut and swinging teasingly under the thin cotton of her sundress.

She unlocks the door to number three-fourteen, shoves it open with her toe and goes straight to the kitchen. She's not watching to see if I follow her in uninvited, which I do. I close the door behind me, set her guitar case on the floor beneath a light switch, just inside the doorway, next to a small square table stacked with sheet music and guitar books and packets of nylon strings. My case goes on the floor next to the entryway to the open kitchen. I watch her jerk open a cabinet next to the refrigerator, pull out a bottle of Jack, twist the cap off, and toss it on the counter. Her fist shakes, and she tilts the bottle up to her lips and sucks three times, long hard drags straight from the bottle. Damn. She sets the bottle down violently and stands with her head hanging between her arms braced on the counter, one foot stretched out behind her, the other bent close to the counter in a runner's stretch. She shudders in a breath, straightens, wipes her lips with the back of her hand. I cross the space between us, and I don't miss the way she tenses as I draw near. She stops breathing as my arm dives over her shoulder, and my hand grabs the bottle. I bring it to my lips, and I match her three long pulls. It burns, a familiar pain.

She turns in place, finally, leaning against the counter edge, staring up at me, eyes wide and searching. She looks like an anime character suddenly, so wide-eyed and full of emotion. I want to kiss her so badly, but I don't. I don't even touch her, even though I'm mere inches from her. I hold the bottle, my other hand propped against the counter beside her elbow.

"Why are you here?" she asks. Her voice is a harsh whisper, whiskey-burned.

I let a lopsided smile tilt my lips. "Here in your apartment? Or here in New York?"

"In my apartment. In New York. In my life. Here. Why are you here?"

"I live in New York. I have since I was seventeen. I'm here in your apartment because I followed you from Central Park."

"But why?"

"Because we weren't done talking."

She scrunches up her nose in confusion, a gesture so absurdly adorable my breath stutters in my chest. "Talking? Neither of us said a word."

"Still a conversation." I tilt the bottle to my lips and take another pull, feeling it hit my stomach.

"About what?"

"You tell me."

"I don't know." She takes the bottle from me, drinks from it, caps it, and puts it away. "About…that night on the dock?"

I shrug, tip my head side to side. "Sort of, but not really."

"Then what *did* you think we were talking about?"

"Us."

Author's Note

If you've read the other books in this series, you're probably expecting a playlist here. I'm not including one, though, because, honestly, you know the songs. It would be redundant, at this point.

The playlist is the same as in *Falling Into You, Falling Into Us, Falling Under,* and *Falling Away.* The songs are the ones he and Nell sang together, the ones Becca and Jason danced to, the ones Kylie and Oz performed together, the ones Ben and Echo listened to.

You know the songs, so I'm not going to list them here, not this time. Dig up your old copy of *FIY*, play that playlist, and think of Colt.

Because this book is, truly, the end of this series. I hope you loved Colt's story, riding with him as he became the man Nell would fall in love with, that you all fell in love with.

Jasinda Wilder

Visit me at my website: **www.jasindawilder.com**
Email me: **jasindawilder@gmail.com**

If you enjoyed this book, you can help others enjoy it as well by recommending it to friends and family, or by mentioning it in reading and discussion groups and online forums. You can also review it on the site from which you purchased it. But, whether you recommend it to anyone else or not, thank you *so much* for taking the time to read my book! Your support means the world to me!

My other titles:

The Preacher's Son:
Unbound
Unleashed
Unbroken

Biker Billionaire:
Wild Ride

Big Girls Do It:

Better (#1), Wetter (#2), Wilder (#3), On Top (#4)
Married (#5)
On Christmas (#5.5)
Pregnant (#6)
Boxed Set

Rock Stars Do It:

Harder
Dirty
Forever
Boxed Set

From the world of *Big Girls* and *Rock Stars*:
Big Love Abroad

Delilah's Diary:

A Sexy Journey
La Vita Sexy
A Sexy Surrender

The Falling Series:

Falling Into You
Falling Into Us
Falling Under
Falling Away

The Ever Trilogy:
Forever & Always
After Forever
Saving Forever

The world of *Alpha*:
Alpha
Beta
Omega

The world of Stripped:
Stripped
Trashed

The world of *Wounded*:
Wounded
Captured

The Houri Legends:
Jack and Djinn
Djinn and Tonic

The Madame X Series:
Madame X
Exposed
Exiled

Jack Wilder Titles:

The Missionary

To be informed of new releases, special offers,
and other Jasinda news, sign up for Jasinda's email
newsletter at http://eepurl.com/qW87T.